A KNIFE IN THE FOG

A KNIFE IN THE FOG

A MYSTERY FEATURING
MARGARET HARKNESS AND
ARTHUR CONAN DOYLE

BRADLEY HARPER

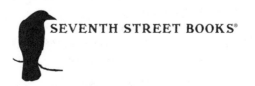

SEVENTH STREET BOOKS®

Cover design by Jacqueline Nasso Cooke
Cover image © Silas Manhood
Cover design © Start Science Fiction

This is a work of fiction. Characters, organizations, products, locales, and events portrayed in this novel are either products of the author's imagination or used fictitiously.

John Tenniel, "The Nemesis of Neglect," published in *Punch, or the London Charivari*, September 29, 1888.

William Henley, "Invictus," written in 1875, published in *Book of Verses*, 1888.

Inquiries should be addressed to
Start Science Fiction
101 Hudson Street, 37th Floor, Suite 3705
Jersey City, New Jersey 07302
PHONE: 212-620-5700
WWW.SEVENTHSTREETBOOKS.COM

22 21 20 19 18 • 5 4 3 2 1

Library of Congress Cataloging-in-Publication Data

Names: Harper, Bradley, 1951- author.
Title: A knife in the fog : a mystery featuring Margaret Harkness and Arthur Conan
    Doyle / by Bradley Harper.
Description: Amherst, NY : Seventh Street Books, 2018.
Identifiers: LCCN 2018016936 (print) | LCCN 2018019554 (ebook) |
    ISBN 9781633884878 (ebook) | ISBN 9781633884861 (paperback)
Subjects: LCSH: Doyle, Arthur Conan, 1859-1930—Fiction. | Jack, the Ripper—
    Fiction. | Physicians—Fiction. | Serial murderers—Fiction. |
    BISAC: FICTION / Mystery & Detective / Historical. | FICTION /
    Historical. | GSAFD: Mystery fiction.
Classification: LCC PS3608.A77227 (ebook) |
    LCC PS3608.A77227 K58 2018 (print) | DDC 813/.6—dc23
LC record available at https://lccn.loc.gov/2018016936

Printed in the United States of America

To Chere,
"The Woman," in my life's story.

CONTENTS

AUTHOR'S NOTE

The period of the Ripper murders in 1888 was an interesting one for Arthur Conan Doyle, both as a writer and a physician. He had a successful practice as a general practitioner in Portsmouth, and some small pieces of historical fiction accepted by minor publications, but nothing that had attracted much notice. His first Holmes work, *A Study in Scarlet*, completed in April of 1886, was his largest and most ambitious work to date. He sent it to various publishers and was hurt by what he described as the "circular tour" of his manuscript. Fortunately, Jeannie Bettany, wife of the editor in chief for *Beeton's Christmas Annual*, plucked it from the slush pile in her husband's office and convinced him to buy it. They offered Doyle twenty-five pounds, which he found insulting, as they also demanded full copyright, but he ultimately agreed. For the remainder of his life, Doyle never failed to mention that those twenty-five pounds were all he ever received for his introduction to the world of his most enduring character.

In July of 1887 he began a historical novel entitled *Micah Clarke* about the English Civil War. When *Scarlet* came out in the *Christmas Annual* it was an instant success, selling out within two weeks after a positive review from the *Times*. Doyle, embittered by his meager pay for the story, labored on finalizing *Clarke*, which occupied him for the next year. The second Holmes novel, *The Sign of Four*, was not published until February 1890, roughly fifteen months after the Ripper's last victim, and nearly four years since *Scarlet*. The Ripper murders therefore took place in the interim between *Scarlet* and *Sign*.

All the Ripper murders occurred in 1888, but there is still debate as to which women slain that year could be attributed to him. There

11

are five all experts agree on, however, beginning on the thirty-first of August 1888, and the final "canonical" victim on the ninth of November. These five murders, over seventy days within the narrow confines of London's East End, were so brutal that they made Jack the Ripper into an immortal figure of savagery and fear.

There is in every one of us a deeply seated love of cruelty for its own sake, although the refined only show it by stinging words and cutting remarks. So let no one think the scum worse than the rest. The scum is brutal, the refined is vicious.
      —Margaret Harkness, *In Darkest London*, 1890

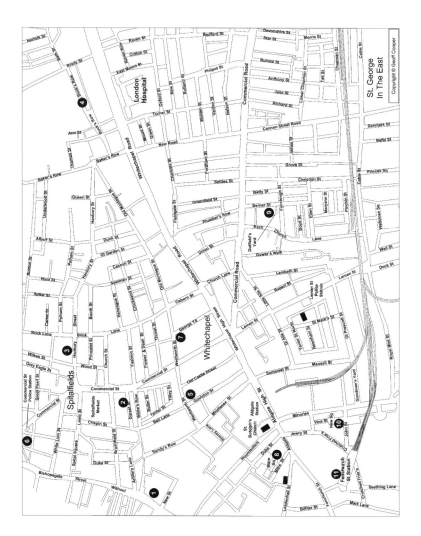

London East End, 1888

1. Bishopsgate Police Station (City of London Police)
2. Mary Kelly
3. Annie Chapman
4. Mary Nichols
5. Goulston Graffito
6. Commercial St. Police Station

7. Martha Tabram
8. Catherine Eddowes
9. Elizabeth Stride
10. Margaret Harkness's apartment
11. Fenchurch Street Rail Station

THE BOX

January 1, 1924, Windlesham

The small cardboard box arrived from Florence last month and sat unopened on my desk until today. Knowing this contains my last communication from one with whom I faced great danger, and who earned my enduring affection, I have been reluctant to confront this final farewell. Foolish of me perhaps, but I can pretend she is still alive as long as the box remains closed. It is as though by opening it now I am consigning her to her grave, though it has already been occupied these past several months.

It is human nature to reflect upon one's life journey when those dear to you pass away, to recount shared experiences, and to contemplate the road ahead without them. While I have never considered myself an introspective man, I find with the passage of time this tendency becomes more pronounced. The comrades to whom I swore an oath of silence regarding the events I am relating here have now, with her death, all crossed over, and I believe when we meet again they shall forgive my desire to recount their courage and nobility of spirit.

My soon-to-be published memoir, *Memories and Adventures*, contains no reference to my involvement in the Ripper investigation, or how it is that I alone now know why he ended his wanton killing of the "unfortunate" women of London as suddenly as he began. I am of two minds as to whether this account shall ever be released, but the arrival of this box has spurred me into recording my memories while I still can. Perhaps, in the end, I shall leave it to my dear wife, Jean, to decide this memoir's fate once I have joined my companions on the other side.

CHAPTER ONE
THE COURIER

Thursday, September 20, 1888

I t began in September of 1888, the month hastening into autumn. I was closing my clinic in Portsmouth for the day when a stranger arrived without an appointment. I asked the nature of his ailment, and he surprised me by responding that he was not there for a medical consultation but was serving as a messenger, handing me his card, which identified him as Sergeant Major (Retired) Henry Chambers, courier.

His erect carriage and regulation grooming were in character with his previous occupation and rank, as were his clothes, which were well-made but unobtrusive. When I requested the nature of his message, he handed over a thick envelope addressed to me.

Within I found a ten-pound note and a letter written on thick bond paper bearing the letterhead of former prime minister William Gladstone.

Dear Doctor Doyle,

Please consider this letter an offer of employment for a period of up to one month as a consultant. The nature of the task I request of you is best discussed in person. As a gesture of good faith, I have enclosed a ten-pound payment that would be yours for traveling to London to hear my proposal. Should you decline my offer, the payment would be yours to keep. If accepted, it would be deducted from future reimbursements.

The courier has no knowledge of the matter but merely requires your response. If you accept, he will telegraph my office with the date and time of your arrival and I will ensure a member of my staff is there to meet you.

I strongly urge you to accept my invitation, sir, as many lives may lie upon its balance.

Respectfully,

William Gladstone

I could not explain how Mr. Gladstone should know of me, or why he would seek me out. I considered myself a capable general practitioner, but gamely admitted there was an abundance of physicians at least as competent as—and certainly more experienced than—myself readily available throughout London. While I was hardly destitute, the promised sum of ten pounds for a journey I could easily make and return from in a single day was enticing. As my wife, Louise, was pregnant with our first child, the funds would be welcome.

After a moment's reflection I agreed, perhaps as much influenced by my curiosity as the ten-pound note, which exceeded a fortnight's income at the time. Besides, a brief holiday from the daily labors of managing my practice would be invigorating.

The courier had a copy of the train schedule, so I selected the train arriving at Waterloo Station at one o'clock in two days. I informed him I would be wearing an oiled canvas coat over a checked vest so that I could be easily identified upon arrival.

I notified Louise of my impending absence, posted a sign announcing the closure of the clinic in two days' time, and arranged for colleagues to see my patients during my absence. Had I known at the time the nature of the request, I cannot say to this day if I would have accepted the invitation. Though my purse would profit significantly, many of my preconceptions regarding humanity and society (humanity writ large), would be lost. What else I may have gained I leave to you, Dear Reader, to conclude at the end of my tale.

I arrived at Waterloo Station punctually at one o'clock, relieved that someone would be meeting me, as at the time I was only vaguely familiar with London. Indeed, for many years I kept a simple post-office map of the city posted above my desk as a reference when writing my Holmes stories. I carried it with me now, and it would become well-worn over the next six weeks.

I noted a pale, well-dressed gentleman of slightly less than average height and in his early twenties who was plainly searching for someone among the disembarking passengers. I opened my overcoat to display my checked vest, and his face brightened when he noticed me.

"Doctor Doyle?" he enquired, with a vague continental accent.

"Indeed," I replied, extending my hand. "Can you tell me what this is all about?"

"I see you are a straightforward man, sir," he responded, grasping my hand a tad over-enthusiastically. "Mr. Gladstone has empowered me to act as his agent in this matter. My name, sir, is Wilkins. Jonathan Wilkins. I am Mr. Gladstone's personal secretary."

"So, Mr. Gladstone is not the patient?" I asked, puzzled by his use of the word "agent."

"I apologize for the vagueness of our correspondence, Doctor Doyle, but it is not in a medical capacity that Mr. Gladstone seeks your assistance."

"Then why in heaven's name am I here?" I asked, irritated by the vagueness of his reply.

Mr. Wilkins looked about, then hoarsely whispered in my ear, "Murder, Doctor Doyle. Or rather, murders . . . the Whitechapel homicides." Then in a normal tone he added, "But I request we delay further discussion until we reach Mr. Gladstone's club, where you shall find the lodgings most agreeable and paid in full."

I walked along in a daze as Mr. Wilkins took my bag and guided me to a waiting hansom. While Portsmouth is not the heart of the British Empire, our local papers had related the grisly doings of the madman at the time called "Leather Apron." It had not occurred to me that I should be asked to assume the role of my fictional character, Sherlock Holmes, as a consulting detective. I resolved to hear Mr. Wilkins out, politely decline, and return home on the next available train. For ten pounds I could certainly give him an audience of a few minutes.

We passed the journey to the club in silence, for which I was grateful, as I was busy mentally composing my eloquent refusal of Wilkins's pending request.

The Marlborough Club was indeed quite comfortable, conveniently located at No. 52 Pall Mall and aptly fulfilling its stated goal of being "a convenient and agreeable place of meeting for a society of gentlemen." Its members consisted primarily of affluent barristers and members of the Stock Exchange. My traveling clothes, when contrasted with their well-tailored suits, seemed shabby. I insisted Wilkins state his proposal before I unpacked, should that prove unnecessary. He escorted me to the reading room, then poured us each a glass of water from a crystal decanter before beginning.

"Very well," said Wilkins. "I could tell by your reaction that you know of the gruesome murders that have occurred within Whitechapel this past month. Three women, Martha Tabram on August the seventh, Mary Ann Nichols on the thirty-first, and a fortnight ago Annie Chapman on September the eighth. All three slain within yards of residents asleep in their beds."

Mr. Wilkins shivered slightly and sipped from his glass before continuing.

"Mr. Gladstone has always been charitable to the community of fallen women in Whitechapel, and a delegation of these ladies approached him with a request for his assistance to end this reign of terror."

"How does this involve me?" I asked, hoping to bring him to the point.

"I read with great interest your story *A Study in Scarlet* published this past December," he continued, not to be deterred. "The use of scientific methods of analysis to deduce the murderer seemed quite sound to me, so I convinced Mr. Gladstone to summon you to serve as our own consulting detective. Your task would be to review the work of the police and propose avenues of investigation they have overlooked."

He took a deep breath and, before giving me a chance to respond, concluded his apparently well-rehearsed offer. "The pay is three pounds per day, lodgings provided here in the club, and any reasonable expenses reimbursed. Do you accept this commission, Doctor Doyle? It grants you an opportunity to test your theories as to the role science could play in combatting crime. The pay is not unsubstantial, and the experience may well guide you in future stories. What say you, sir?"

I sat there stunned, overwhelmed by the scope of the task laid at my feet. I have always seen myself as a champion of justice, but I did not wish to assume a competence beyond my abilities. Were I to fail, as was most likely, my reputation would suffer and my clumsy efforts might impede the work of others more capable than myself. I saw no reason to accept this strange commission, and several to refuse.

"I am sorry, Mr. Wilkins. Your cause is just, but I am not Sherlock Holmes," I replied. "He is a fictional character, with knowledge and skills I do not possess. My inspiration for this person is my old professor of surgery, Joseph Bell. Although I carefully studied his techniques, I lack his keen intellect and ability to deduce the great from the small. I recommend you contact him, though I doubt he will leave his practice in Edinburgh for such a quixotic quest."

Mr. Wilkins leaned back in the comfortable leather chair and pondered my words with a worried frown on his face. I confidently awaited my dismissal, when his reply caught me off guard.

"Very well, sir. Knowing how keen Mr. Gladstone is to resolve this matter, I extend the same offer to Professor Bell. Please understand, I am offering this to the both of you as a team. Professor Bell may have the deductive skills, but you are his voice. I will only accept the professor if you agree to work alongside him. Having a colleague to discuss his findings may make a team that is stronger than the sum of its parts. Is that agreeable?"

I recall my thoughts quite clearly at that moment: Surely Professor Bell would never agree to this; thus, I would be excused from taking it on myself, allowing me to walk away ten pounds richer without angering a powerful man. I had to suppress a smile while congratulating myself on my clever escape.

"Agreed," I said with false heartiness. "I shall telegram Professor Bell at once. As today is Saturday, I do not expect a response before tomorrow, or perhaps not until Monday. The lodgings are quite acceptable; I assume the daily stipend begins now?"

"It does," replied Wilkins.

"Then I have a telegram to compose and bags to unpack. How shall I contact you when I receive the professor's answer?"

"The doorman of the club has three street Arabs he uses as couriers; he will ensure any messages for me are sent straight away. Mr. Gladstone prefers not to meet with you until this matter is concluded. Please understand, his enemies have already made far too much of his Christian charity toward these women over the years, and he does not desire to detract from the current investigation by drawing attention to you."

"Very well then," I replied. "Expect my message within the next forty-eight hours."

Wilkins departed, and I applied myself to the wording of my telegram to Bell. I finally settled on the following:

GREETINGS FROM LONDON STOP IMMEDIATE CONSULTING OPPORTUNITY THREE POUNDS PER DAY STOP UNABLE TO DISCLOSE DETAILS HERE BUT OPPORTUNITY TO SAVE SEVERAL LIVES AND SERVE JUSTICE STOP REPLY SOONEST WITH RESPONSE AND ARRIVAL TIME AND PLACE IF AGREED STOP DOYLE

I felt as though I had been sufficiently faithful toward my potential new employer, and with a clear conscience I spent the remainder of the day walking through London's buffet of sights and sounds. Although in later years I found the great metropolis wearisome, on that day I agreed with Doctor Samuel Johnson that when a man is tired of London he is tired of life. Thus it was with a light heart that I returned to the club in time for dinner, to be stopped at the door with a reply from Bell:

INTRIGUED STOP MUST WIND DOWN MATTERS HERE
STOP ARRIVING MONDAY THREE O'CLOCK KINGS
CROSS STATION STOP BELL

I read this several times, brief as it was. No matter how I analyzed it, there was only one possible explanation: Bell was coming. I was in for it now!

I reluctantly sent a message to Wilkins that Bell had agreed, ate a dinner I do not recall in the slightest, and went to my room. Shortly before retiring I received Wilkins's reply:

Excellent! Will meet with you for breakfast at eight tomorrow to help you begin your investigation. J Wilkins.

I feared I would have little appetite for whatever breakfast had to offer, and I spent a restless night pondering how fate and a single flight of fiction had led me to this moment.

CHAPTER TWO
FIRST IMPRESSIONS

Sunday, September 23

Breakfast with Wilkins the next day was enlightening. He was the kind of officious person who attach themselves to great men. They can be useful, such as a guide dog for a blind man, but make poor mealtime companions. I ate of the generous offerings, while Wilkins sipped tea and talked in what I was growing to realize was his usual efficient fashion.

"Here is a note signed by Mr. Gladstone dated yesterday saying you are acting as his agent regarding the Whitechapel murders, and any information shared will be kept in strictest confidence. He trusts you will avoid notice by members of the press as to your, and by inference, Mr. Gladstone's involvement in this matter."

I nodded my agreement.

"As we await Professor Bell's arrival, I suggest you meet with some people who will be useful to help you get your bearings, both geographically and as to the status of the investigations. As for geography, I have the address of a Miss Margaret Harkness. She has agreed to see you this afternoon for tea. She is one of the new breed of 'emancipated women,' a female author. She currently resides within Whitechapel to become familiar with the daily lives of the working poor portrayed in her novels."

Wilkins's eyebrows lifted in mild distaste. "She lodges in a tenement building, living side by side with daily laborers who can afford only those meager lodgings. I have no familiarity with the East End personally, but after reading her most recent work, I believe she will make an acceptable guide. I met with her briefly yesterday, and I've contracted her services for a tour to familiarize you with the area. I strongly suggest you not wander about after dark in that neighborhood, at least not alone."

Wilkins saw my discomfort at the thought of visiting the residence of a single, unaccompanied woman, and a slight smile at the corner of his mouth betrayed amusement at my sense of propriety. He spoke before I could voice my objection, "She has a lodger and has reassured me this woman will be joining you for tea."

Such sensibilities seem quaint now, but I was very much a man of my era. The thought of being alone with a woman in her residence, other than my wife or family member, was unacceptable. The matter resolved, Wilkins continued.

"The second person I suggest you see is Inspector Abberline from Section D, or the Criminal Investigation Department, as he is responsible for leading the pursuit within Whitechapel. He has been temporarily reassigned to Division H in the East End, due to his intimate knowledge of the area and contacts within the criminal class. He will be able to get you into the morgue and to see any crime scenes should, God forbid, there be additional murders."

"I'm impressed the police commissioner would invest such resources just to stop the murder of a few streetwalkers, no matter how brutal."

Wilkins shrugged. "There has been a recent influx of Jews from the Continent, and they have found a cold welcome in the East End. Some within Whitechapel, with no evidence to back their claim mind you, say a Jew must be responsible. The authorities fear large-scale riots in the East End if the murders continue."

Wilkins then handed me a sheet of paper torn from his notebook with the address of the Division H police station on Commercial Street within Whitechapel, and Miss Harkness's residence on Vine Street. I glanced at the addresses briefly, then tucked the paper into my jacket as he continued.

"I suggest you arrive at his office either very early or very late, for he will be on the streets most of the day. I doubt he is at home even today, but you may wish to wait until Professor Bell's arrival to call upon him so that he may meet you both at one time."

"How may we stay in touch?" I asked. "I am very much in terra incognita here in London. Would a telegram suffice, or would you prefer more direct communication?"

"You can correspond with me as before via the doorman here at the club. I will expect an update on your progress once a week, though any suggestions or requests for additional resources may be sent at any time."

He reached into his coat and produced a bulging sealskin wallet, declaring to me that Mr. Gladstone was either a very generous or very trusting employer, and with a satisfied air he counted out the remainder of my first week's payment.

"Here are twenty-six pounds, eleven pounds for you which, plus the ten pounds you have already received, totals twenty-one, and fifteen for Professor Bell. I shall pay you in advance each week on Saturday. That will allow a recurring face-to-face meeting to update me on the progress of your investigation. You may, of course, share your insights with Inspector Abberline, but anything you wish to send to higher authorities should be handled through me. I know best whose ear to whisper into while avoiding public attention. It is my raison d'etre as it were."

Mr. Wilkins was thorough, if not charming. After his summation, he provided me with his card, an elegant creamy pasteboard with the name *J. Wilkins* in filigreed gold lettering and an address in one of the poshest areas of London, which I assumed represented Mr. Gladstone's residence.

Wilkins advised me to present his card as needed to establish my bona fides in addition to the note, but to use them sparingly to limit the knowledge of Gladstone's interest in this matter.

I required nothing further from him at the moment, and he departed.

I fear I did not give the most excellent kippers the full attention they deserved, for my mind was still attempting to grasp all that had happened within the past three days, beginning with a mysterious summons from a man thrice privileged to lead Her Majesty's government.

Frankly, I did not feel myself up to the task, but I have always possessed a robust curiosity, so I decided to give the investigation a week. If nothing else, I was already twenty-one pounds richer for the experience, and this firsthand exposure to police investigations could serve me well should I decide to pen any further crime stories. They were quite the rage at the time, and in truth such tales have never waned in their power to grasp the public's fancy. It says much about human nature, I fear. None of it good.

After composing a letter to my wife, Louise, informing her of my continued stay in London, I found myself some six hours before tea time, so I decided to explore my surroundings.

I did not disregard Mr. Wilkins's warning about wandering the Whitechapel neighborhood unaccompanied, but it was Sunday, the sun was out in full force, and I felt robust enough in spirit and appearance to offer no temptation to anyone intent on villainy. I enjoyed long walks and thought it time to merit my second helping of kippers. Apparently my earlier fear that this adventure would lessen my appetite had been unfounded.

To describe the East End of that day to those born in this more genteel twentieth century is a daunting challenge. The year prior, in June of 1887, our nation had celebrated the fifty years our Glorious Monarch Queen Victoria had so magnificently occupied her throne. The sun never set on the British Empire, and the wealth of distant lands poured into our nation. Every British citizen saw prosperity as their inalienable right. The West End of London teemed with shops, comfortable establishments, and even more comfortable residents.

The East End, by comparison, was the dumping ground for the poor and dispossessed. This area on the fringes of London and "polite" society contained upward of seventy-six thousand inhabitants. The population consisted of a mix of Irish and British poor, in addition to a recent substantial influx of Jews from Eastern Europe fleeing persecution in their homelands. There was much tension between the East End and the rest of London, exceeded only by the hostility the Irish and British poor showed toward their newly arrived Jewish neighbors.

Among the various slums, Whitechapel was the worst, with the severest overcrowding and highest death rates. The 1891 census listed the population density of outlying communities at twenty-five people per acre, and the prosperous West End at fifty. Whitechapel had a density of eight hundred residents per acre. I will repeat that number so that the implications may be fully understood: eight hundred. The image brought to mind is of an enormous ant colony.

This astonishing density of humanity was only possible because roughly half were children, and because of the packing of people into every conceivable space, often with up to eight people per room. Those with a steady if meager income could rent a corner of one room. Some lodging houses catered to those working irregular hours and charged by eight-hour increments. They proudly declared that the bed would still be warm from the previous occupant as an inducement to their potential customers to favor their establishment.

Most of the inhabitants spent their nights in common lodging houses with varying rates. Eight pence procured a double or matrimonial bed, while four pence rented a single. For a tuppence one could be propped up against a wall, a rope run across the body to stay erect, and you slept as best you could. It was not uncommon to see an entire family dozing fitfully together like soldiers, derelict in their watch. Those who could not afford even these meager accommodations would spend their nights tramping the streets to keep warm, finally sleeping in doorways or stairwells when exhaustion overtook them.

Obviously not all eight hundred people could be on the street at the same time. Still, I cannot fully describe the bedlam that ensued during the day when the majority of the residents were about, arguing over right-of-way, buying and selling, or going to and from work while sharing the streets with various horse-drawn conveyances. All in all, it made the undetected murders in the midst of this multitude that much harder to comprehend.

Even before the arrival of the man subsequently called the Ripper, the consensus among the Metropolitan Police was that Whitechapel contained a level of vice and villainy unequaled in the British Isles. I am ashamed to say I saw poverty and human degradation on those streets that I did not know existed in my native land. Had I been taken blindfolded and then exposed to these scenes, I could have easily been convinced I was in Moscow or Krakow.

Prostitutes abounded of every age, coloration, and language, yet all sharing the hollowed eyes of desperate souls. Public houses were open continuously, serving the vilest gin to any with a copper in their pocket. Alcohol was widely believed to offer some protection against venereal disease, and it was heavily consumed by the ladies of Whitechapel.

I had set off with the intention of getting my geographic bearings regarding the hunting grounds of my adversary, but the emotional impact of human suffering on such a grand scale left me dazed.

While the thought of tea was most welcome, to partake within the boundaries of this wretched community was decidedly unappealing. I gathered my resolve, however, and after a couple of wrong turns found myself before a dilapidated and foul-smelling tenement that matched the address of Miss Harkness on Vine Street.

I took a deep breath. No turning back now. Time to meet my guide.

CHAPTER THREE
POCKETS

Sunday, September 23, cont.

I had no firm idea what kind of woman would willingly choose to live amid such squalor, but I envisioned a stern-faced spinster with thick pince-nez glasses; I was skeptical a lady of letters could be of any use to me in this environment. The best I could hope for was a detailed map and some history of the events surrounding the murders; I had no intention of burdening myself with the responsibility for her safety while traveling through the darkened alleyways and courtyards of Whitechapel.

There were no postal boxes or names in the entryway, so I trudged up the dark and slippery stairs to the third floor and knocked on an unassuming door that corresponded with the address 3A.

"One moment," said a muted voice on the other side. I heard the rattle of a bolt, and an eye peered through the slit allowed by a heavy chain. "Who is it?" asked the same voice, now clearer.

"Doctor Doyle," I replied.

The door closed, the chain rattled, and the door reopened. The back of a slender figure proceeded ahead of me into the soft light and, without pausing, instructed me to secure the portal behind me.

I fastened the door nervously, unsure of my reception or of who was receiving me, and entered a small and dimly lit sitting room. On the far side, if a room so small can have a "far" side, a woman sat quietly. She could have been anywhere from thirty to sixty-five, the marks upon her face revealing a life of hardship. She held a yellowish, stained rag over her mouth and a partially knitted sock and her needles in her lap. Beside her stood a slender young man of average height, dressed in working man's clothing, and wearing a battered bowler hat. The woman looked at me with mild interest, but the young man's piercing gaze apparently found the stout gentleman before him rather amusing, while I perceived him to be quite rude.

"Pardon my interruption," I said, doing my best to appear calm, "but I understand a young woman named Margaret Harkness lives here. She was expecting me."

"Quite so," replied the young man. "I am she."

My reaction must have been what she was expecting, given the smirk on her face. Nowadays a woman dressed as a man would cause others to stare, but at the time it was scandalous.

"Forgive my bit of fun, Doctor Doyle," she began, "but my work often requires me to travel these streets at night and alone. I have found that dressed as a man, I can move about unnoticed, thus more safely. Do not be embarrassed by your reaction. I am quite accustomed to it when men first meet me 'undressed,' by which I mean not traditionally attired."

My face must have been quite scarlet by this time, yet she was not the least bothered by my embarrassment. To move our conversation forward and not linger on my discomfort, I turned to the woman beside her.

"And you, madam, you h-have the advantage of me," I managed to stammer. The woman nodded slowly, lowered the rag from her face, and grimaced a smile, revealing a festering wound on her right jaw.

"Molly," she replied slowly, taking care to articulate each syllable.

"Miss Jones is my lodger, my touchstone, and friend," replied Miss Harkness. "She listens to my writing and tells me if it rings true. I in turn grant her a safe place to sleep and a fair share of my meager meals. She worked in the match factories until she developed phossy jaw. We met during the Matchgirls' Strike in July of this year."

Miss Harkness and her lodger exchanged glances before continuing.

"I cannot afford the surgery required to excise the rotting bone within her jaw, but I can give her shelter and friendship. This is the world you have entered, Doctor Doyle, and I am to be your guide within it."

She smiled at me, and I wondered if she was having similar thoughts toward me such as I had when I imagined her as a middle-aged spinster in need of my constant protection.

"I am a writer, sir, as I understand you are," Miss Harkness continued. "Perhaps you have heard of my most recent novel, *Out of Work*, or my work published last year, *A City Girl*?"

I shook my head, still astounded to find myself casually conversing with a woman attired as a man, as though it were in no way out of the ordinary.

"You are in the majority," she shrugged. "To expand my circle of readers, I have published my last two works under the nom de plume John Law. It seems most men feel either threatened, contemptuous, or both when confronted by a capable woman with strong opinions. For the most part, I make my living as a journalist, paid piecemeal by various newspapers for reporting on happenings here in the East End, as no 'respectable' journalist dares come here. Indeed, there are some streets within Whitechapel even police officers fear to tread if less than four in number, while I, in my poor attire, pass ghostlike among them.

"Be assured Doctor, despite my current attire I have no desire to be a man; the only thing I envy the male gender is the abundance of pockets your fashion allows." She jutted her chin out as though daring me to criticize her "undress," but I held my tongue and she continued.

"My experiences here are being stored away for future use in works of a hopefully more enduring nature. Currently I am researching the Salvation Army in preparation for my next novel." Then she locked eyes with me and challenged me, "And what of you, sir? Are there any of your writings I may have read?"

Her impudent tone soured our initial encounter, I'm afraid. I replied that I had written a crime story, which had led to my being asked to look into the Leather Apron murders. I was unaccustomed to being so roughly cross-examined by a woman, and I felt she was taking undue liberties with a gentleman she had just met. I began to question Mr. Wilkins's wisdom in choosing her as my navigator, but I resolved to keep the tone civil.

"Leather Apron, eh? That explains it. Mr. Wilkins said only that a gentleman, a writer from outside London, would be working a few weeks in the East End, and that he would pay me two pounds to show you around and introduce you to some of the tarts. I have become acquainted with several streetwalkers while researching my Salvation Army story, and as two pounds is nearly a fortnight's income for me, I asked no more questions. A lady, or ladies," she swept her arm to include Molly, "have to eat."

I started when she mentioned Wilkins's requirement that I meet with a streetwalker. "What purpose would that serve? I can't imagine what we'd have to talk about."

Miss Harkness smiled at my obvious discomfort. "I can't answer for the man, but you'd be surprised what you'd learn of life in the East End if you listened."

She adjusted her sleeves. "Well, shall we take a stroll?"

"Now?" I replied. "It will be getting dark soon, and I would not place you at risk unnecessarily."

She laughed. "You, dear sir, shall be much more at risk than me. Your accent, comfortable waistline, and well-tended clothes all declare you an outsider. It is rather common for our benevolent neighbors in the West End to visit us for the pleasures of the flesh. Few prosperous gentlemen are willing to explain to their wives how they came to be robbed within our alleys, so they often refuse to report a theft.

"I shall serve as your guide and interpreter, so let me do the talking unless I prompt you. Come!" She beckoned, as though we were about to go to the theater. "The East End at night is the world you must enter if you are to understand the lair of this monster."

I agreed with reluctance. While not wanting to place a lady into such a dangerous environment, I had to admit she most likely had the right of it as to which of us was in greater peril. Still, while serving as a young ship's surgeon on the SS *Hope* during an arctic whale-and seal-hunting expedition, I had earned the respect of seasoned sailors by my ability to blacken their eyes in sparring matches. As I was still not quite thirty years old, I had confidence I could give a good accounting of myself should it become necessary. I was determined not to show any reluctance in the presence of this rather rude woman, and so would follow where she led, if only to show my nerve was equal to hers.

I soon learned what a high standard I was setting for myself.

CHAPTER FOUR
WELCOME TO
THE EAST END

Sunday, September 23, cont.

We set forth as the lengthening shadows announced sunset. Miss Harkness's apartment on Vine Street was near Fenchurch Street Railway Station, and we bore in a northeasterly direction toward Whitechapel Road. She explained this was the main artery in the East End. By knowing that roadway, she said, I would always have a reference point within the labyrinth.

As we walked I learned something of her personal history. She told me she had grown up in Worcestershire, the daughter of a conservative clergyman. She came to London as a young woman to become a nurse, eventually becoming a dispenser of medications on the wards. After a couple of years, however, she found the life planned out for her by her father too restricting, so she struck off on her own to pursue a career as a writer, working as a freelance journalist and author. Miss Harkness assured me, with no trace of regret, that her current career was not approved by her conservative, middle-class family.

I would have inquired further as to how a woman with such a proper upbringing could have found herself wandering the East End in male attire, but the more personal my inquiries, the faster her pace, and I soon had little breath for conversation.

Some of the prostitutes gave a quick nod to Miss Harkness as we passed, while giving me a curious stare. Apparently she was acquainted with many.

"Tarts see everything," replied my companion when I remarked upon this. "They are always searching for a possible customer and assessing danger. I predict our Leather Apron fellow, when caught, will reveal a rather unassuming man of meek demeanor. Otherwise, these ladies would not so quickly agree to join him in a darkened alleyway or unlit staircase for a 'four-penny knee trembler.'"

I was grateful our need to navigate the crowded streets kept Miss Harkness from seeing the vivid color her last comment surely inspired. I was quite unused to such language from anyone, least of all a lady of respectable class and education, as she obviously was. The contrast between her evident good breeding and casual use of such coarse references left me speechless, but also intrigued. I could see time in her company would not be boring.

"Look about you, Doctor." Miss Harkness waved her arm before her, indicating the jammed mass of ill-fed humanity. "The East End is starving. Those in the West End are mad not to see it, but someday these unfortunates will turn upon them like abused dogs, and it will take the army to put them down!"

I saw desperation and resignation on the faces of the men, women, and children about me—not defiance. I suspected it would take at least three hearty meals before they could find the strength to rebel against anything. We passed children playing in garbage, blood from nearby abattoirs staining their bare feet. The smell of unwashed humanity, mixed with smoke and cheap gin, pervaded. I struggled to imagine what their daily lives must be like, and I confess it was quite beyond me. In retrospect, perhaps that was more due to a lack of will than imagination.

Time has blurred much of what Miss Harkness showed me, but I do recall asking to go to the sites of the two most recent murders. I realized any possible clues had been washed away long ago, but the writer in me wanted to visualize as clearly as possible the moment of the killer's action, and the sort of place he would choose to attack his victims.

My guide readily agreed. "As you say, not much to see now, but for two pounds I'd walk to Cornwall and back. Follow me."

We were approaching the Royal London Hospital by this time, so we proceeded on to the site of Mary Nichols's death in nearby Buck's Row.

Enough time has passed since the alleys of London ran red with the blood of murdered women, that most of you reading this would not have lived through those terrible times, so permit me a moment to recount the circumstances of her death.

At three-forty on the morning of the thirty-first of August, a carter named Charles Cross discovered a small bundle in the roadway near the old Boarding School, which still stands today. It was lying in a gateway on his left, and thinking it a discarded tarpaulin and perhaps useful, he approached and discovered it was a woman lying upon the ground.

As Cross stood over her, he heard footsteps behind and turned to find a fellow carter, Robert Paul, also on his way to work. Cross called him over. Together they found the woman on her back, her dress pulled up around her waist. Cross later said her face was warm, though her hands were cold. Paul testified he thought he felt weak respirations from her chest. They pulled down her skirt to preserve her decency and, feeling they could do no more for her, each went his way, promising to notify the first policeman they encountered. Later examination of the body made Paul's belief that Mary Nichols was still alive doubtful, as her throat wound was so severe she was nearly decapitated.

Within moments of their departure, Police Constable John Neil independently discovered her corpse. He later stated he had passed by the area thirty minutes prior, and that both then and at the moment of discovery he'd seen no one else there. With the aid of his lantern, he noticed the wound to the throat and found her arm still warm above the elbow. At that moment he spied Police Constable John Thain passing by the end of the street, and flashed his bull's eye lantern to summon him.

A series of events then happened in rapid succession: Thain went posthaste to fetch Police Surgeon Llewellyn; as Thain departed, PC

Mizen arrived after being told of the body by the two carters. Neil sent Mizen off to gather reinforcements to secure the area and fetch the police ambulance.

Doctor Llewellyn arrived at around four o'clock, only twenty minutes after the initial discovery by the first carter. Llewellyn pronounced the woman dead and noted that, while the hands and wrists were now cold, the body and legs were still quite warm. He surmised that the time of death was not more than thirty minutes prior.

News of the murder rapidly spread through the neighborhood. One spectator of interest was Patrick Mulshaw, a night watchman from the nearby sewer works. He stated that at approximately four-forty, a passerby had remarked to him, "Watchman, old man. I believe somebody is murdered down the street," and Mulshaw immediately went to Buck's Row. Later attempts by the police to locate this mysterious informant were unsuccessful.

The gathering crowd made Doctor Llewellyn uncomfortable. With the arrival of the police ambulance—a lofty title for a simple wooden handcart—he ordered the body removed to the morgue, where a proper examination could be made without boisterous comments from onlookers.

Only after the corpse arrived at the morgue, and after examination by Inspector Spratling, was it discovered that the victim had been disemboweled. I credit the covering of the abdomen by the two modest carters and Doctor Llewellyn's desire to remove the body quickly from a growing crowd for this lapse. During the inquest, however, the coroner was unsympathetic regarding the delay in the discovery of the abdominal wounds, and cited it as evidence of the general incompetence of both Doctor Llewellyn and Inspector Spratling.

Miss Harkness and I arrived at the location of the murder at around eight o'clock, by which time the sun had fully set, and it was not difficult to imagine movement in the shadows. Looking about, I was struck by the nerve of the killer to perform such a vicious attack in an area so heavily populated. The fatal injury must have been inflicted with such savagery and accuracy that it immediately rendered his victim incapable of sound or resistance. I stared long at the battered cobblestones so recently covered in a woman's blood.

We were about to go to the second spot when our evening took an unexpected turn, and I saw another side of my well-educated and published companion. A large man suddenly appeared out of the shadows I had found so threatening just moments before. I smelled him at the same instant, reeking of gin and of body and clothes that had not seen hot water for at least a fortnight. He held a straight razor in his right, slightly shaking hand, his intent obvious even before he spoke. His pale face was distorted by a leer made even more disturbing by his gray complexion in the darkness.

"Good evenin', gents! Here to smell a little blood and get some shivers, are we? How about you both hand me yer wallets, and you'll be havin' a grand story to tell your mates when you get home. If not, things may go ill for you, and you'll be tellin' no tales at all!"

I started to step forward to place myself between this scoundrel and Miss Harkness, when she moved past me in a blur. She pressed a small handgun up against his neck so quickly that to him it must have appeared by magic.

"Allow me to introduce you, sir, to my good American friend, Mr. Derringer. He only knows two words, but at this distance one should prove enough. I suggest you leave now before he speaks his mind. Oh, and you can drop that razor, which you apparently rarely use, as a token of your goodwill."

Our erstwhile assailant dropped his blade to the pavement with a stricken look on his face, mumbling some vague apology. Miss Harkness stepped back and watched him until he disappeared once more into the shadows. After he was gone, she bent over to retrieve his weapon, folded it with care, and placed it in her pocket before turning to me.

"Well, Doctor Doyle," she said, "You have now had a proper East End welcome. I suggest we adjourn for the evening, as I believe you've had a full day."

I asked to see the weapon she had used to thwart our robbery. I had little personal experience with firearms, and I was fascinated by this diminutive version.

Miss Harkness explained it was a .41-caliber, double-barreled pistol, commonly known as a "muff gun," as it could be easily concealed within a lady's fur hand warmer. When questioned on her possessing such a small, yet lethal, weapon, she merely shrugged and said it was prudent when wandering the East End at night to "take precautions."

(Writers are the most shameless of thieves. I was so entranced by the expression "take precautions" associated with carrying a firearm, that in later years I made it the code phrase Holmes would use in telegrams to Watson, directing him to bring his service revolver.)

Our traditional roles of man as protector and woman as the protected were reversed for the remainder of the evening (though thinking back, they had been all along), as Miss Harkness led me to the nearest place a cab was available. Perhaps I should have been ashamed at being rescued by a woman, but at that moment my only emotion was gratitude. I comforted myself with one thought as we made our way back to Whitechapel Road: Miss Harkness was definitely not boring. Once I was safely aboard, she bowed slightly, maintaining her masculine facade, and slipped back into the dark, noisome warren of the East End as though she had never been.

CHAPTER FIVE
REINFORCEMENTS

Sunday, September 23,
to Monday, September 24

As I traveled out of the East End, I pondered its endless labyrinth of darkened streets and courtyards. I shook my head as I contemplated the task of locating a killer who could flourish in such a vile and complex environment.

When I arrived at the club, I procured a chair beside the fire and a brandy as soon as possible. I then buried myself in the welcome embrace of my bed, and promptly fell into a deep slumber.

I awoke later than normal the next day and decided to have a quiet morning before meeting Professor Bell at three o'clock. Perhaps I was a bit shaken after the previous night's adventures, but I told myself I had gone as far as I could without his perceptive assistance. One can easily manufacture a host of reasons for whatever course of action one chooses, so permit me the more honorable explanation this time.

Perhaps now is the proper point in my narrative to explain why I had gone to such lengths to secure the aid of my old professor. Professor Joseph Bell, Fellow of the Royal College of Surgeons and Surgeon in Attendance whenever Her Majesty visited Scotland, had been a lecturer in surgery at my medical school when first we met in 1877.

He was a marvel at physical examination and diagnosis! I shall never forget his famous quote: "the basis of all successful medical diagnosis [lies in] the precise and intelligent recognition and appreciation of minor differences." He was famous among the medical community for his ability to correctly diagnose a patient by merely observing them as they entered the examination room, while also identifying their trade or profession as well as their recent travel history. I knew that if I were to be of any use as a consulting detective, I would need his astute powers of observation to see what others had overlooked.

Although it had been over five years since I had last seen him, I had no doubt that I would recognize him immediately. Thus, when I saw a slender gentleman of average height with a high forehead, silver hair, and an aquiline nose (I have elsewhere described him as having an "eagle" face), I was certain it was him. Professor Bell was an avid tennis player, and he moved with the grace and surety of an athlete. He was an imposing man, not because of his size, which was modest, but due to his quiet and thoughtful demeanor. One immediately sensed that his words were carefully considered and well-intended.

He noted my quick approach and extended his hand as the gentleman he was, for now I was no longer his student, but a colleague.

"So, Doyle," he began, "what manner of mischief have ye been up to?" using a slightly teasing tone of voice I had not heard before.

"Professor," I replied, "it's best we adjourn to our lodgings before we discuss the matter, for this topic is not for idle ears."

"Well, you've got my interest," he answered. "I'll stay the night at least. I'll promise no more till I know what this is about."

Once we arrived at the Marlborough, I had his scant baggage moved to his chamber, and we sat by the fire, each with a whiskey and soda in hand. I told him of my strange contract with Gladstone, what I had accomplished so far, and my shameful rescue by the "undressed" Miss Harkness the evening before. Upon hearing the last, the corner of my companion's mouth twitched a bit, hinting at a smile at my expense.

"The woman seems most formidable indeed, Doyle, to pluck you out of that situation unscratched, and with a straight razor as a trophy! Or did she keep it as her rightful spoils of war?"

"She claimed it as her due, and she is right welcome to it," I answered, earning a nod from my colleague.

"Then we've naught to fear, Doyle. Between my cane," he raised his silver-headed ebony walking stick, "your vigor, and Miss Harkness's armory, I feel we shall be well equipped for whatever danger awaits us."

"Then you'll agree to work with me on this?" I asked, unsure which reply I preferred.

"Indeed I shall," he responded. "My father was a forensic surgeon. I would be proud to follow in his path, at least in this instance, to help bring this monster to justice. As long as I feel useful, and more pressing obligations do not interfere, I'm your man. Her Royal Highness travels to Balmoral Castle in a fortnight, and I shall be required to keep myself near to hand during her stay there, but I shall be as available as possible otherwise."

I believed that gave us ample time to discover whether we could be helpful to the investigation, as well as give the police the opportunity to catch the killer, be it with our assistance or not, so we shook hands upon it. I should have been disappointed, as I now had no honorable means to escape my agreement with Wilkins; yet to my surprise, I was relieved. There was nothing more to be said: the hunt was on. Later, however, I had reason to question who was the hunter and who the hunted.

It was approaching five o'clock and would be dark within the next two hours, but Bell was all for a meeting with Inspector Abberline as soon as possible. As Wilkins had said he was only to be found either early or late in his office, this seemed as good a time as any to introduce ourselves. I was uncertain how our "assistance" might be received, but I decided that if we were denied cooperation with the Metropolitan Police it was best to know now and proceed accordingly.

Soon we were traveling toward the heart of the Ripper's hunting grounds, to meet with the huntsman leading his pursuit.

CHAPTER SIX
AN UNEASY ALLIANCE

Monday, September 24, cont.

Though not luxurious compared to the West End, the neighborhood surrounding the Division H police station in Spitalfields had a more genteel poverty than Whitechapel, sporting a few hotels and non-alcohol-related businesses. The police station was well lit and maintained, and upon asking the desk sergeant where we might find Inspector Abberline, he nodded to a passageway behind him to his right.

"Third door on your left down the hallway. T'was his before he went to Scotland Yard and his upon return." I thanked him, and we proceeded as directed.

The door was open. A heavy-set balding gentleman of middle age, dressed in well-worn brown tweeds and sporting impressive sidewhiskers, was deep into a document when I knocked on the door frame. He looked up when I asked "Inspector Abberline?" and this badger-like figure sighed wearily.

"Who are *you* and what do you want?" he asked.

"Sir," I replied, trying to be as inoffensive as possible, "I am Doctor Conan Doyle. My companion is Professor Joseph Bell. We were directed to seek you out by our employer. We are here regarding the Leather Apron murders."

My introduction seemed to inspire resignation rather than enthusiasm, judging by his weary reply, "I don't give out interviews. There are plenty at Whitehall and Scotland Yard all too happy to see their name mentioned kindly in the press, but I have work to do, and unless you have something to tell me to help find this madman, I'd rather not be bothered."

I extended the letter from Gladstone and replied, "Hopefully, sir, we may be able to do that very thing. If you could take a moment to read this letter of introduction, I think our position will become clear."

Abberline accepted the letter with reluctance and, after reading it, showed no more interest than before. "This gentleman has no authority in this matter, and I have no intention of allowing voyeurs to hinder this inquiry." A light then seemed to dawn upon his face. "Bell, did you say? Any relation to the forensic surgeon in Edinburgh?"

My colleague inclined his head. "My father," he replied.

"Are you a forensic surgeon as well?" asked the inspector.

"I have done official inquiries from time to time, though it is not the focus of my practice," Bell responded.

Abberline sat back in his chair and surveyed Bell with new respect.

At that moment, I felt inconsequential. I would soon become accustomed to the sensation.

Abberline shook his head with a grimace. "The coroner has been extremely unhelpful in the investigation thus far, preferring to mock our efforts to the delight of the press. To be honest, some unbiased or at least non-hostile professional advice would prove useful." Then, arching an eyebrow, "Perhaps we may come to an arrangement, gentlemen, so pay attention. I will allow you to consult on this investigation if you agree to the following stipulations, so don't answer me until I've had my say.

"First: you," (here he swept his arm to indicate the two of us), "are under no circumstances to speak with any newspapermen. If any do approach you, deny that you are present in any official capacity; you are an extra set of eyes, not another voice."

Wagging his finger and warming to the topic, he continued. "Second: if I tell you to come, come; if I tell you to go, go! I'd rather not be explaining your presence to my superiors. Whatever your expertise, there are many of the high and mighty who look unfavorably upon Mr. Gladstone and his views. The last thing I need is for politics to muck this up worse than it already is.

"Third," he said, with a humorless smile, "lacking any better advice, do as I say! You will be allowed to observe and comment entirely upon my good graces. Currently I am not feeling very graceful, so do not try my patience. Are we understood?"

Though not the most elegant invitation I have ever received, I sympathized with this hard-working public servant, and the professor and I agreed to his terms without hesitation.

"Perhaps we might begin with the current state of the investigation," I ventured, trying to regain some control over the conversation.

At this, Abberline sighed and pulled out a well-worn short briar pipe, inspecting it carefully before continuing. "Ah, if there were only one. Let me educate you two gentlemen on the patchwork quilt that constitutes the law enforcement community here.

"There are two police agencies within the great city of London. Currently you are in Spitalfields police station, manned by the Metropolitan Police headed by police commissioner Sir Charles Warren. He has taken much abuse regarding these murders, and he's keen to see this matter resolved as soon as possible."

"I was told you are assigned to Section D," I prompted. "What is that, exactly?"

"Section D is our Criminal Investigation Department, commonly known as Scotland Yard," he answered as he filled his pipe.

Inspector Abberline smiled with well-deserved pride as he told us he had been assigned to Section D after many successful years in Spitalfields, but he'd scarcely occupied his new office when fatal assaults on prostitutes began in April. Given his familiarity with the East End and contacts among the criminal underworld, he was sent temporarily back to Spitalfields to lead the investigation on the ground. Currently he had no other duties save the Leather Apron murders.

He swiveled in his chair and pointed to a large map on the wall behind him, then explained that the East End was made up of two divisions: Division H, headquartered in Spitalfields, and Division J in Whitechapel. Each division had its own inspectors doing their own investigations; Inspector Abberline's role was to orchestrate this vast enterprise. Commissioner Warren had appointed Chief Inspector Swanson as the senior officer in charge of all aspects of the investigation, however, so Abberline sent his summaries to him, "in his very comfortable office in Whitehall, where he is bravely 'leading' our efforts," he explained, in a slightly mocking tone.

"You stated that there are two police agencies in London," I prodded. "What then, is the second one?"

"Oh yes, that would be the City of London Police," the inspector snorted, while lighting his pipe. "Their jurisdiction is, as you would expect, the heart of the city around the financial Square Mile. Frankly, we in the Metropolitan Police do not see them as 'real' police officers, but rather as ornaments for the mighty, there to comfort the comfortable as it were. Given the inhabitants of their district, they do a fair amount of investigation of financial crime, requiring green eye shades more than a cudgel. Bookkeepers with badges, if you ask me."

As the smoke of his tobacco filled the office, Inspector Abberline complained of the many amateur detectives now wandering the East End, hoping to catch the killer. A fortnight past the director of the Bank of England had been apprehended dressed as an ordinary laborer after streetwalkers reported him as a suspicious character.

"Last night we detained a journalist dressed as a woman," he smirked. "He claimed he was in women's clothing hoping to encounter the murderer! I suspect the interview would have been a brief and one-sided affair. These blasted newspapermen are a sharp thorn in our side, reporting every rumor as though it were fact, as well as everything the police are doing. Our villain is informed daily on the status of our hunt, and he must take great comfort in that intelligence."

He looked at us with eyes full of weariness and frustration. "I tell you straight, gentlemen, he shall strike again. Our enemy is quick, ruthless, and knows what he's about. He's got his blood up and won't stop until we catch him."

"And what of the *nom de guerre* of the murderer, Leather Apron," I asked. "How did he acquire that name?"

The inspector sat back in his chair, watching the smoke trail up to the ceiling before answering. "After the murder of Mary Nichols in late August, we made the rounds of the prostitutes in the area, asking them if they had noticed anyone suspicious. Several mentioned a chap they called Leather Apron, for he was always wearing one. He was, or still is as far as I know, a ruthless extortionist who assaults any who will not pay him a fee.

"Sergeant Thicke, one of our police sergeants, believes he knows the man they spoke of, a poor piece of work named John, or Jack Pizer." Clamping down hard on his pipe stem, he snorted. "As has too often happened in this affair, a local paper, the *Star*, published the fact that we were seeking 'Mister' Pizer. There's been no sign of him since, and Commissioner Warren now forbids us from talking to journalists to prevent other 'interested parties' from learning of our plans."

"I have heard some believe a Jew must be responsible," I prompted. "Why so?"

"Ah, that bit of foolishness." He winced. "The article in the *Star* went on at some length to describe Pizer as appearing Hebrew. That has greatly inflamed our Gentile inhabitants, for many of the Jewish tradesmen wear leather aprons for their work."

He shook his head. "We've taken Jewish tradesmen into custody more than once—not to arrest them but to protect them from angry crowds seeking out the first foreign-looking man they saw wearing a leather apron."

"What is your opinion on the matter, Inspector?" Bell asked. "Surely you do not take these accusations at face value?"

Abberline stated with conviction, "As to a Jew being the killer, ask any police constable, and he'll tell you this is very unlikely. The Jewish immigrants we have here came mostly with their families, know a trade, and were trying to escape hard times back home. On the whole, they are more law-abiding than the poor Irish and English residents, and all their rules regarding blood and corpses make me very doubtful a Jew could perform murders as vicious and bloody as these. I would wager a month's pay we'll not find a Son of Abraham as our monster.

"Luckily I'm not alone in this opinion. A group of local businessmen has formed the Mile End Vigilance Committee. The president, a local builder named George Lusk, has been petitioning the Home Office to offer a reward. So far, the Home Secretary has refused, saying, quite rightly," (he emphasized with the stem of his pipe), "that rewards only bring out folks with more avarice than information."

Then, fixing us with an intent stare, "I fear if he strikes again with no suspect in custody, we might see riots such as have been all too frequent on the Continent recently. The East End is a tinderbox, gentlemen. It matters little which match sets it ablaze; the result would be terrible beyond anything I have ever witnessed. I labor day and night with that vision in mind. If there is anything you can do to avert such a tragedy, give it your best! I would consult an oracle at this moment, if I thought she could help."

I was shaken by the image of the East End erupting into flames set by angry mobs, and realized that, as important as it was to stop this madman from taking more lives, the danger extended far beyond the few prostitutes he could personally murder. His shadow loomed over an entire community.

The evening was now fully upon us, and as Professor Bell was tired from his journey to London we sought to leave. Inspector Abberline dashed out a brief note stating we were acting as consultants in the investigation and granting us access to any evidence that came into police custody. Before leaving, we arranged to return the following day to review photographs of the two most recent victims.

During our return to the club, I mentioned to Bell that we could visit the site of the third murder the following day in the company of Miss Harkness, while en route to Spitalfields. This would place us at the scene in the safer hours of daylight, though I did not mention the latter fact to Bell. He merely nodded in agreement, his weariness evident.

"It appears you've signed us up for quite an adventure," is all he had to say.

Despite his outward calm, however, I could tell by the wrinkles on his forehead that he was worried by the enormity of the task before us.

CHAPTER SEVEN
A COOL RECEPTION

Tuesday, September 25

As the meals at the club were ample and well-prepared, it wasn't until half-past nine in the morning when we arrived at Miss Harkness's tenement. Bell was withdrawn though not unfriendly, and I could tell by the glint in his eyes and the set to his jaw that he was as fixed upon the scent as a bloodhound. His presence and calm determination had done much already to steady my nerves and to give me a sense of purpose in our endeavor.

The monosyllabic Miss Jones greeted us at the door, and when we asked about Miss Harkness, she removed the blood-tinged rag from her mouth and remarked curtly, "Out. Back soon."

Professor Bell asked if he might examine her mouth, and after he explained he was a surgeon she agreed. After peering into her mouth for perhaps thirty seconds, he told her gravely her case was a serious one that required excision of the necrotic bone.

She nodded, clearly aware that, untreated, her case would prove fatal.

I was impressed by her stoic acceptance of this fact and wondered if I would be capable of the same were I in her position. We accepted her invitation for tea and were perhaps ten minutes into our chipped cups when Miss Harkness, "dressed" for the moment in a plain, though clean, dress of faded blue cotton, came bursting into the apartment with two loaves of bread and a quarter wheel of cheese.

She was surprised by our presence and did not mince words about it. "What are you doing here?" Then nodding toward Professor Bell, she added, "And who is he? I thought our contract complete. You have enough for your story now, don't you?"

I suddenly realized I hadn't fully shared the reason for my previous visit.

Bell was smiling, amused by her blunt demeanor, while I, caught off guard by her reaction, was surely blushing once more. This woman seemed to have that effect on me.

"I am sorry, Miss Harkness," I began, trying to soothe her irritation at our unexpected visit. "I have not been entirely forthcoming. What did Mr. Wilkins tell you? Then perhaps I can answer your very pertinent questions."

She looked at me, weighing how best to respond, then shrugging her shoulders, replied, "He said one to two gentlemen would visit me, needing to be shown around the East End a bit. That one of you was a writer interested in the Leather Apron murders, and Mr. Wilkins would pay me handsomely for my time. I did, and he has. I do not see we have any further business to conduct."

"And whom did he say he represented?" I inquired with caution, not seeking to anger her further.

"He didn't say, and I didn't ask. The money was good, the work quick and honest, and little travel involved. A woman in my situation finds curiosity an expensive luxury. As I see it, you got what he paid for, so finish your tea and be off with you."

"Please allow me to explain," I pleaded. "I have as I told you, written a crime story. The detective I created, Sherlock Holmes, used a means of observation and deduction to arrive at the identity of the killer. My companion is Professor Bell, a professor of surgery at Edinburgh, and a master of the skills I credit to my detective. Mr. Wilkins has convinced his employer, a man of some influence, to engage us as consultants to the Metropolitan Police. Our purpose is to provide alternative explanations to their evidence, as scanty as it is, to help them catch the killer.

"We have an appointment this afternoon at Spitalfields to view photographs of the victims, leaving us time to visit another murder scene beforehand. The first murder, that of Martha Tabram, I understand occurred some distance from the police station, so I ask you to take us to the scene of the third, that of Annie Chapman, which I understand is conveniently nearby. After that we shall bid you good day and good fortune. If you require additional payment, I am prepared to pay it, as Mr. Wilkins has assured me he will reimburse any reasonable expenses."

Miss Harkness watched me intently throughout, searching for any evidence of falsehood. Apparently, my sincerity allayed her suspicions, and she nodded twice with conviction. "Very well then. Two pounds for another tour, and I will then escort you to the police station. Should you require my aid in future, my rate will remain two pounds per day. If I could afford it, I'd pay as much to you to help put that monster away, but we have to live in the real world."

I paid her two pounds, noted the expense in my ledger, and, after finishing our tea, we set off.

"Your itinerary is most convenient," Miss Harkness explained, "for the site of 'Dark' Annie Chapman's murder is but a brief walk from Spitalfields Police Station on Commercial Street. We could spend the next hour walking north if you gentlemen prefer, but if your generous Mr. Wilkins's purse allows, I suggest we take a brief stroll to the rail station and hire a growler. One of the reasons I chose this location is that Fenchurch Street Railway Station is one of the few places in the East End where they are reliably available."

I agreed, and we made our way there.

In the modern London of the twentieth century, its citizens do not grasp that during the reign of Queen Victoria we were still a society of horse. The Underground was yet in its infancy; the working class rode horse-drawn trolleys, while people of means had two choices of cabs. The first and most common was the hansom, a nimble two-wheeled carriage drawn by a single horse, with the driver seated above and behind his two passengers. The doors were opened and closed by a lever operated by the driver, and in general, passengers were not released until the fare was paid. The seating was sufficiently intimate that ladies would be scandalized if asked to share a ride with a man other than their husband or close relation.

For groups over two, or when more proper transport was required, a Clarence cab was called for. This four-wheeled conveyance was fully enclosed, seated four in two facing seats, and was drawn by one or two animals. It was slightly more comfortable than a hansom, and therefore more expensive. A Clarence was commonly referred to as a growler due to the noise its wheels made going over cobblestones.

Miss Harkness gave the driver the address of 29 Hanbury Street, at which the driver tightened the grip on his reins. He said nothing for a moment, then replied, "That'll be half a crown then, sir. Not a penny less. That's an evil address to be sure, and I'll not linger no longer than it takes you three to alight."

I sighed and paid (as it was now my habit to do), and after boarding made a quick addition to the expanding list of expenses in my ledger.

To pass the time as well as become better acquainted with her, I asked Miss Harkness how Wilkins had known to contract her as our guide.

"He said he had read *A City Girl*," she answered, "and was so taken with my description of the East End and the working poor, he tracked me down via my publisher. He was, needless to say, surprised to learn that *I* was 'John Law.' After overcoming his initial shock, however, he hired me anyway, saying you'd benefit from having an educated person as a guide.

"He paid me the moment I agreed, saying he'd rather not make a return trip. He's a fastidious little man, isn't he? My understanding was there was only to be the one tour, though we didn't meet any streetwalkers that night as he requested," she smiled, "Due to unforeseen circumstances."

Bell chuckled at her last remark; I gritted my teeth and said nothing.

"If you're willing to pay for my time," she continued, "we can rectify that whenever you'd like."

Soon after, we stopped abruptly and disembarked before a row of faded brick four-story tenement houses. Gesturing toward number twenty-nine, Miss Harkness remarked, "These are designed for eight people per flat but are often occupied by up to twice that number. As the residents work all hours, the doors are usually left open, so the streetwalkers often pass through to the backyards to ply their trade; on rainy nights, they use the stairwells. Follow me please."

Miss Harkness took on the manner of a docent leading visitors into an art gallery. I was learning that, with experience, even the most horrible events could be discussed as calmly as cricket scores. She had evidently gained such experience in the East End and was as matter-of-fact as any of my professors at the dissecting table.

The tale she related gave us needed insight into our foe, and reinforced the challenge we had agreed to.

CHAPTER EIGHT
THE THESPIAN

Tuesday, September 25, cont.

"**A**s I am a woman who often goes out alone at night, you can understand my personal interest in these murders," she began. "I follow the reports closely in the newspapers, and as a journalist myself, I take every opportunity to speak with my colleagues following the case."

She indicated the opening to number twenty-nine. "Let us begin, then . . . On the night of September seventh, eight days after the previous murder, Annie Chapman was trying to pass the night at Crossingham's Lodging House. The night porter allowed her to sit by the fire in the kitchen when she said she lacked money for a bed and was weak from consumption, having been discharged that day from hospital."

"She would still be quite feeble," said Bell. "The demand for beds is such that patients are rarely fully recovered before required to surrender theirs to another even more gravely ill."

Margaret nodded in vigorous agreement before continuing. "Around midnight, the porter went to the kitchen and found her the worse for drink. He told her if she could find money for gin, yet none for lodging, she had to leave. As she left she told him to save her a bed and she would return soon with payment. He last saw her headed toward Spitalfields Church, tipsy but not inebriated.

"A barman at the nearby Ten Bells recalled a woman answering Annie's description drinking in the bar at five o'clock when a small man in a 'little skull cap' stuck his head through the door and called her outside. That sighting is unverified, but we do know that she arrived here by five-thirty. Follow me."

I hunched my shoulders as one does before going out into a storm. I recalled the events of my last visit to a murder scene with Miss Harkness, but I did my best to appear as though this was nothing more than a casual stroll, and I suppressed a slight shiver.

Bell and I followed as she led us through the front entrance, past the stairwell reeking of cabbage and humanity, and on into the back. A pale young man with blond, dirty hair partly covered by a gray wool flat cap came down the stairs as we passed. He was dressed in well-worn but serviceable trousers, a shirt with a tattered black wool vest, and a cravat. He stared at us for a moment, apparently taken by surprise, then accosted us as we entered the backyard.

"'Old on there!" he cried. "This 'ere's private property! If you wants to stare about, it'll cost you each a copper. For that you can stay as long's you like, and I can tell you all I knows about the murder."

We three exchanged looks. Margaret gave a curt nod, and I counted out three coppers into the enterprising young man's hand.

Satisfied, he swung his arm around, encompassing the area and said: "'Ave a looks about, and when you're ready, I'll begins me recitation."

It appeared he had performed as a guide before, for he took on a professional air once paid.

The back plot consisted of a small courtyard with grass growing between large paving stones and a locked cellar door, to the right as one looked away from the building. The sides and back were bordered by a dark-brown wooden fence five feet high with no gate; the entire space was not much larger than a boxing ring. There were three clotheslines in the left-hand corner running along the back fence for about six feet, currently devoid of laundry.

After we had looked around I indicated we were ready, and he began enthusiastically.

"Laydy 'n' gentl'men, allow me to introduce meself. Me name is John Richardson, son of Amelia Richardson, who lives upstairs. On the day of the murder, I was 'ere a little before five in the mornin' to check on the cellar door, you sees to the right. I was on me way to work, but I check the lock each morning 'cause it'd been broken into some time back. All was well, and as me right boot was pinching, I sits down 'ere." He indicated the steps leading down from the residence. "to trim it with me knife."

Young Master Richardson spread his arms wide, as though to emphasize the seriousness with which he trimmed his boots. I decided he had missed his true calling as a mummer.

"After it fit right, I went to work. 'Bout half past fives, Mr. Cadoche, a carpenter who lives next door, went out to his backyard for a mom'nt. When he turns to go back in he hears a woman's voice say 'No.'

"He weren't sure but thought it was from 'ere." He indicated our location. "He returns three or four minutes later when he hears somethin' falls against the fence 'tween us. He din't look over the paling, but at the inquest said: 'It seemed as though somethin' touched the fence suddenly.' He then sets off for work, and when he reached the Christchurch Spitalfields clock tower along the street, he said it showed five thirty-two." Whereupon he pointed dramatically down the street to the clock tower, which was plain to see from our location.

"About the same time, Mrs. Eliz'beth Long was walkin' along Hanbury Street on 'er way to market." He fixed us with what I am sure was a practiced gaze and pointed in the opposite direction from the clock. "She 'eard the brewery clock chime five thirty just before she passes outside our flat and sees a man 'n' a woman jawin' away. She din't get a good look at his face, but said 'e was 'foreign lookin' with a dark complexion, shabby, yet genteel. Much like meself, I s'ppose," he added with a wink and a grin. "'E looked to be 'bout forty and a bit over five feet, wearin' a dark overcoat and brown deerstalker cap."

"The carpenter's report of the time and Mrs. Long's can't both be correct," I said. "It's not possible the victim was seen outside this building at five thirty, and then slaughtered in the backyard several minutes before five thirty-two."

Our narrator straightened to his full height and placed his hands upon the lapels of his vest. "I'm only reporting what they said," he replied. "Ye'll have to ask 'em yourselves about that if ya can find 'em."

"Don't be surprised by this, Doyle," Bell said. "I'd be suspicious if everyone agreed. Please continue, Mister Richardson."

Our guide gave me a glare, then resumed.

"The woman was facin' 'er way, so Mrs. Long got a be'er look at 'er and later when she sees photographs of 'Dark' Annie said it was 'er. At the inquest she said the couple was talkin' pretty loud and the man said, 'Will you?' in a funny accent, and the woman said, 'Aye.' Sad to say we often see couples 'ere about at odd hours, so she thinks no more 'bout it and gone about 'er business."

He went on to describe with many flourishes how shortly before six o'clock Mr. John Davis, an elderly resident of his building, came downstairs and discovered a woman's body in the backyard. He went running into the street calling for help, and convinced three men to follow him immediately. After passing through the house they saw the mutilated body of Annie Chapman lying upon the ground between the steps and the wooden fence.

Our guide indicated the spot, some six feet from the steps and beside the paling, the innocent-appearing paving stones now well-scrubbed of any residue. He then resumed his narrative. "'Er head was turned toward the 'ouse with her dress pulled up to the waist, showin' 'er red 'n' white striped stockings, and an 'andk'chief tied round the throat."

Her hands and face were covered in blood, and the hands outstretched, giving the impression she'd struggled with her assailant and had fought to protect her throat.

After taking in the scene before them, the three men sprang off to summon a policeman. The first quickly changed his mind, however, and summoned a brandy at a nearby pub.

The second raced to Spitalfields Market, where he found a constable on fixed-point duty, but the constable refused to follow, stating it was against procedure.

The third went directly to Spitalfields Police Station and Inspector

Chandler accompanied him with the nearest constable at hand. By the time they arrived a large crowd had already formed.

The inspector ordered the scene cleared of onlookers, then sent the constable back to the station for reinforcements and Doctor George Phillips, the police surgeon.

Our guide struggled to describe her injuries, when Miss Harkness intervened. "The body was terribly mutilated with early rigor mortis present and the throat deeply severed. The postmortem revealed the uterus had been neatly excised."

Mr. Richardson seemed to take offense at Miss Harkness's unasked-for assistance, glaring at her for a moment, then shrugged and warmed to the next part of his recitation.

"Three brass rings she always wears were missin', but the strangest things is, 'er pockets had been emptied out 'n' everythin' in them, far as we know, was laid at 'er feet in a row."

"Over there." He pointed to the corner opposite the clotheslines. "Were a washed leather apron that belongs to me. I weren't asked 'bout it until it already been in the papers."

"Many took the apron as proof the murderer was a Jew," added Margaret.

Our guide nodded, resigned to her additional comments.

"Only a very robust police presence prevented riots when this discovery was announced," Margaret continued. "The uproar over the apron was so bad, additional police constables from other parts of London were temporarily reassigned here, both to aid in the pursuit of the killer and to prevent large-scale attacks on the Jews."

"Thank you, Miss Harkness and Mr. Richardson," said Bell. "I think we have profited all that we may from this sad place. Doyle and I are off to view the photographs of the two victims. If you would direct us to the entrance of the police station, Miss Harkness, you may go."

Richardson shed his thespian persona, tugged on his cap, and was off in an instant, intent perhaps on investing his three coppers.

Margaret meanwhile looked first at Bell, then to me, and, after a thoughtful pause made an unexpected request. "Doctor Doyle, if you do not mind terribly, I'd like to accompany you to view the photographs. As I mentioned before, I am a single woman living amidst this horror, and any intelligence I can gain from them may help me."

I was taken aback by this unusual request and could not understand how a lady could ask to view such terrible images.

"Professor Bell and I were only granted permission yesterday," I replied. "I do not have the authority to grant you access we have only recently received ourselves."

Miss Harkness fixed me with a look of determination I was learning should not be ignored. "Very well then, I would be *content* to wait outside so we could discuss them afterward while the photographs are still fresh in your mind."

I could find no argument against this, and was reluctant to incur her displeasure, so I nodded in agreement.

Shortly after leaving the scene of the killer's latest atrocity however, we would encounter the second monster Abberline had warned us about; the many-headed beast known as the Mob.

CHAPTER NINE
LEGION

Tuesday, September 25, cont.

We were scarcely one street from the murder site when we heard the frenzied shouting of several angry, male voices. The streets in this residential area were sparsely occupied at midday, so we quickly noted the crowd of young men behind us, headed our way, chasing a middle-aged smallish man clutching a pair of boots. He was being quickly overtaken, and as he drew near I saw the yarmulke on his head and, unfortunately for him, a leather apron. I noted the boots were newly resoled. A cobbler.

"Come here!" Bell commanded, and the frightened man halted in our midst, Bell to the right, I to the left, with Margaret and the cobbler in the middle.

The mob, composed of seven young working men, halted, puzzled by this turn of events.

The leader, the largest among them, as is usually the case, could not have been above nineteen years, his fellows anywhere from sixteen to twenty. Young toughs, eager to prove themselves to their fellows.

"Stand aside!" their red-faced captain commanded. "'Less you wants some of what's coming to 'im! We don't want his kind about, and it looks like he needs a lesson!"

"Turn around," Bell said, ice to his fire, "Or you may be the student. Go about your business."

"Go on, Tommy!" urged one of the mob, one in the back I noticed, as is also usually the case. "Show 'im what for!"

Tommy, with his followers at his back, found himself in a tight spot. Pummeling a single, relatively helpless man was one thing. Confronting three men and a woman was quite another. Though they still had us outnumbered by nearly two to one, the odds had changed.

Mobs are ugly things, even one as small as this, and I have come to appreciate that those who incite them quickly become their prisoner. Tommy could not back away now without losing his authority. He was as trapped as the cobbler in this tragic farce.

I saw the look of determination in his eyes, and stepped forward to meet his advance, resolute to protect my friends with all the strength I possessed.

I had not sparred in four years but my opponent, while young and strong, was untrained. I knew to watch his shoulders and hips to predict his next move, so I easily avoided the energetic but wild "haymaker" aimed in my general direction.

A blow has a very small area where it may be effective; if you step back, it quickly fades in power as your opponent loses his balance. If you step into it, you dilute its force as it is still gaining momentum. I am pleased to say that my return blow to his midsection was perfectly timed and placed. Tommy collapsed on the cobblestones, his face gone from red to purple, as he struggled to find his breath.

The remaining hooligans were not deterred by their leader's quick defeat, but were sufficiently impressed that they began to encircle us. Bell used his cane effectively, applying his backhand to deliver a smart blow to the elbow of his closest adversary, driving him back as he howled in pain.

Two down. Five to go. The odds were looking better by the moment. The remainder of this sorry lot decided the cobbler or the woman among our party were the easier targets. They surrounded us and began, one at a time, to make quick advances only to back away again, attempting to draw Bell or myself out enough so that others could attack our center.

Another came within my reach and attempted a feint with his right fist, then lashed out with a kick. His hips gave him away, however, and I staggered him back with a well-aimed blow to his right ear. I could not subtract him from the total, though he moved further back. He would not be quick to resume the attack.

I do not know how much longer we could have kept at this without one of them getting through our defenses, when the toughs and I jumped at the sharp report of a pistol. Margaret held her derringer aloft, smoke curling from its tiny barrel.

"I have one bullet left. Who wants it?" She said, as though discussing the remains of a meal.

Our adversaries looked at one another, perhaps considering whom they would volunteer, when police whistles sounded from the direction of the Spitalfields police station, three streets away.

Our enemy ceded us the field, gathered up their injured fellows, and ran or staggered as best they could away from the approaching constabulary.

I turned to my comrades and was relieved to see that none of us, including the cobbler still clutching his boots, appeared injured.

While violence was common in the East End, gunfire apparently was not, for a squad of six panting constables quickly arrived, accompanied by an inspector in a loud checked suit. Bell briefly related our encounter and the reason for the gunshot.

The inspector, who I subsequently learned was named Thicke, nodded when Bell mentioned the name "Tommy."

"Aye, I know the lad, and the pack that follows him." Turning to the cobbler, who had yet to speak a word, he asked, "Would you be willing to testify, Mister Rubenstein?"

"Yes, Sergeant, of course. They must learn a better way. I am happy to help if I can."

The inspector tugged his flat cap, then, leaving a bobby to accompany us to the station, went off with the remaining members of his band to begin Tommy and his mates' instruction.

Mister Rubenstein turned to us and, bowing slightly, said, "David Rubenstein. I am in your debt."

I introduced the three of us. "We were on our way to the station in any event," I said. "I am sorry you must be delayed by this incident, and also have to go to the station."

Mister Rubenstein smiled, color returning to his face, and said, "How odd, as I was also on my way to the station. I have a loyal customer there, and I am the only person he entrusts with his boots."

"It's a small world we live in, Mister Rubenstein," Bell said. "So small, in fact, I believe I know whose boots those are."

"How could you possibly know this?" the cobbler asked. "I didn't mention his name."

"Consider. The boots are well-made, calfskin in fact, therefore expensive, but have seen heavy use. Am I correct that this is not the first time they have been resoled?"

"Correct," confirmed the cobbler, more confused than ever.

"Then from what I see of their use and quality I can deduce that these belong to an inspector whose salary allows some small indulgences, yet earns his pay by the energetic execution of his duties. Given their size, I nominate Inspector George Abberline as the demanding owner of this footwear. Am I correct?"

The cobbler's eyes were now as wide as when I first saw him, fleeing a gang of hooligans. "Yes, Professor. You are as apt with your mind as you are with your cane."

Bell nodded, smiling at the cobbler's kind words, and we set off once more toward the station. It was time to return our attention to the single-headed monster . . . Leather Apron.

The constable took us to a back office where we gave our accounts of the assault in the street, then the four of us found ourselves before the stolid desk sergeant of the day before.

He glanced up at us with a resigned sigh, and before we spoke announced, "Ah yes, Drs. Doyle and Bell. Inspector Abberline is expecting you, and you as well, Mister Rubenstein. Go straight back; you know the way. You Miss, please take a seat over there," pointing to some benches by the entrance.

Miss Harkness gave me a long sideways glance, then straightened her shoulders and sat where the sergeant had indicated. She surprised me by pulling some knitting out of her bag, then began to work studiously on an unrecognizable article of clothing.

I thought to myself that after her demonstrated abilities with her derringer, I would have been less surprised if she had produced a Scottish dirk. The woman was unlike anyone I had ever met.

Or ever would.

CHAPTER TEN
FACES OF DEATH

Tuesday, September 25, cont.

Inspector Abberline, enveloped in a dense cloud of tobacco smoke, was in the midst of composing a report for his more comfortable colleagues in Whitehall. He smiled broadly, however, when he saw the cobbler with his repaired boots.

"Mister Rubenstein! I'm right glad to see you intact. I would have felt terrible if you'd gone to grief on account of my boots.

"As for you two," he said, turning to Bell and myself, "We didn't start off on the best foot, but right now I'd make you both honorary constables."

Abberline accepted his footwear with reverence and, with a look of utter bliss, replaced some battered brogans with the calfskin boots the cobbler had guarded with his life. "Thank you, Mister Rubenstein," he said. "Better than new."

The cobbler smiled, obviously pleased at his customer's reaction. "A good walk requires good shoes. I sleep better at night, knowing you're on the street. And oh, I wouldn't make them honorary constables, Inspector. They and their lady companion handle themselves well in a fight. You should put them on the force! Good day, sir." And with that the cobbler bowed slightly and made his way out with his head held high, glowing from the inspector's joy at his craftsmanship.

As I watched Mister Rubenstein depart, I considered that he walked with as much grace as any head of state. It occurred to me that, ultimately, dignity was not a product of social station; it was a gift available to anyone, but one that only we could bestow upon ourselves.

The inspector then turned to the business at hand, and pointed with his pipe to a thick manila envelope on one corner of his desk.

"I have the photographs of the two latest murders here, gentlemen," he said. "Take as long as you like, but nothing leaves this room. If you have any questions, feel free to ask them at any time. Any respite from this clerical duty is most welcome."

I pulled out a stack of well-executed photographs consisting of two bundles, each held together with a paper clasp and a small piece of paper attesting to the date and murder victim's name. As a photography enthusiast myself, I was impressed with the technical expertise of the photographer and the lighting of the bodies. Turning to the top bundle, I read the paper note: M Nichols, Aug 31, 1888.

"I didn't know it was customary in London to take photographs of murder victims," Professor Bell commented. "They should be extremely helpful."

Abberline looked up and gave a grimace that may have been intended as a smile. "We only began this past year, Professor. We have no staff photographer as yet, but pay commercial photographers for the service. It ensures the latest equipment is available to us, but sadly it is also a source for additional images sold to the press."

The body was washed and posed so the injuries were clearly evident. The camera seemed about six feet away, though close-ups of the more severe wounds were from about half that distance.

Bell peered closely and noted, "Look at the throat, Doyle. One forceful incision did this. Often with suicides who slash their wrists, you see multiple incisions of varying depth, what we call 'hesitation marks,' as the person works up their nerve to make the fatal cut. No hesitation here. The initial wound was sufficient such that none other was required."

I was impressed, if that is the right word, with the decisiveness of the throat wound. The larynx and major vessels were clearly exposed by the incision. A cadaver in an anatomic theater could not have had its vital structures more clearly displayed.

"The loss of blood was so immediate, her ability to resist would have been completely neutralized," Bell continued. "The severing of her larynx made her incapable of crying out. This man knew what he was about; when you consider he did this in the midst of a city with people sleeping nearby, his nerve is faultless."

He looked up at Inspector Abberline and mildly inquired, "I note the pictures are all of the body after it was thoroughly washed. It would be instructive to see photographs taken at the site of the murder before the body was moved, as well as images of her clothing. I am familiar with the protocols of the Edinburgh police, and they routinely examine clothing and corpses in the condition they are found before being cleansed."

Abberline flinched at this, and I thought the mention of the Edinburgh police was impolitic given our tenuous status in the investigation.

With a sigh he replied, "Good police protocol, wherever you are, Professor. The body arrived at the morgue before the police surgeon. Two paupers who are paid to tend the bodies washed her corpse and disposed of her clothing before they were examined, in direct violation of the orders by the senior inspector on the scene."

"Yet I see that the second body is also undressed and washed," Bell observed.

Abberline grimaced and said with an edge of irritation in his voice, "That would be Miss Chapman. When her body arrived at the morgue, Inspector Chandler saw that Robert Mann, one of the two who had washed Annie Nichols, was waiting to receive the body. Chandler ordered Mann's removal and left strict instructions the body was to remain undisturbed until both Chandler and Doctor Phillips had examined the corpse and clothing."

Abberline's irritation at Bell's comments made me nervous, fearing Bell's observations might spur the inspector to end our collaboration before it had fully begun, but before I could redirect the conversation, Abberline continued.

"Despite his efforts however, when Chandler later returned he discovered that two nurses acting on instructions of the clerk of the morgue had already washed the remains. If there is another murder, and I have every reason to expect one, I shall have a police constable posted beside the corpse from the moment of discovery until the post-mortem is complete."

Bell nodded with sympathy, implying that he too, had dealt with bureaucracy and all its faults. He resumed his scrutiny of the photographs, saying nothing more until he completed his examination.

Turning to me, he gestured with his free hand toward the close-up image of Chapman's neck injury. "Again, you will note a single deliberate stroke. There is some tearing of the skin along the edges that could imply the knife was not as sharp as it could have been, or that she was turning her head as he made the incision. I suspect the tearing is due to movement, however, for when you note the abdominal incisions," at which point he picked up an adjacent image of the abdomen, "no tearing here. I doubt he would use more than one knife. Also, note that the uterus was neatly excised with no tearing of the adjacent viscera."

I peered closely at the photograph in Bell's hand. "It appears he knew exactly what he was looking for," I said. "and how to reach it. The first victim was disemboweled—any hunter or butcher's apprentice would be capable of that feat—but an exact dissection to a single structure in the brief time available tells me this man has a strong familiarity with human anatomy."

Bell nodded at my insight, and I was encouraged by his agreement. Bell was ever the professor, and I would always be the student, but it appeared I was still a capable one.

"So, gentlemen," Abberline asked, "What can you tell me that I don't already know?"

"The killer has killed before, I am certain," Bell declared. "There are no wild or unnecessary strokes. He kills with rapid precision, then dissects his victim without wasted motion. He hates women, or street-walkers at the very least, as he is willing to risk discovery by taking the additional time required to remove their organs. I would enquire with your colleagues throughout Britain, Inspector, as well as other countries if possible, to discover if they have had cases similar to these murders. He did not acquire these skills suddenly."

Abberline noted Bell's observations into a small black notebook while maintaining a grim expression, not looking the least encouraged by the professor's insights.

"I suspect you are right about him being no novice, Professor, but there are no means I know of to ask around unless I am willing to telegraph or write to every police superintendent in the Commonwealth. I can only hope someone may read of our troubles and, if it reminds them of previous murders, they will contact us."

"I think," Bell said, "we have gleaned all we may from this evidence, Inspector. Unless you have any other issues to discuss with us, we'll depart to rejoin our companion and determine our next step."

At the mention of a "companion," Abberline raised his eyebrows and frowned. "What's this then?" he asked. "I will repeat myself, gentlemen, if any of the information we share with you appears in the press, and I determine you to be the source, I shall terminate our arrangement immediately!"

"Please sir," I responded. "Our companion is a lady who is serving as our guide within the East End. She was the woman Mr. Rubenstein referred to when he spoke of our encounter. I take full responsibility for her discretion."

"Very well," the inspector replied. "You know where I stand. Don't make me regret my decision. Let me know if you develop any additional insights into our killer. I have your address; if anything new develops, I'll send a constable round."

We took our leave, and at the entrance I spied Miss Harkness knitting as though she hadn't a care in the world. I felt a duty to share what we had seen, and what Bell had deduced, but was reluctant to do so there, still feeling the glare of Inspector Abberline.

CHAPTER ELEVEN
I ACQUIRE
A NEW NAME

Tuesday, September 25, cont.

Returning to her cramped tenement was unappealing, so we settled on the Ten Bells, a nearby pub, and where the late Annie Chapman probably had her last drink. Although midday, it was well attended. Fortunately most patrons contented themselves at the rail or nearby tables. I was relieved to find they served something besides gin, so I ordered three ales, and we went to a table in a far corner.

Miss Harkness was bursting with curiosity. We had no sooner received our drinks than she sought to satisfy it.

"What did you see and, more importantly, what did you make of it?" she demanded.

"Before we can share anything, Miss Harkness," I began, "I must have your pledge of complete confidentiality. I do not doubt your character, but you are a journalist, and Inspector Abberline has forbidden us from sharing any details of the investigation with members of the press."

I saw a glint of anger in her eyes and color in her cheeks, the latter oddly pleasing to me. Then she relented, the color passing as quickly as it came.

"You have my word," she said. "I pledge not to divulge anything I learn, but consider myself released once this affair is complete and the killer either captured or the investigation concluded. Will that do?"

I agreed, distracted for the moment, the image of her flushed face fading more slowly than the color itself, and nodded to the professor to proceed.

Bell, in his detached, clinical manner, described the images we'd reviewed. In an anatomical theater surrounded by colleagues, I would have thought nothing of it. Inside a public house in a disreputable part of London with this young woman as our table companion, it struck me as surpassing odd.

Miss Harkness seemed unaffected by the hideous nature of the injuries, but quite indignant at the careless manner by which the bodies had been cleansed of potentially vital clues.

"Shameful," she muttered as she shook her head, while Bell, his eyes glowing as he re-visualized the corpses' injuries, nodded his agreement.

When he had completed his descriptions, she leveled her gaze at him and asked, "And now the most crucial part. The reason you are here, sir. What can you deduce from all this?"

Bell thought for a moment, fumbled for his pipe, and as he absently placed it unlit into his mouth, began to speak slowly and deliberately. "A man. I am sure we are dealing with a man, though I agree with your observation that he is most likely not physically intimidating. Though probably at or below average height, he contains a terrible rage against women that, when released, gives him a momentary strength that belies expectations."

"Why do you say he directs his rage against women?" Margaret asked. "Perhaps he enjoys killing for its own sake, and chooses these women simply because they are the easiest to kill?"

"Note how he left the two women's bodies in humiliating positions, their genitals exposed," Bell responded. "Had he covered them with their skirts, as he could easily have done, I could deduce some shame or remorse at his actions; but no, they were displayed. The third victim, Chapman, had her uterus removed; so, not only was she murdered, but her very Womanhood taken from her."

Miss Harkness shivered at this last revelation, and Bell paused, perhaps thinking this was more than she could bear.

She took a deep breath, however. "Go on," she insisted. "If I weren't prepared for the answer, I wouldn't have asked the question."

"The second woman was disemboweled," Bell continued, his eyes losing focus momentarily as he recounted the images of the slain women. "And I speculate he may have intended to remove her womb as well, but on hearing someone approach, fled before he could complete the act. The third time he was in a more secluded area, and feeling more secure, he took the time to achieve his goal.

"He feels wronged by women and is exacting revenge. Perhaps he has at some point been harmed by a venereal disease or betrayed by a lover. Choosing prostitutes as his victims may simply be because they are the easiest class of women to victimize, or perhaps they are his preferred targets due to the venereal disease scenario. He also has a solid knowledge of female anatomy."

"A doctor, you think?" mused Miss Harkness. "That would explain his anatomic expertise."

"I shudder to think he may be a member of my profession, though it is possible," Bell responded. "But a morgue attendant or casual student of anatomy may also possess such knowledge. One possible explanation for the disembowelment of the second victim is that it was done to verify knowledge acquired from anatomical drawings."

"And what of his being undetected?" she queried. "How could anyone commit such a wanton murder in a crowded city, and yet no one notice?"

The professor took a sip of his ale. "Well, he certainly knows the East End well," the professor said, lowering his tankard.

"His ability to move about without drawing attention speaks of a man who knows where he is going and how to get there. If only I could have seen the injuries firsthand; I might have been able to discern if he were right- or left-handed, as the depth of the incision where he initiated the wound would be deeper than the finish. But the photographs had no scale to demonstrate such differences. If he is right-handed, we should be none the wiser, but if we can deduce that he is left-handed, then we should be well on our way to finding him."

Miss Harkness absorbed these insights as intently as a medical student in a lecture hall (perhaps more so than some of my classmates), and she brightened when Bell mentioned he supported her supposition that the killer did not look intimidating.

When he finished we all took another, slow draught from our ales. "So, what do we do now?" Miss Harkness asked, gently dabbing at her lips.

"We?" I asked, irritated. "I recall you specifying ours was strictly a commercial relationship. Two pounds a day when called. I do not know that *we* have anything more to do together."

She shook her head smiling, expressing her amusement at the foibles of men. "There are few advantages, God knows, to being a woman, but one of them is the right to change her mind. You have taken me into your confidence. You treat me with respect and as someone gifted with intelligence despite my gender, and you are doing important work. The opportunity to collaborate with you would inform me as a writer, as well as give me insight into this deductive reasoning Professor Bell has mastered. I waive all future fees if you allow me to participate. Do we have a deal?"

"Miss Harkness," I replied, flummoxed by her request, "while I do not envision us personally chasing this killer down the dark streets of Whitechapel, we may be going into harm's way. I could not in good conscience allow you to share in that danger."

At this, she laughed long and hard, such that tears formed at the corners of her eyes. The rough-looking patrons at the bar gazed at us curiously for a moment before returning to their gin.

Finally, after regaining her composure, she smiled. "My dear sir, I reside in the East End and walk alone at night through the most dangerous neighborhoods in the British Empire. I assure you, sir, I am constantly in harm's way. I believe I have more than once demonstrated that I am quite capable of protecting myself, as well as my companions if necessary."

I turned to Bell, who smiled and said, "Welcome to our enterprise, Miss Harkness! If we are to be the Three Musketeers, I nominate Doyle as Porthos. I will let you decide if you prefer the persona of Aramis or Athos. Shall we finalize our partnership?"

We raised our tankards and, with perhaps a bit too much bravado, intoned in unison, "All for one and one for all!"

Our words were lightly spoken, but in the end, proved true.

CHAPTER TWELVE
A WELL-DRESSED
YOUNG GENTLEMAN

Tuesday, September 25,
to Wednesday, September 26

After depositing Margaret (whom I was now allowed to address by her given name) outside her tenement, we returned to our lodgings for the remainder of the day. Although I could not point to any tangible progress in the investigation, I believed that things were going well. We had proven ourselves in battle and earned the cooperation of the senior investigator on the ground.

We also had a better understanding of the enemy we were confronting. I believed we had taken the measure of our foe, and had therefore begun to encircle him. A most reassuring thought, but, as time was soon to tell, a false one.

The following morning, when Bell and I met for breakfast, it was apparent our run of fair weather had expired. Autumn was beginning to assert itself with blowing rain and chilly temperatures. I had little desire to go out into the cold, wet air unless I had a clear destination and purpose. "Where to today?" I asked.

"The morgue," Bell replied, "would be worth a visit, as it would inform us as to the quality of the work done there, and thus the information it provides."

I sighed, inspected my oiled canvas coat carefully for defects, and agreed without enthusiasm. "Should we take Margaret along?"

"Aye," replied Bell. "I'd rather not go astray in this weather, so her guidance may save us a soaking. Besides," and here Bell surprised me with a wink, "I find her company most refreshing. She asks hard questions and expects hard answers. She would have made an excellent medical student. Besides, all for one and one for all, eh, Porthos?"

I was having difficulty reconciling the stern professor of surgery with this far more congenial colleague, but my respect for him only grew as I saw his admiration for Margaret. Even now, in the 1920s, you would be hard-pressed to find a surgeon or any professional man willing to consider that a woman might be his equal, despite women having acquired universal suffrage. Some men are products of their time, while others exceed them. I was growing to appreciate that my old professor was one of the latter.

Not wishing to wander to Margaret's tenement only to find her out, I dispatched one of the doorman's couriers to ask her to meet us at Fenchurch Street Station at one o'clock, and the messenger returned with an affirmative.

Having three hours before we needed to depart, I paid the doorman two pounds (noted in my ledger) to procure newspapers from the first of the month so I could read about the inquests of the three victims. He was diligent and seemed not the least bothered by my request. I promised myself to join a club as soon as my finances allowed.

I found an article in the *East London Observer* dated September second concerning the inquest of the victim murdered in late August. It was evident the coroner used every opportunity to disparage the efforts of the police in investigating the murder of Miss Nichols, berating them for not discovering her abdominal injuries at the scene.

I passed the paper over to Bell and, after reading the article, he remarked, "It appears Coroner Baxter is more intent on looking clever than assisting the police in finding her killer. I see now why Abberline was willing to accept our assistance."

I resigned myself to facing the unpleasant weather outside. I pulled on my oiled canvas coat, wrapped a dark-green scarf around my neck, and reluctantly followed the professor out into the rain.

Margaret was not immediately apparent when we reached the station, and, as I peered out, a young man in a coat similar to mine and a dark bowler hat suddenly wrenched the door open and sat down facing us.

"I beg your pardon," I said in a stern tone.

Suddenly Bell began to laugh deeply. I turned to see him wiping tears from his eyes, as he said, "Woe unto those who have eyes yet do not see."

"Good afternoon, Doctor Doyle," said Margaret.

Bell, still smiling, shook his head slightly from side to side, "This won't do, you know, won't do at all."

Margaret gave Bell a look I was certain was to be followed by a fierce argument, but held her tongue when Bell unwound the scarf from my neck and gently placed it on hers.

"We are about to visit an experienced police surgeon," Bell said. "I would not hazard him failing to notice your lack of a prominent larynx, as one would expect in a slender young gentleman of your age. I assume this is in reaction to being excluded from Inspector Abberline's office yesterday?"

Margaret nodded, giving Bell a look of respect and gratitude. "Precisely so, Professor," she answered. "If you will humor me, I'd like to pass myself off as your personal secretary. That ruse will allow me to accompany you without question. Are you agreeable?"

Bell nodded, smiling. "I've always wanted a private secretary. Agreed!"

I gave the driver the address, and in the wet and cool of an autumn afternoon, we three set off for the first time as a team.

As we traveled, Bell asked Margaret why so few streetwalkers inhabited brothels. "As sordid as such a life might be, it would afford the women protection from the elements and make it more difficult for the murderer to visit them unseen. A cry would more likely be heard, and the Madame at the very least would be able to describe the victim's last customer."

Margaret shook her head angrily, "Oh there are brothels about to be sure, but a good deal fewer than before, thanks to Mr. Frederick Charrington." She enunciated each syllable of the gentleman's title and name with heated emphasis. "Mr. Charrington's a wealthy heir to a brewing fortune, and whether through an excess of ill-informed good intentions or sheer embarrassment, he's taken it upon himself to close as many of these establishments as possible. His goal, simply put, is 'Rid the East End of Vice.' Unless or until he endeavors to rid it of poverty, he is on a fool's errand."

"How can a private citizen go about closing brothels?" I asked, surprised to find myself discussing brothels with this woman as calmly as though we were debating the merits of various pubs. My topics of conversation were certainly expanding.

"He uses the Criminal Law Amendment Act of 1885," Margaret explained with some feeling, "which allows any citizen who reports a brothel to the police to receive a reward. Armed with that scrap of paper, he's gone on a crusade to close them all down."

"A man with such a fixation on courtesans merits suspicion," Bell observed. "Forcing these women out of doors makes the killer's hunt easier."

"Whatever his intentions," Margaret said, "many women have been displaced out into the streets or common lodging houses to ply the only trade they know. Leather Apron could not have a better ally than Master Charrington. There may be no blood on his hands, but that's how it usually is with the well to do, isn't it? Those who die of exposure are just as dead as those slit open by this madman. If there is justice in the next world, I expect this pious gentleman to be greatly surprised by what awaits him."

Just then we arrived at the morgue, and Margaret stated flatly, "Well, we're here, and I've had my say."

We alighted from our carriage in silence, Bell and I digesting Margaret's words. I have learned some things are best left unsaid, if for no other reason than that you lack the words.

The morgue was in a modest brick building just off Whitechapel Road, where I was about to see another side of my distinguished colleague, and Margaret was about to acquire a new name.

CHAPTER THIRTEEN
CORPSES . . .

Wednesday, September 26, cont.

We were immediately accosted by the supervising clerk, who ruled his small kingdom behind a raised desk.

"Who might ye be and what do ye want?" asked this minor deity. "You don't look like ye came here to deliver nor pick up no body, and the press ain't allowed lest they be accompanied by an inspector. I knows all the inspectors in the East End, and I don't know a one of you!"

Bell straightened to his full-though-modest height, and the stern professor of surgery suddenly reemerged, "I am Professor Bell, Professor of Surgery at Edinburg University. I am not here to deliver anyone into ye'r care but wish to speak with any of your surgeons who examined one of the Leather Apron victims. I am here as a consultant for the Metropolitan Police, and I assure you that neither my personal secretary," he indicated Margaret, "nor, my colleague, Doctor Doyle, have any relationship with the *prress*. I am willing to wait here should ye care to summon ye'r surgeon or advance if ye will direct me to his office."

Bell's Scottish brogue became more pronounced when he became emotional. I understood it signified at this moment that he was exceedingly irritated with the clerk's attitude. The man before him did not comprehend what the trilled "r's" conveyed, however, and I was not disposed to warn him.

The clerk's scowl showed he was unaccustomed to having his

authority challenged, but this small gnome-like man with a thinning pate and ample side-whiskers was a British public servant, the most immovable of objects, while Bell, I already knew from our acquaintance in Edinburgh, was an unstoppable force.

I watched in fascination as the battle of wills ensued.

"Ye're in luck," the clerk said, his tone still officious. "Doctor Llewellyn is examining a corpse that was brought in this morning. Ye can wait here, and I'll have him brought out when he's done."

Bell wordlessly produced the letter from Inspector Abberline stating we were granted access to all evidence pertaining to the Leather Apron investigation.

After reading the note, the major domo of the charnel house bowed his head ever so slightly to acknowledge his defeat, and with the hint of a sneer, turned to Margaret. "If yer stummach ain't too queasy, lad, ye can all go in and speak with 'im while he finishes up. Hope ye don't mind the smell!"

Margaret nodded, and we proceeded into what Dante may well have envisioned in his Inferno.

Smells can evince powerful reactions. A whiff of an apple tart may bring memories flooding back of your grandmother's kitchen on a rainy day; lavender may take you to a summer sojourn in Provence. For me, the smell of decaying flesh shall always revive the images of the poor and destitute lying about in various stages of their return to the dust from which we all emerged.

Margaret brought my scarf up over her nose, but otherwise marched on and showed no sign of distress. Bell, having done more than a few postmortems himself, was entirely unaffected. As for myself, it had been some years since I had labored, anatomy atlas in hand, within the dissecting theater. I bore it as best I could, but was grateful we had not recently dined.

Doctor Llewellyn was slender, nearly to the point of emaciation, his face revealing its skeletal foundations. The sight of him carefully poring over the remains of the gray body of an elderly woman was suggestive of a corpse examining a corpse. The long coat he wore over his garments may have once been white, but it was now thoroughly tinged with every fluid a human body may contain. He was animated enough in his movements, however, and turned at our approach with a curious look.

He bowed slightly, and said in a soft voice, "Good afternoon, gentlemen, how might I help you?"

Bell introduced himself, and upon hearing the name Bell Doctor Llewellyn quickly made the connection between my colleague and both the professor's distinguished career and that of his father.

"An honor, sir. And who are your companions?"

"Doctor Doyle," I said, "A former student of the Professor's."

Llewellyn then looked at Margaret with raised eyebrows.

"Professor Bell's secretary . . ." I began. At this moment, I realized we had not settled upon an alias for Margaret.

She noticed my hesitation, and in a convincing tenor said, "Pennyworth. Joseph Pennyworth." She started to offer her hand, then after considering where his hands had just been, merely nodded.

"A pleasure, gentlemen. What brings you to this abattoir?" Llewellyn asked while gesturing broadly at the surrounding carnage.

"We are serving as consultants to the Metropolitan Police," Bell answered. "I would like to hear your version of events relating to the Mary Nichols murder. You were the police surgeon summoned in her case, were you not?"

Llewellyn narrowed his eyes, "Am I to be replaced? Has Inspector Abberline lost faith in my competence? If so, you are welcome to assume my duties immediately. I can seek employment elsewhere." Llewellyn's veins became more prominent, illuminating his pale visage. Bell raised his hand in a placating gesture.

"I assure you sir, we have no desire to either supplant you or cast aspersions on your efforts," he insisted. "But sometimes fresh eyes may see what tired eyes do not."

Llewellyn took a deep breath. "Forgive me," he responded, calmer now. "We have all been under tremendous demands to solve this case. And . . . I sometimes do not feel up to the challenge.

"Your fresh eyes are welcome, sir," he added, resuming the friend-lier tone of his greeting. "If you would care to wait for me at the public house across the street, I can meet with you in twenty-five minutes, after I complete my examination and clean up."

I concluded from the perspiration forming on her forehead that Margaret was for this course of action. As was I.

Bell nodded, so we passed back through the entrance where the senior clerk stared us out the door. We quickly located the public house Doctor Llewellyn had mentioned. As tea was not available I gratefully ordered a brandy for myself and Margaret, while Bell contented himself with ale. I wiped some perspiration from my own brow with my hand-kerchief, and finding it now reeked of the morgue, left it on the table.

We were eager to hear what the police surgeon could tell us of the murderer's victims and, thereby, of the killer himself.

CHAPTER FOURTEEN
. . . AND CRICKET

Wednesday, September 26, cont.

"Pennyworth?" I asked Margaret, bemused.

"The phrase, 'in for a penny, in for a pound' suddenly occurred to me," she replied, smiling, enjoying her masquerade, "and that name just came out. I briefly considered using my nom de plume, John Law, but I did not want to chance some well-read inspector making a connection with my works."

The police surgeon was as good as his word, arriving well within his self-allotted time, and, after collecting an ale, he joined us at a back table. He ducked his head as he sat down.

"Carefully notice the gentleman in the checkered coat at the far side of the bar," he said in his soft voice. "He is a journalist for the *Star* and makes it a habit of loitering about in hopes of another Leather Apron victim being brought in before his colleagues get wind of it."

I glanced casually over to the bar, as I was facing it, and noted a short, stout man in a loud checkered suit coat and dark trousers with greasy, long, dark hair. He appeared somewhat tipsy, and was staring into his glass of dark liquid, oblivious to our presence.

"His name is Collier," Llewellyn said, "and he is a rather poor specimen of humanity. I have given strict instructions to the clerk that no strangers are to enter the morgue without authorization, as Collier has in the past gone in to make sketches of the victims of accidents and murders to sell to his paper. His unauthorized artwork has, of course, sold many issues, while causing much distress to the families of the deceased. I warn you not to let him learn of your presence or purpose, lest everyone in the East End who can read will soon know of it and dog your steps wherever you go."

I was beginning to appreciate the degree to which the press was an active participant in the Whitechapel murder investigations. They hired detectives, performed in-depth interviews with neighbors and friends, and did everything conceivable to be the first to report the latest developments with little regard to their veracity.

Although I have over the years contributed various articles and letters to newspapers, I have never been a working journalist, so the ferocity of their competition was new to me. At times it seemed that newspapermen, like streetwalkers, could be found at every street corner, and were no more virtuous (perhaps less so).

It was only some years later, however, during a trip to America, when I came to appreciate that the entire world had been following the tragic murders within this one blighted district of London. I think this must have been the first crime to have ever gotten such global attention, due both to the sensational nature of the murders and the increasing use of the telegraph.

"To save time and reduce our chances of discovery by Mr. Collier," Bell began, "let me start by saying we have been thoroughly briefed by Inspector Abberline about the killings. I have only a couple of questions for you, and then we may go our separate ways."

Llewellyn nodded his agreement, and Bell continued. "What kind of knife do you think the killer used?"

"Certainly over four inches in length, but it wasn't the knife that killed her. All her wounds were postmortem, I believe. Her tongue was swollen and protruding, and her face was gray. It is my opinion that the killer suffocated her, and once she had expired he lay her body down and had at her with his knife. There was ample blood beneath her head certainly, but the severing of the major vessels on both sides of her neck with her legs raised facilitated the free flow of blood onto the ground.

Her wounds elsewhere had no signs of bleeding into the surrounding tissue or on her dress, which explains how her abdominal incision was missed at the scene."

I recalled that during the inquest Coroner Baxter had heaped scorn upon the police and Doctor Llewellyn for initially missing the abdominal wounds. I could understand Llewellyn's desire to explain to a colleague as distinguished as Bell how that happened, and why he had become so defensive when Bell first described our function.

The professor nodded his understanding. "Your colleague Doctor Phillips conducted the postmortem on Miss Tabram, the woman murdered in early August. He concluded two knives were used, most wounds caused by a short-bladed knife, perhaps a clasp knife, but that the deep wound in her left breast was inflicted by a longer-bladed weapon, possibly a bayonet or sword. Did you see anything in the Nichols case to suggest the killer used more than one knife?"

"None," answered Llewellyn confidently. "Although I respect my colleague very much, I find his opinion that a second blade was used inconclusive. Soft tissue is easily distorted by force, and since the breast is mainly adipose tissue, if the murderer had been holding the breast in his right hand while thrusting with his left, an injury track much longer than the actual blade may result."

At the mention of the killer holding the weapon in his left hand, Bell brightened. "Do you believe the entrance wound was on the inside of the breast then?"

"Indeed I do, sir," replied Llewellyn. He took a long draught of his ale, then placed the tankard down with perhaps more force than he intended, given his warnings of the esteemed journalist. "Phillips told me the marks left by the knife guard were noted on the medial surface of the breast, indicating the blade's entry point."

"Excellent!" Bell exclaimed. "Looking for a left-handed killer simplifies our task enormously. But earlier you said Miss Nichols was suffocated. Not strangled? Wouldn't strangling have been easier?"

"I am positive she was asphyxiated, sir," replied Llewellyn, shaking his head. "As you know, manual strangulation usually results in a fracture of the larynx, or at least the trachea. Both structures were pristine. A sober person might easily resist or call for help, but our victim was quite intoxicated, as was evident from the smell of gin about her corpse when I examined it. A man of fixed intent and forceful grip could have easily overpowered her. I am as sure of her cause of death as I am that I am sitting here with you."

"Thank you, Doctor," Bell replied, a faint glow in his eyes I had often seen when presented with a challenging case. "Is there anything else we should know?"

"I can think of nothing now," he answered. "If I do, or if we get another victim, how might I contact you?"

I gave him our address at the Marlborough Club, and Llewellyn was standing to depart when Mr. Collier pulled his head out of the fumes in his glass long enough to recognize the surgeon. He staggered over to our table.

"Good afternoon, Doctor," he said to Llewellyn, his breath and body odor saying far more than his words.

I noticed a sketchpad like those one often sees art students carry about, sticking out of his coat pocket. What little I saw of a female nude demonstrated more skill than I would have credited him, based on his appearance and odor.

"And who might these gentlemen be?" he inquired, at what I assumed was an effort to be charming.

"Colleagues of mine, Mr. Collier," Llewellyn answered coolly. "From Scotland."

"Sorry, I didn't catch their names," Collier said, his bloodshot eyes glinting.

I desired no entanglement with this man whatsoever. Were he to quote us in any way regarding the murders, it would give Abberline grounds to terminate our access. Besides, I found him quite offensive both in manner and hygiene, and wished for fresher air as soon as possible. Still, it would do us no good to ignore him, as that would only heighten his interest, so I gave him the first name that came to mind. "Watson," I answered.

"Holmes," Bell responded, his quick wink and use of the name of my consulting detective revealing he had read my story.

"Pennyworth," Margaret replied, puzzled by our private joke.

"We were discussing the cricket match held last week between the Australian national team and Surrey," I said. I still played regularly myself and could discuss the strengths and weaknesses of all the major teams with ease. "The Aussies acquitted themselves very well, wouldn't you agree?"

I have learned over the years that people either adore or detest cricket. I was gambling, given what I could deduce of Mr. Collier's character, that he was one of the latter. Apparently I judged him correctly, for I saw a look of mild panic appear in his eyes. He mumbled his apologies and returned to the rail and his glass of dark liquid.

Llewellyn gave me a slight bow and departed, while Bell and Margaret lifted their glasses in a mute toast to my subterfuge.

"Well played," Margaret mouthed silently, and we exchanged grins like two errant children who had just poached a pie from a windowsill.

I felt a thrill pass through me to see her gaze at me so, and our eyes lingered a bit longer perhaps than was seemly, and the image of my devoted and pregnant wife, Louise, sprang to mind, and I looked away.

"Come," Bell said, "we should retire before Mr. Collier bestirs himself again. It is getting late, and I have no desire to linger here this damp evening. Let's be off."

We had to walk to Whitechapel Road before finding a cab. While we walked, I returned to Doctor Llewellyn's assertion that the killer asphyxiated his victims before slitting their throats. I asked of no one in particular, "I wonder why that wasn't mentioned at the inquest?"

"There are many possibilities," answered Bell, still smiling, I assumed, at the ease with which I had driven away the malodorous Mr. Collier. "The police may have wished to prevent the killer from learning how thoroughly the corpse had been examined, thus making him careless. Llewellyn may have been overruled by his superiors, who thought that with the wounds to the throat there was no need to speculate further.

"What matters to me is knowing something the killer doesn't know he has revealed; the wound to the left breast was inflicted by the left hand. It was the deepest wound, so it stands to reason the killer would have used his dominant hand. I think our visit was most profitable."

At one point, I thought I saw a man in a checked suit following us, but when I stopped to get a better look behind me he was gone. Collier, perhaps? I said nothing to my companions, though I did quicken my pace, and thus theirs. I was uncertain of what I had just glimpsed, but I was sure of my desire to depart the area promptly.

"What next?" I asked Bell as we sought a growler.

"I should like to spend one night 'walking the beat,' as it were, to complete my orientation to Whitechapel.

"Then," Bell continued, "if there are no new developments, I will return to Edinburgh next Tuesday Never fear! I shall come back quickly should another murder occur. I am very keen to examine one of Leather Apron's victims before the evidence is lost."

We finally hailed a cab, and once inside agreed to meet at a coffeehouse adjacent to Fenchurch Street Station at one o'clock the next day. After dropping Margaret off outside her tenement, Bell and I continued to the club.

"I didn't know you'd read my story," I said to Bell as we rode along, fearful of his opinion yet desiring it fiercely.

"Aye, Doyle," he replied, smiling. "I know naught about Mormons, but the reasoning behind your detective's deductions seemed sound to me. I enjoyed it very much."

His words filled me with pride. I believed my best work lay in historical fiction (and some critics would agree with that), but were I to write only one detective story, it should be a good one.

I felt an intense need to bathe before dinner, and to send my clothes off to be laundered, and I noticed Bell was in a different suit when we dined. We had two more days until Bell would be introduced to Wilkins, and we could present our findings. Hopefully, Wilkins would be satisfied with our report. Then we could both return to our previous lives, and I could set aside my ill-fitting role of consulting detective.

CHAPTER FIFTEEN
HOUSE CALLS

Thursday, September 27

Today we were to meet with Mr. George Lusk, head of the Mile End Vigilance Committee. Mr. Lusk was a local builder chosen by his neighbors to organize the community to aid the police and augment the security of their district. Professor Bell thought it helpful to learn what actions were being taken to thwart the killer should he strike again. We had until one o'clock to loiter about the club, and I took the opportunity to update my knowledge of the official investigation.

A cartoon in *Punch* caught my eye. Labeled "The Nemesis of Neglect," it portrayed a ghostlike figure drifting along a dark alleyway, a naked blade in its right hand, the left extended like a claw, and the word CRIME written upon its forehead. Beneath the apparition was the following inscription:

> There floats a phantom on the slum's foul air,
> Shaping, to eyes which have the gift of seeing
> Into the Spectre of that loathly lair.
> Face it—for vain is fleeing!
> Red-handed, ruthless, furtive, unerect,
> 'Tis murderous Crime—the Nemesis of Neglect!

From what I had recently experienced in the East End, I heartily agreed with the sentiment of the cartoon and accompanying legend. I shook my head sadly, then turned to the cricket scores.

At length the time came for us to be off. I had no scarf to shield Margaret's modest larynx, what with the day being mild, but she greeted us clothed in a workingman's attire and vest. She had wrapped a clean rag about the neck as was commonly worn by those of that class, and completed her wardrobe with a billed wool cap. Bell and I had grown accustomed by now to the vagaries of her dress, or "undress" to use her phrase, and neither of us batted an eye at her masculine ensemble.

"So, Porthos," Margaret teased, "whither today?"

I chose not to bristle at this gentle dig at my circumference. Bell had so named me already, and a woman who wields a derringer as aptly as a knitting needle should not be lightly crossed.

"Mr. Lusk, of the Mile End Vigilance Committee," I answered. "It would be helpful to know what actions the locals are taking, and I recall you mentioning, when we first met, that you would introduce me to one of the streetwalkers, per Mr. Wilkins's instructions."

"Done and done!" replied Margaret cheerfully. "Lusk first. The ladies will still be sleeping off last night's activities."

I told myself I would not blush when the subject of sexual commerce came up, but under Margaret's calm gaze, I felt my ears warming. Again.

"Well, then, let's be off!" I muttered, perhaps more brusquely than I had intended, but sly smiles between Bell and Margaret told me my discomfort was apparent to them both.

Mr. Lusk resided on Alderney Street in Mile End, which borders Whitechapel on the eastern side. Inspector Abberline had sent him a message that we would be paying him a call. His exact phrase, as I recall, was that we were "sanctioned" consultants.

We found Mr. Lusk at home and patiently awaiting us. He had my name and Bell's, but looked quizzically at Margaret, whom we introduced as Mr. Pennyworth, our local guide. That was only half true, of course, but I digress.

Mr. Lusk appeared as one of those hail-fellow-well-met chaps one often finds in the mercantile class, yet the bags under his eyes testified to some restless nights of late. Portly, with broad shoulders, I imagined he had once been an active participant in his construction business, though now with increasing age and responsibility, he left the actual labor to others.

He was subdued for the most part as he led us into his parlor, though with occasional bursts of what I assumed was his usual optimism breaking through, speaking forcefully one moment and hesitantly the next. While I was certain we had nothing in common, I respected him due to his common decency and desire to aid his neighbors.

"Good day, gentlemen!" he said. "The inspector sent word of your coming. I've no idea how I can help, but ask me anything—George Lusk is an open book. Me and me neighbors are anxious to put this terrible matter to rest, and if I can help you, I'll do what I can."

Bell had grown accustomed to taking the lead in these interviews, so I was content to sip the excellent tea Mr. Lusk provided and let the professor get on with it. By allowing him to carry the conversation, I was free to sit back and observe, an aid to both a consulting detective and a writer.

"Thank you for seeing us, Mr. Lusk," Bell began. "How did your Vigilance Committee come into being, and what steps are you taking to protect your neighborhood?"

"How is easy enough," said Lusk. "I've always been a loud speaker and organizer. More than once a Jewish man has been taken into custody by the police, not because they are suspected of being the murderer, but to protect them from hooligans who'll attack any man who appears Semitic. I've known many of these businessmen since they first arrived, and I'm happy to represent them." He made a fist as he spoke of the "hooligans," and though somewhat advanced in years, I had no doubt of his willingness to raise that fist against them.

"As for what we are doing to prevent further killings, we are petitioning the Home Office and even Her Majesty to offer a reward for any information that could lead to Leather Apron's arrest. The police have resisted, saying it would only encourage riffraff and soothsayers to lay false trails they would be obliged to follow, yet we feel anything that increases the odds of his capture is worth trying."

Mr. Lusk's tone changed when he referred to Her Majesty. His softer, reverential tone revealed his simple faith in the goodness of our monarch and her love for her people. I have found deceitful people suspect duplicity in others if only to justify their own, while decent folk expect the same from their fellow man. It was evident to me to which point of view Mr. Lusk subscribed.

"Currently," he continued, "we're raising our own reward fund, and we've taken to posting watchmen in pairs to patrol the neighborhood. They are not to confront any suspicious characters they encounter, mind you, but to summon a constable should they feel the need. They walk their beats from eleven o'clock until two; when the streets are believed to be most dangerous. It's been three weeks since the last murder, so we're hopeful our measures are having an effect."

"Have these killings impacted your trade?" Bell asked.

"No sir, but I have friends and family who inhabit this neighborhood. I would be a poor Christian indeed if I did nothing to stop these murders if there were aught I could do."

At this he clenched his jaw and looked every inch the "British Bulldog" I am sure he felt himself to be.

Lusk was about to say something more when there was a knock at his door. He went to see who it was and returned puzzled, with a young police constable who was red-faced from exertion and out of breath.

"Doctor Doyle and Professor Bell?" the constable wheezed. When we acknowledged our identities, he took a deep breath before gasping out, "Inspector Abberline sent me round! He hoped you might be here as you weren't at your club and he gave you this address. He asks that you come with me. Immediately!"

Given the urgency of his voice there was nothing for it but to wish Mr. Lusk a good day. So off we went with the constable to the now familiar Spitalfields station, where I heard the name Jack the Ripper for the first time.

CHAPTER SIXTEEN
DEAR BOSS

Thursday, September 27, cont.

We found the inspector in his office with a worried expression, studying a document on his desk. When we entered, he stood and gestured to Bell to take his seat, whereupon he handed the professor the object of his intense scrutiny.

Bell sat down, and Margaret and I crowded close on either side and leaned over his shoulders so we could view what turned out to be a letter dated September twenty-fifth addressed to the Central News Agency.

"This letter was received two days ago," Abberline explained. "After some discussion, they forwarded it to us. I want your opinion as to whether it is genuine, and if it contains any useful information."

The paper was of inferior quality, and the ink was red, making it difficult to read, but the contents were chilling.

Dear Boss

I keep on hearing the police have caught me. but they wont fix me just yet. I have laughed when they look so clever and talk about being on the right track. That joke about Leather Apron gave me real fits. I am down on whores and I shant quit ripping them till I do get buckled. Grand work the last job was. I gave the lady no time to squeal. How can they catch me now. I love my work and want to start again. You will soon hear of me with my funny little games. I saved some of the proper red stuff in a ginger beer bottle over the last job to write with but it went thick like glue and I can't use it. Red ink is fit enough I hope ha. ha.

The next job I do I shall clip the ladys ears off and send to the police officers just for jolly wouldn't you. Keep this letter back til I do a bit more work, then give it out straight. My knife's so nice and sharp I want to get to work right away if I get a chance. Good Luck.

Yours truly

Jack the Ripper

Don't mind me giving the trade name

Wasn't good enough to post this before I got all that red ink off my hands curse it No Luck yet.

They say I'm a doctor now. *ha ha*

Bell sat silent for several moments as he studied the letter, the only noticeable sound in the room Abberline's pacing.

Finally the inspector could bear it no longer. "Well, Professor, what do you make of this?" he asked. "Do you think it genuine or no?"

Bell answered slowly, "The writer is well educated, though trying to appear less so. The words are correctly spelled and no words are crossed out, so it was all written in one go without any wavering in the lines, demonstrating confidence in his writing ability. Some contractions lack the apostrophe but others are correctly written, hence my supposition he is attempting to hide his knowledge of proper grammar. The phrase 'I gave the lady no time to squeal' is interesting. Perhaps he is alluding to the throat being slashed, which is assumed by most to be the cause of death, or perhaps it is a reference to her suffocation, which few other than the killer would know.

"I believe the writer was either born in England or came here at an early age, as his use of English is colloquial, for example, his phrase 'til I do get buckled' and 'just for jolly.' Therefore I can safely exclude a recent immigrant or anyone who arrived in England as an adult. I would say this was written by a man who is either British or well acquainted with British culture, with an above-grammar-school education."

Abberline took a deep breath before asking, "Is this from the killer, sir? Does this help us in any way?"

"I can't say with certainty if this is from our murderer," Bell answered with candor, "but I can say it is consistent with what we know about him already. He is alluding to further murders soon, and unless we are extremely fortunate, we can only wait and see if the next victim has her ears removed."

Abberline snorted at this. "A proper method that is!" he exclaimed. "I shall be sure to include that in my next report to my superiors: 'We should wait patiently for the next murder to see what we learn!' I do not believe that would be well received. Well, the intelligence the writer has some formal education lets us rule out most of the poor men who live in the East End, as well as the more recent immigrants. My official report then shall be I doubt its authenticity, but I shall privately act as though it is genuine."

Bell spread his hands. "How may we help?" he asked.

"I think it time for me to pull some night duty," Abberline said, with a degree of resignation. "For the next few nights I'll sleep here in my office. Should there be another murder, I want to arrive at the scene before it has been all trampled over. You two gentlemen are welcome to join me, but you," here he indicated Margaret, "in my excitement I failed to ask who you might be. How is it that you are accompanying my 'consultants,' eh?"

"Pennyworth, sir," replied Margaret in her boyish tenor, respectfully tugging at her cap. "I have been contracted by Doctor Doyle as his guide in the East End. You might say I am a consultant to your consultants. I apologize for not introducing myself earlier, but you and these gentlemen were so excited I dared not interrupt."

Margaret's meek reply did little to allay Abberline's suspicions as he continued to view her with narrowed eyes.

"I haven't seen you about before," he said. "You're obviously well educated, and you must know the East End well, or you could not serve as a guide. How do I know you're not the killer? You certainly seem to fit the professor's description of the man who wrote this letter."

"I can vouch for him," I said, just catching myself from saying "her" at the last possible second, so there was a slight catch in my voice when the word "him" came out.

Abberline turned his gaze upon me. "And how can you do that?" the inspector inquired, eyeing me now with those same narrowed eyes.

"He—" (again a near fumble) "was referred to us by our employer. We would be quite lost within this maze without him." I could feel my palms moisten with Abberline's gaze, and I hoped despite my inner unease, that I returned his look with a convincing innocence.

"Well, *Mister* Pennyworth," Abberline remarked, "I will let it pass for now. No word of this letter is to escape your lips or we shall have further inquiries as to your affairs. Do I make myself clear?"

"Indeed, sir," Margaret answered. "I shall be as inscrutable as the Sphinx."

The inspector nodded, somewhat puzzled by this reply, but let it pass, mollified for the moment.

"So, gentlemen, care to spend a night or two as guests of the Metropolitan Police? I could arrange a pair of cots in our conference room down the hall. I promise not to disturb you unless a report I feel merits my attention calls me out. The holding cells are on the other side of the building, so our regular guests should not disturb you. Are you up for it?"

"And what of our companion?" I asked. "Does your invitation include him as well?"

"This is no walking holiday," replied the inspector. "You will be accompanied by myself or a police constable at all times. You'll have no need for your guide, and the fewer 'consultants' I have mucking about, the fewer I have to manage. No gents, I am sorry, but he's not welcome."

Margaret nodded her acceptance without expression. I awaited Bell's reply.

"Very well, Inspector. In for a penny," he added with a quick wink to Margaret. "Expect us at ten this evening. We have some errands to run and a change of clothes to procure, so unless there is something else, we'll be off."

Abberline nodded, "Until ten, then."

Once outside, Margaret fumed at her exclusion, "I am quite disappointed, Doctor Doyle," she complained, turning her frustration upon me, "that you did not support me before Inspector Abberline. You and the Professor shall go off to examine the murderer's next atrocity while I, the helpless maiden, await your attention and rescue. I have spent most of my life rejecting the role men would choose for me, and I do not willingly accept it now. I have stood mutely loyal throughout our investigation, yet now, at the first sign of reluctance to include me, you yield immediately. I deserve better of you, sir. I deserve more."

Bell came to my rescue. "Miss Harkness," he began with his calm and reasoned voice, "Doyle and I, despite the rescue of the cobbler and his boots, are on thin ice with the inspector. I do not in the least discount your contribution, and I know you are capable of far more than society has allowed. I respect your opinion and assistance. Please trust me when I say I shall seek to include you as much as is within my power to grant or to negotiate throughout this affair, for however long as I am involved. I cannot do better than that, and it would be disrespectful of my integrity and your intelligence to promise more."

Margaret sighed. "Well said, sir. I withdraw my complaint, if not the feeling behind it."

It was now approaching five in the evening. We had five hours to return to our lodgings, sup, and return to pass the night at the Spitalfields police station.

"Well," said Margaret, "I suppose we have time to visit one of the streetwalkers I know, though most, when asked their profession, will answer 'laundress.' Mr. Wilkins was rather insistent you do so."

"Are you sure we have time?" I asked, my reluctance no doubt obvious.

"Just," replied Margaret, unswayed by my lack of enthusiasm. "Luckily, she resides in a rented room off Miller's Court nearby, on the other side of Spitalfields Market. We can be there within ten minutes' brisk walk. Let's be off!"

CHAPTER SEVENTEEN
THE LAUNDRESS

Thursday, September 27, cont.

"**W**ho is this person?" I asked, uneasy at the prospect of going to a place of sexual commerce.

"Her name is Mary," Margaret replied, as Bell and I labored to meet her hurried stride. "We became acquainted during my time with the Salvation Army. As she is one of the few tarts with a fixed address, I thought she was the easiest to present to you. I told her we might come by since we were assisting the police in the Leather Apron murders, so she's expecting us."

Margaret suddenly stopped and turned to address us with a stern expression. "I expect you gentlemen to treat her with the respect due all humankind. If you open your minds, you will find her a noble spirit trapped in demeaning necessity."

Bell and I nodded agreement quickly, like the two scolded children we suddenly felt ourselves to be.

The shadows were already lengthening, and my apprehension growing, but I wisely kept my reluctance to myself. Off we went to Miller's Court and a meeting with the young prostitute.

"She's better off than many," commented Margaret as we walked. "She has a stable roof over her head, she is younger than most of the ladies here, and she's in good health. She shares her room intermittently with a fishmonger who provides her some protection, but she has had to walk the streets to pay the rent as he gives her no financial support.

In the hierarchy of streetwalkers within the East End, she is near the top of the heap."

I was soon to learn what a very shallow "heap" that was. We passed through a narrow and dark brick-lined archway into the open space of Miller's Court. The courtyard was teeming with children playing noisily, the air thick with the smell of cooking cabbage and fish. Margaret headed for the flats at the far end, which were notable for the bricks having been recently whitewashed. The door to the woman's residence was on the ground floor, adjacent to a larger entrance to apartments upstairs, so it had windows on two sides. As we came closer, I noticed the window around the corner from the door was broken and stuffed with odds and ends to block the wind.

I confess to being nervous, meeting a harlot in her living quarters. I was uncertain what manner of person we might encounter, but I was not prepared for the pleasant young woman who awaited us.

She had a fair complexion with light brown hair, and was neatly dressed in a clean brown frock with a white apron. Her accent declared an Irish heritage, and her age appeared to be around twenty-five years; the harshness of the East End had yet to leave its mark upon her. Indeed, she could easily have passed as a milkmaid in any artist's depiction of simple country life.

Her small single room was furnished with a double or "matrimonial" bed, a small night table, a larger table with two chairs in one corner, a chamber pot beneath the bed, and a wash stand. She noticed my eyes straying to the window with the broken pane.

"From a row with me mahn," she said, with a charming blush.

I saw now that the gap was covered over with newspaper, rags, and an old coat. Her man was currently not in residence she explained, as he assisted a greengrocer during the day.

"Mary", said Margaret, "these gentlemen are aiding the police hunt for Leather Apron, as I told you. It might help us to understand how to stop him if you could tell us about your work as a laundress. How do you choose your customers? Where do you take them?"

Mary smirked when Margaret used the word "laundress," apparently having no false modesty as to how she paid her rent.

"It's hard enough," she said, "making yer way as it is. But with Leather Apron about . . . every time you go out at night, ye take yer life in yer hands. Oh, I'm lucky to have a man in me life to look after me, though he chafes about bringing customers here. I'll not do business in an alley when I've a proper bed to go to." She pointed with satisfaction to the plain black iron bedframe and rumpled mattress. I tried not to look too closely at the stains, my imagination furnishing vivid explanations for their origin.

"The time it takes to bring 'em here gives me a chance to sort 'em out, else they don't get in. I'm safer here than anywhere else. After a while, ye get a sense of who's dangerous and who's just anxious to be done with it. I get 'em to talk a bit, and if I can get 'em to laugh, then I know they're no danger. You can tell a lot about a man from his laugh."

"What manner of 'clients' do you have?" I asked, overcoming my reluctance.

"Oh, all types! Dandies from the West End, clergymen, sailors. Sailors are the best! They have a pocket full o' coin and haven't had a woman in weeks; like crowns falling from the sky!"

I blushed at this but stammered my thanks as manfully as I could. I confess I was fascinated with this young courtesan, as women in my social circle were entirely mute regarding sexual relations. I found it stimulating to encounter a woman who could be so frank about this fundamental aspect of humanity.

The young "laundress" made a profound impression on me, and to my surprise I found I respected her. She was doing what she could with what she had to make her way in the world. I found no "fallen woman," as was so popularly portrayed in the literature of the time, but a brave soul who stared unflinchingly at the worst life could throw at her and carried on.

There are many forms of courage, and I reckoned hers no less than that of a guardsman on the field of battle, except her battle was daily.

Though not the typical streetwalker, since she had a fixed residence, her procuring of clientele was no different and exposed her to the same dangers. A survey conducted by the Metropolitan Police two weeks later concluded there were over twelve hundred active prostitutes in the East End. That level of competition made the ladies not overly selective of their customers, for there was literally a competitor on every street corner.

Our killer could not have fashioned a more abundant hunting ground, nor prey so eager to seek a private audience with him. As the ladies of the night typically plied their trade in the back streets and alleyways, they knew better than anyone the darkest and most secluded places to lead their executioner.

Bell asked, "Wouldn't you prefer to work in a brothel?"

"Not for me life!" she declared. "There, yer take whoever the Madame sends your way, and work the hours she says. Here," she extended her arm to encompass her meager room, "I work the hours I want and bring only the customers I think fitting. I get to sleep with me own mahn when I'm not working, and as long as I keep the landlord happy, I can do as I please. Aye, there's some girls that like to get tucked into bed, but there's plenty enough of us what like to have a proper say as to who we do it with, and how it's done."

I had to suppress a smile, for I had similar thoughts regarding having an employer, even one as intermittent as Mr. Wilkins. I admired her entrepreneurial spirit and admitted to myself that we had something in common.

"So, gentlemen, you working with the police and all, what's a working girl like me to do to save herself from this bahstard?"

"The best advice I can give you," I said, "is that this man is far more dangerous than he appears. Don't be taken in by someone who looks harmless."

"Then you'd be asking me to starve." Mary snorted. "I can't be turning away those what don't scare me now, can I? What's the point of that? Well, good day to you then, unless yer've another reason to stay?" She patted the well-used mattress. Smiling at me, she asked, acting coy, "Need yer laundry done, luv?"

Margaret giggled in delight at my startled reaction. While I am proud to say I did not bolt out of the flat, I took my leave rather hur-

riedly, to the clear amusement of the young prostitute and my companions. As we reached the archway at the far end of the court, Margaret
took my arm and said Mary was waving us goodbye, and I turned to see
her waving from the door. As I raised my hand halfheartedly to wave
back, she blew me a kiss. At that moment I believe my face could have
warmed the entire courtyard, as her neighbors all turned to see who
was Mary's most recent paramour.

Bell and Margaret were in a very jolly mood as we sought a cab,
though I failed to appreciate the source of their good humor. It is the
only time I can recall walking faster than Margaret.

"What did you think of Mary?" asked Margaret, once we were
underway. "Was she everything you expected?"

Bell had been silent since we left the residence at Miller's Court,
but spoke out now with heartfelt emotion. "She is like a fire walker
dancing upon the coals, always one false step from calamity. There was
a desperation yet defiance at the same time, which I found quite noble."

There was little more to be said, though I saw a tear in the corner
of Margaret's eye when she disembarked, and I found myself in sudden
need of a replacement for my recently discarded handkerchief.

"Goodnight to you both, gentlemen," Margaret said huskily then,
with more feeling than normal, "and thank you. For seeing, for listening, and for caring. Please be careful tonight. Leave the heroics to
the police."

Bell and I arrived at Spitalfields police station as the market clock
struck ten. Abberline showed us to the back room and our cots, which
were adorned with rough gray wool blankets and lumpen pillows.

"We keep these handy should the cells fill up," the inspector said all
too jovially, apparently enjoying the thought of us sleeping so roughly.
There was nothing we could do but make the best of it, so we settled
down for, well, anything. At least it was better than standing all night
propped up against a wall with a rope running across my body.

I composed a letter to Louise, but left the details vague. It being
her first pregnancy, she was understandably nervous; so I thought it
my husbandly duty not to give her additional reasons to worry. My

sister Lottie had kindly moved in with us to assist Louise, and she was a welcome addition to our household. My mother-in-law arrived the week of my departure. I feared Louise suspected my reasons for accepting this unusual consultancy were not entirely monetary but also to avoid protracted conversations with her mother. I therefore considered regular correspondence with my wife an insurance policy of sorts, to maintain domestic tranquility.

Once I had completed my letter, and with the hour being a little past eleven, I undressed to my shirt and trousers, removed my shoes, and made myself as comfortable as possible. I am not an unusually modest man, but I saw no need to demonstrate my taste in undergarments to my old mentor. Also, being only partially undressed in this fashion would allow me to accompany the inspector rapidly should he be called out.

Bell put away a recent copy of the *Lancet*, and we bade each other goodnight; neither of us entirely sure if a good night's rest would be a relief or a disappointment.

CHAPTER EIGHTEEN
THE CALM BEFORE THE STORMS

Friday, September 28, to Saturday, September 29

Inspector Abberline woke us promptly at six o'clock as we had requested. His rumpled appearance testified to his long night dozing in his office, and he informed us that nothing untoward had happened during our watch. He invited us back that evening should we wish.

Bell nodded and said, "If it would be convenient."

Abberline could tell by my face I did not find it "convenient" in the slightest. With a smile, he replied, "Oh quite convenient, sir. No problem at all."

Soon enough we were back at the Marlborough Club, which at that moment seemed one of the most delightful places on earth. I washed the grime from my face and hands before we broke fast together. Afterward, I made up for my poor night's slumber by retiring to my chambers for a "brief lie down," which lasted four hours.

Bell seemed impervious to fatigue, a prerequisite for a surgeon it seems, and after breakfast announced he was off to the Royal London Hospital in the East End to consult with colleagues. He wondered if any of them might have treated a patient recently of unstable mental condition whom they would consider a candidate for our murderer. Margaret had an appointment with an officer of the Salvation Army related to research for her next book, so I was left to my own devices for the day. When it appeared I could sleep no more, I dressed for a leisurely day indoors and went to the reading room to see what could be gleaned from the various newspapers there.

A British club is a delightful oasis; here men may excuse themselves from the hustle and bustle of the world and female companionship, and relax in the company of fellow males. Proper etiquette is, of course, always expected, but privacy is respected. Food and drink are plentiful, and comfortable bedchambers are readily available. A man may think, write, read, eat, or nap, in any sequence and as much as he desires. If we can choose our heaven when we finally cross over, I could do far worse than to spend eternity in a celestial version of the Marlborough.

I found before me a wealth of daily papers of various quality and every political persuasion; they seemed to be waiting patiently to share their contents with me. What bliss! Perusing my treasure horde, I came upon an article from the *Pall Mall Gazette* that recapitulated the Lipski murder that occurred in June of the previous year, and which was used by many as an excuse to believe Leather Apron was Jewish.

Israel Lipski resided in an attic on 16 Batty Street, off Commercial Street, when he poisoned a fellow lodger, Miriam Angel, with nitric acid. Lipski hanged for the crime, but since then the cry of "Lipski!" was often on the lips of those who attacked Jewish-appearing residents in the East End. There had been a growing anti-alien sentiment in the poorer neighborhoods of London, which was worsened by growing unemployment. Many of those who lacked jobs blamed their worsening economic condition upon the recently arrived Jewish immigrants who had fled the growing anti-Semitism in their homelands.

The *Times* had an article that summed up the findings of a recent select committee within the House of Lords investigating the so-called "sweating" system in the East End. Employees were crammed into tiny, foul-smelling, and frequently unhealthy workshops to work up to sixteen hours a day, usually seven days a week. The wages were barely enough to sustain life. One quotation, from a Mr. Arnold White, a leader in the anti-alien movement, was especially odious:

The poor Russian Jew laughs at what he hears of English poverty and scanty fare. He has a false notion that the English artisan is generally overfed, and easily discontented, and that the Jew can live easily where an Englishman would starve!

It concerned me greatly that such language would not only be published in a respectable newspaper, but that such words should be uttered in the House of Lords without rebuke. I began to grasp the powder keg of anti-Semite hostility Inspector Abberline was desperately trying to prevent from exploding.

Bell returned after five o'clock, looking as fresh as though he had just awakened from a long nap. As a general practitioner, I was used to established clinic hours. A surgeon however, especially one on staff at a teaching hospital, was accustomed to working all manner of hours, often through the night, only to see their clinic patients the following morning. I could never match their fortitude, and suspected they evolved from some other branch of human ancestry.

"Any luck?" I asked.

"None, and too much," he said. "London, as you would suspect, has no shortage of lunatics, and more than a fair number with violent tendencies. Sadly, however, my colleagues could not name one who had the capacity for violence coupled with the cunning to escape detection repeatedly. I suspect our killer is quite insane, yet sufficiently aware of his insanity to avoid letting his homicidal nature become known. Such men know how to feign normality quite convincingly. Hmm . . . he will not give himself away easily, I fear."

We passed a quiet evening. Bell read, and I prepared a summary of our activities and expenses for Wilkins. When nine o'clock drew near, I sighed, gathered my basic toiletries, and we made our way back to our post.

Inspector Abberline looked up as we entered. He smiled, perhaps with a touch of pity, before stating there was nothing new to report, and he wished us goodnight.

I grimaced, nodded in reply, and trudged to the waiting rack.

The next morning, when he woke us, Abberline appeared to have slept poorly. When he asked if he could expect us again that night, I told him I couldn't say until after a conversation with our employer. As we had an appointment with Wilkins at nine o'clock at the club to present our report and settle accounts, we departed promptly.

We arrived after seven, giving us ample time to bathe, dress, and eat before his arrival. I introduced Professor Bell, and when they shook hands Bell remarked upon his accent.

"Your speech, sir, is intriguing. You have attended British public schools, but I detect a slight cadence that reminds me of—"

"That would be the influence of my late mother," replied Wilkins quickly, slightly flushed by Bell's comment, and he resumed speaking in an impeccable public-school accent. "She was from Prussia and was quite insistent I learn her language as well. I spent my early years between England and her native land, and, although I am fully fluent in both languages, I tend to lapse into a slight accent when I speak English under duress. I am blessed with being the product of two great cultures, my father being British. He was a member of the British diplomatic corps, and I was privileged to attend his alma mater, Christ Church College at Oxford. Sadly, my English classmates made rather merry with my heritage at my expense. As children are apt to do," he said with a faint smile.

"You, sir, are as observant as Doctor Doyle claimed. I did not begrudge your fee from the start, but now I see what a valuable contribution you can make in this ghastly affair."

A few more pleasantries followed, then we settled comfortably into a small meeting room off the dining area.

"So, gentlemen," Wilkins continued, steepling his fingers and gazing over them like a headmaster, "what have you to report?"

Bell and I had previously agreed I was to do the bulk of the talking, as I had dealt with Wilkins before. I gave him a written summary of whom we had met, along with their addresses and what information we had gleaned from them.

Wilkins became animated when I recounted the letter from the person calling himself Jack the Ripper.

"Do you consider this to be genuine?" he asked Bell.

"I am uncertain," the professor answered. "All I can say is it's possible."

Bell's deductions of its contents made Wilkins pensive. "I agree with you," he said after a moment. "We can only wait to see if events prove out the letter's authenticity, and I believe the inspector is correct that we haven't seen the last of this man's handiwork. We shall know soon enough if it is genuine."

Wilkins wrinkled his nose with mild distaste at my mention of our meeting with the young prostitute. "It must have been awkward for gentlemen of your station to meet with a lowly whore in her den," he said with a sour look on his face. "My patron is more sympathetic to their plight, but *entre nous*, I fail to see the reason for his compassion. They plainly merit their station in life, and their betters," he swung his arm to include the three of us, "should take little account of them. Still, I serve one in a higher station than my own, so will labor in whatever vineyard he assigns." I noted Bell's ears turning bright red, though he held his tongue, ceding me the floor.

I responded in a firm voice that we had not been alone. Miss Harkness had accompanied us, and if he found our meeting with her so disagreeable, why had he insisted on it in the first place?

At this Wilkins screwed up his face as though he had bit into a lemon, "Frankly, Doctor, it wasn't my idea at all; Mr. Gladstone believed it might impress upon you the seriousness of your task. He wanted you to experience their fear for yourselves, as an incentive to give this your all. As for Miss Harkness, I am surprised to learn she continues to be associated with this inquiry. Surely by now, you gentlemen can find your own way about?"

"She has provided us with invaluable insight into the milieu in which we find ourselves," I said firmly. "The society of the East End is terra incognita for us. Observation without context can be misleading."

Wilkins continued to scowl but said nothing until I presented him my ledger with expenses for the past week. It included ten pounds for Margaret's assistance. Although she had voluntarily waived her fee, I strongly believed she deserved it, and had no qualms presenting a bill for her services.

Wilkins sighed, grudgingly paid me the full sum, then remarked, "Be advised, sir, that I shall not disburse any additional funds for this woman. She has served her purpose. Given our desire to keep Mr. Gladstone's participation from the press, the fewer involved, the better."

I agreed, knowing full well Margaret would accompany us regardless, but that the payment I had secured for her would be most welcome.

"What next, gentlemen? I stand ready to disburse twenty-one pounds to each of you for another week's labor."

"I can promise you only three days more," answered Bell. "I have many responsibilities in Edinburgh at both the university and in my surgical practice, which includes my duties as the Surgeon in Attendance to Her Majesty during her pending stay at Balmoral. When I came here, I was unaware of the task I'd be facing, so I did not adequately delegate my duties to allow for a longer absence. I may return in future, if necessary, but will not accept more than three day's fee now."

Wilkins seemed disappointed but nodded in acceptance. He turned to me and asked, "What of you, Doctor Doyle? Have you grasped enough of the professor's methods to continue in his absence?"

"I may observe a falcon soar," I replied, "yet never learn to fly." My colleague bowed his head slightly.

I continued. "The killer could strike again tonight, in a fortnight, or never. There is no way to know. You never expected us to apprehend the murderer ourselves, but to review the evidence collected by others and give an independent evaluation. Either or both of us can return within a day's travel should the need arise.

"Inspector Abberline has assured us the bodies of any further victims will be carefully attended until our colleagues and ourselves can perform a thorough examination. He has invited us to stand watch again tonight in Spitalfields, and I think we should accept the invitation to maintain our good working relationship. Barring any new developments, we'll go our separate ways on Tuesday."

Wilkins accepted our pending departure as graciously as he

could, then paid us each nine pounds more, remarking he would settle accounts for our lodging and meals on Tuesday morning. "If there is nothing more, I shall be off to inform Mr. Gladstone of your findings. Until Tuesday next, gentlemen."

After Wilkins had departed, I turned to Bell. "What did you make of him?"

"He is very meticulous. As he grew up in two cultures, it's hard to tell how much of his mannerisms are a result of that experience, and how much reflect his true nature. He is certainly unsympathetic to the streetwalkers, and it must gall him to labor so to protect them. I would find his prolonged presence rather tedious and thus prefer to move on to more engaging topics."

He stifled a yawn, revealing even he was not entirely impervious to fatigue. "We have the day to refresh ourselves before we return to the unyielding cots of Spitalfields station. I applaud your collection on Miss Harkness's behalf, by the way; it is well deserved. Perhaps we two could decrease our income so we could pay her fee with her being none the wiser?"

I agreed. I did not exaggerate Margaret's usefulness in navigating both the geographic and social morass of the East End. I also freely admit I felt safer with her at my side, shameful as it may appear to most men. I would be dishonest to deny it. The nagging guilt I had at my growing infatuation with her was shoved firmly into the back of my mind, though I knew it would not stay there long.

CHAPTER NINETEEN
A POETRY READING

Saturday, September 29, cont.

"**M**argaret will be curious to know how we have passed the last two nights," I said, "and I am anxious to deliver her payment. If you agree, I'll send a messenger asking her to meet us at the train station. We have no appointments today until ten o'clock, so we might as well invest some of Mr. Gladstone's payment in a pleasant meal outside of the East End, and perhaps take in some light entertainment."

Bell was amenable, so I had the now indispensable doorman dispatch one of his urchins to Margaret's residence with the following message:

> Dear Miss Harkness,
>   Would you be kind enough to join Professor Bell and myself at Fenchurch Street Station at one o'clock for a meal, at the place of your choosing outside the East End? We could then enjoy an early evening's entertainment before the Professor and I resume our post in Spitalfields. I hesitate to mention it, but please come "dressed" for the occasion.
>   Sincerely,
>   Doyle

We retired to our rooms to augment the meager sleep of the previous night on our merciless cots, which in my case was further affected by Bell's prodigious snoring.

The doorman's courier returned with a note from Margaret expressing her delight at a brief escape from the East End. She promised to come appropriately dressed, adding, "I may have something that will serve."

Midday came too quickly, and after packing a small valise for our overnight stay in Spitalfields, we were off to our rendezvous with Margaret. As we left the Marlborough, I noticed a man in a checked suit leaning against a street lamp, apparently engrossed in the newspaper he was holding before him, shielding his face. Coincidence? I feared I was becoming obsessed with random men in checked suits and I boarded our ride without mentioning my observation to Bell.

Margaret was dazzling in a dark-blue gown with white lace collar. Her attire was not too elegant for the afternoon, but certainly of sufficient quality to freely admit entrance to any of the finer restaurants in London. I noted the absence of jewelry and concluded that walking abroad in the East End with adornment, even in broad daylight, was not advisable; yet her appearance did not suffer in the least.

Given her voluminous skirt, I could easily conjecture a vast armory sequestered within those folds. She seemed delighted and relieved to see us uninjured, taking Bell's hand in one of hers and mine in the other and grasping them both warmly for a moment. Once inside the carriage, we asked her to choose the site of our luncheon. After she had directed the driver to a popular bistro in the West End, her bright eyes fastened upon mine, and she demanded I recount our evenings' adventures.

"Nothing of consequence, Margaret," I replied, teasing, "although I did discover that Professor Bell's snores can frighten the most hardened criminal into silence, as none dared disturb his slumber." Margaret and Bell laughed together at my jibe as I pulled out my wallet. "Our conversation this morning with Mr. Wilkins was fruitful, however." At which point I carefully placed ten pounds into her hands.

"What's this?" she asked, and my pulse quickened at the smile she gave me.

"Your payment," I replied with aplomb, savoring the moment. "We impressed upon Mr. Wilkins the value of your guidance, and thus, here is your salary for the five additional days you helped us."

Margaret clapped her hands, and for a moment, I forgot what I was about to say as I watched her eyes sparkle with joy.

Finding my bearings, I continued. "The professor and I have informed Mr. Wilkins that unless something new arises, we shall both depart in three days. We feel we've done everything possible for the moment, and rather than wait aimlessly for the killer to strike again, we'll return to our humdrum lives until there is a new development."

Margaret's smile faded before she shrugged and asked, "So my friends, what now?"

"We are free until ten o'clock tonight," I said, trying to sustain her smile. "We have some of Mr. Gladstone's crowns in our pockets and wanted to celebrate our small successes with you."

Margaret laughed at this. "Thank you, sir," she countered. I believe she would have curtsied, were it possible inside the cab, such was our mood. "You are most generous with your compliments and the coin of another, and I gratefully accept both."

We passed a carefree afternoon and early evening eating an enjoyable meal and attending a subsequent poetry reading at the Old Vic. The poetry was not to my taste, but Margaret was quite persuasive, and we men chivalrously yielded to her wishes. I recall neither the poet nor the poem; and I may have dozed off, for at one point I noticed Bell's elbow nudging my ribs.

As we left, I saw a poster regarding an upcoming performance by the American writer Samuel Clemens, known more widely as Mark Twain. He was to give readings of his works on three successive nights, from the tenth until the twelfth of November. I had read his novel *Huckleberry Finn* and found it to be two-thirds of a great work. He wrote movingly of the condition of the slave Jim, treating him as fully human with many admirable qualities, only to fall into a trite tale at the end with Tom Sawyer's arrival and subsequent pranks. As I had not yet written two-thirds of a great novel, however, I was obliged to consider him to be much the superior author.

My own trite tale of my fictional detective and Mormon revenge I described in *Scarlet* had done well enough in the popular press, but it revealed no great insights into humanity as did *Finn*. I regretted circumstance would prevent me from hearing him tell his extraordinary tales in his own voice.

We returned Margaret home ten pounds richer and half a bottle of wine happier than when we had met that afternoon, before reporting for our vigil at the station. Inspector Abberline played the part of innkeeper well, conducting us to our quarters and bidding us goodnight.

My spirits had been buoyed by the pleasant company and wine, but now, confronted with the military-style pallet awaiting me, I sighed. I partially undressed as before, and endeavored to fall asleep before Bell could add his cacophony to the night.

I grumbled to myself that thus far his snores had been the most dangerous part of our nights in the station and wished heartily for something to break the monotony.

If only my wishes were routinely granted as abundantly as they were that night.

CHAPTER TWENTY
A BLOODY NIGHT

Sunday, September 30

I dreamt I was wandering somewhere very dark and damp. I heard the scurrying of small feet in the blackness surrounding me. Yellow eyes glowed, and I knew the teeth beneath those eyes were sharp and ravenous.

"Wake up!" shouted the inspector. "There's been another murder; come with me now!"

I responded groggily, in the world somewhere between waking and sleeping, and dressed like a wind-up toy.

Bell seemed in much the same state, but we staggered with a will behind the inspector and through the police station, now full of activity.

My pocket watch read one-thirty as we headed for the exit.

"We just received a telegram that a woman's body has been found with her throat severed," Abberline informed us tersely. "It's in a court-yard off Berner Street. Time to earn your keep, gentlemen. Let's go!"

The night air brought us more fully awake as we were herded into the enclosed police wagon that was to take us to the site. Although I could not see outside, the pace of the hooves and swaying of the wagon told me we were moving at a rapid pace, matched only by my racing pulse.

"What do we know?" I asked Abberline, who sat beside me in the darkness.

"First reports are always wrong," replied the inspector in a tight tone. "Best we wait and see for ourselves. Besides, I'd rather not prejudice you before the facts are in."

It appeared we "consultants" were now truly in the thick of it. My heart pounded with the excitement of the chase, and at the prospect of seeing a victim fresh and at the scene before incompetent, if well-meaning, functionaries obscured all useful information.

After fifteen minutes of nausea-inducing transport, I was relieved to escape the close space of the wagon and step out onto the street. Although still not quite two o'clock, a crowd had already gathered at the entrance to Dutfield's Yard, a courtyard outside a stable where the murdered woman awaited us. A carriage wheel was affixed to the wall beside the gate, serving as a traveler's aid in locating the establishment; an adjacent window had a black sign with white letters proudly advertising Nestlé Milk.

Abberline shouldered his way through the crowd, bringing us in tow. The gates to the yard were secured and guarded by a police constable, who reported to the inspector that all onlookers within the yard were confined pending their examination. He let us in at Abberline's order, then re-secured the entryway after we passed.

The sound of the gate closing behind us gave me a slight shiver. I realized I couldn't leave until permitted to do so.

The sight that awaited us was in stark contrast to the Nestlé sign suggesting milk for growing children or steaming tea. Police Constable Henry Lamb had been the first authority summoned to the site, and it was he who greeted Abberline with a grateful sigh. With some thirty onlookers milling about, Lamb appeared overwhelmed with the responsibility of preserving the scene while managing the crowd.

The pale remains of a woman of middle age were lying in a pool of blood, the moon faintly reflected in the dark fluid surrounding her. A man was bending over her, but it was difficult to see the body or the man clearly, as they both wore dark clothing. And the buildings surrounding the court cast them in dark shadow, broken up only by the bobbing beams of light given off by the constables' bull's-eye lanterns.

"I arrived a little after one, and her face was still warm, but there was no pulse. I summoned Doctor Blackwell, a physician who resides nearby." The constable indicated the man bent over the body. "He pronounced her dead around half-past one. Now that you've arrived, I'd like to examine the Working Men's Club here." He jerked his head toward a small two-story brick building adjacent to the yard. "And clear it of anyone inside."

"In a moment," replied Abberline, "and my men will assist you, but first tell me what you know and how you came to be here."

I was anxious to hear Lamb's recitation, but I was also keen to view the body and speak with Doctor Blackwell.

Bell was aquiver with anticipation for the latter, so with my eyes I indicated to the inspector we medicos wished to confer with our colleague. He nodded agreement. We wasted no time, and it was only later in the day that Bell and I heard of the events leading to the body's discovery.

"Doctor Blackwell. Bell, Professor of Surgery, Edinburgh, and my colleague Doctor Doyle. We're with Inspector Abberline," the professor had begun, when the man straightened and turned around. From pictures in the various newspapers that had reported the inquest of Annie Chapman's murder, I immediately recognized the bewhiskered stout gentleman as Doctor Phillips, one of the police surgeons for Division H.

"Good morning, gentlemen," Phillips said briskly. "I'm Police Surgeon Philips, and ordinarily I'd be pleased to meet you. Doctor Blackwell responded to the police constable's summons to see if there was anything to be done for the poor woman. He correctly identified her as deceased and has been dismissed." Doctor Phillips had a soft voice that was hard to understand above the mutterings of the crowd, who by now were finding the entertainment of the body fading as their confinement wore on them. He borrowed a lantern from one of Abberline's constables, then gestured for us to come closer as he bent over the body.

With the aid of the lantern's light, we could see she was lying upon her back, her dress respectfully draped across her. It appeared to have been undisturbed. Tied around her neck was a checked silk scarf, the bow upon the left-hand side pulled tightly.

"The cause of death, gentlemen," Phillips remarked dryly as he revealed a deep gash across her throat that cleanly severed her windpipe. "Before his departure, Doctor Blackwell told me he believed the scarf was used to pull her backward, though neither of us is certain whether her throat was slit while standing or once she was on her back."

Bell asked for the lantern. He bent over and slowly scanned the throat, the upper body of the deceased, and the surrounding ground. I noted the ear on the right side was intact, as I recalled the message signed "Jack the Ripper."

"I believe her throat was cut once she was on her back," Bell said, after his examination. "Blood loss would have been immediate and brisk. Note here the bloodstains on the dress over her upper body end at her collarbones. I see no blood on the dress below them. Blood spurting out from the supine position would be unlikely to travel far enough to reach her breasts. The distance required from the standing position is irrelevant, however, as gravity would assist the blood's journey down her upper body. That there is no blood on her clothing below the neckline therefore suggests she was supine.

"The knot of the scarf around her neck is certainly tighter than would have been bearable in life, and I agree the killer probably grabbed her by it. I believe the most likely scenario is he suddenly grabbed the scarf from behind, then continued to garrote her until she lost consciousness, cutting her throat once she was down. If he had tried to wield the knife while she was standing, the scarf would likely have been severed. What other injuries have you found?"

"None, sir," replied Phillips. "None whatsoever. I'm uncertain if we are dealing with the same murderer."

"I rather think we are," replied Bell. "The asphyxiation before cutting her throat is his calling card, so to speak. There is nothing in the papers mentioning this peculiarity of his, so, unless he is running a school for assassins, we are dealing with Leather Apron's handiwork."

Bell straightened, and after casting about the body with the bull's eye lantern for another moment, suddenly bent over and with a cry pointed to the victim's left hand.

Phillips kneeled. Opening her hand, he discovered a small paper packet. In one of my fictional accounts, this would have proven to be a crucial clue, a note from the killer, or directions to a rendezvous. But this was real life (or death, in this case), and the packet proved to contain nothing more than cachous, or breath fresheners.

"Nothing extraordinary in itself," Bell said, "but it does speak to the suddenness of the attack in that she hadn't the time to drop this packet to defend herself."

It was now approaching three o'clock, and I was about to ask one of the numerous inspectors about the premises what they knew of the body's discovery, when Abberline suddenly came at us out of the darkness at a dead run.

"Come with me now!" he ordered. "There's been another murder!"

Perhaps it was the early hour of the day, or, more likely, the shock of a second atrocity that turned my thoughts inward, for I became ill at the thought of another whirl-about within the police wagon. Abberline, after noting my expression, relented and allowed me to sit up with the driver. Doors secured, the horses were given their heads, and we were soon speeding through the deserted early morning streets. A sense of foreboding built within me, for the surroundings grew more and more familiar as we barreled westward, first along Commercial Street, then Aldgate High Street. Soon, Saint Botolph's Church loomed on our right, marking where one would turn left to reach Margaret's tenement; my hands began to sweat, and my chest tightened as we drew near the turn.

As we reached the church, I clenched my eyes, praying we go on. And we did, veering to the right onto the following Duke Street. I let out a long exhalation, realizing I must have been holding my breath for several seconds.

The fright I suffered thinking Margaret might be the next victim revealed how dear this unconventional woman had already become to me. I never shared my solitary ordeal atop the racing police wagon with

Bell, though my face must have shown the strain of my momentary terror, for he gave me an odd look on our arrival.

Abberline launched himself immediately into the gathering of police inspectors huddled together in a far dark corner of what I subsequently learned was Mitre Square, only three streets away from Margaret's tenement on Vine Street. I quickly understood by the heated tone of the conversations that this murder scene lay within the jurisdiction of the City of London Police. I recalled Abberline's disdainful description of his neighboring colleagues as "bookkeepers with badges," so I had no doubt as to his intense desire to assume the role of senior officer on the scene, the niceties of jurisdiction be damned.

Doctor Phillips had remained behind to see to the other victim's secure transport to the morgue, where a more thorough examination could be conducted and photographs taken, before an awakened London could produce a crush of onlookers. The body of the latest victim in Mitre Square had already been removed, so Bell and I found ourselves with little more to do than walk around the square to acquaint ourselves with its surrounds.

"Bad news for Abberline," I ventured. "It is an unnecessary complication to have jurisdictional challenges on top of everything else."

I was pondering how we could be of use without a body to inspect, when a police constable suddenly arrived as fast as he could go and went directly to the gathering of senior officers. There was a brief though loud outcry from the group, before Inspector Abberline emerged and came straight to us.

"As there's no corpse here for you to examine, you gentlemen are released. I must leave immediately to investigate the site where a torn-off portion of this victim's apron was found. There is also a message written in chalk on the wall adjacent that we believe to be from the murderer. I can write it down and share it with you later."

"Please, Inspector," Bell said. "I would like to accompany you. I may be able to deduce as much from the manner it is written as from the actual contents. You saw how I could analyze the message signed Jack the Ripper. Perhaps I might do as well this time?"

Abberline seemed of two minds, but lacking time for debate, relented. "Fair enough, Professor. Lord knows there will be plenty of folks about unknown to my superiors. The message is located squarely within the jurisdiction of the Metropolitan Police, so there'll be no doubt as to who's in command there. I'll have to give the driver instructions, Doctor, so you'll have to ride inside."

My stomach turned at the thought, and I asked if I could follow on foot.

Abberline had no time for niceties. "Come as you can, then. The address is on Goulston Street, by the entrance to the Wentworth Model Dwellings, about a half mile to the northeast. Oh, and before we go, you gents may be interested to know that the lady murdered here had both her ears nicked."

Abberline's revelation was like a splash of freezing water to the face, but before I could respond, they were gone. Now I was the man of two minds, for I wanted desperately to go after Bell and the inspector, but I felt a duty to Margaret, who had been excluded thus far.

Her tenement was but five minutes' walk from where I was standing, so I turned round to rouse her and bring her along. Besides, I told myself, I would like as not become completely lost and not find the address on my own. Also, after my fright on the police wagon, I was anxious to see her.

The door to her flat opened a crack within seconds of my knock, revealing Margaret already in her Pennyworth attire, and I had to just look at her for a moment before I could speak.

"What's wrong, Doyle," she asked, troubled at the early hour of my visit and the wild look in my eyes. "You look like you've seen a ghost."

"Almost," I said. I swallowed. "Almost."

"Is the professor all right?" Margaret asked, clutching her chest in sudden concern. "Why isn't he with you?"

"Two murders tonight," I gasped, more out of breath than I should have been, given the short distance I had walked. "Bell is at the Wentworth Building, Goulston Street, examining a message from the murderer."

"I know the place," Margaret said. "Let's go!"

On the way, I asked her why she was up so early and dressed as Pennyworth. She explained that she customarily rose at four o'clock, to write until six, then went out for bread. Not knowing when we might summon her, she was for the moment dressing mostly as a man.

She was full of questions, but she soon realized we could either walk briskly or I could talk.

I promised to share our adventures as soon as I was able, and we proceeded purposefully toward Goulston Street and the message from the killer's bloodstained hand.

CHAPTER TWENTY-ONE
A GRISLY CORRESPONDENCE

Sunday, September 30, cont.

Iheard a church clock strike five as we arrived and found Abberline in another heated debate. Bell noticed our approach, however, and motioned us to the sheltered entrance to the Wentworth Dwellings.

"Here." He gestured to a small dark smudge on the landing. "This is where the fragment of the victim's apron was found by a police constable. And here," he said, gesturing to the wall above, "is our mysterious message."

I had been up most of the night, walked far more than was my routine, seen violent death, and been terrified that this last victim was a woman I had grown quite fond of. I was tired and in need of a pause in the nonstop barrage of shocks to my system. So, with that in mind, perhaps you can realize the effect the message had on me after having withstood so much in such a brief time. The graffito was written in chalk in this manner:

The Jewes are
The men that
Will not
be Blamed
for nothing

"Who discovered this?" Margaret asked.

"Police Constable Long," Bell said, indicating a young constable standing apart from the crowd. "I haven't had a chance to interview him. Perhaps we should do so now, before the police need to be summoned to quell a riot amongst themselves."

PC Long was looking on at the heated arguments between the senior officers of the two police forces with a look of frank amusement, perhaps enhanced by his own role in the matter, when we approached.

"Constable Long," Bell asked, "would you mind telling us how you found this graffito?"

"Who are you three gentlemen?" Long answered, annoyed at our interruption.

"Consultants to the Metropolitan Police," I told him. "Inspector Abberline will vouch for us."

"If he doesn't get a broken jaw, first," Long responded, his good humor returning. "All right then, I'll keep it short. I was walking my beat just before three. I ain't usually assigned here, but I was brought over a month ago from my usual beat by Paddington Station. So, I walk slow and careful. The lot around here are a fair bit shabbier than what I'm used to, and I mind me steps."

The noise level from the scrum of inspectors had subsided for the moment, while Abberline was pointing out that we were now clearly in his jurisdiction. A quiet voice is more compelling than a shouted one, but as soon as the City police began their angry rebuttal that this evidence pertained to a murder in their jurisdiction, Long turned his attention back to us.

"I make my rounds every half hour. I saw nothing unusual before, but this time there was a rag, still wet with blood and a long mark which I reckon was from the killer wiping his blade down, lying in front of the doorway here." He indicated the entrance to the Wentworth Building. "It was as though dropped by someone just before they walked inside. I didn't know about the murders, so when I saw the rag I feared someone had been attacked and was lying nearby dead or injured on the staircase at the entrance. As I stood up after finding the rag, I saw the message written on the wall right in front of me. Well, it took me a few seconds before I could find enough wind to blow my whistle, I can tell ya that!"

"Anything else, Constable?" I asked.

"Well sir, the blood on the rag. I'm told the rag came from the lady's apron—it had a fair amount of shite smeared on it, too. I reckon he must have gutted her like he's done before."

"Thank you, Constable Long," Bell said. "I believe your deduction is correct. Farewell."

"This could hardly be worse," said Margaret, once we turned away from PC Long, allowing him to return to his former diversion. "Mitre Square is but one street over from Bevis Marks, where the Great Synagogue lies, and the bulk of the residents here and in the surrounding two streets are Jews."

"What do you make of this?" I asked Bell. "The meaning is unclear to me."

"Consider," he replied, "our killer has just sated his blood lust. He has found a secluded spot to wipe his blade, apparently on the apron fragment, and perhaps to hide the knife. He has eluded detection, and before going to ground, is inspired to taunt his pursuers. He leaves this obvious clue of the blood-soaked apron fragment to draw attention to his message. Part of him is cold and calculating, yet another part is savoring the havoc he is wreaking on society. He is clearly following everything written about him in the papers, and so is well aware of the growing tendency to scapegoat the Jews for his murders."

Margaret and I exchanged glances, and I believe her pale expression mirrored mine as we recalled Abberline's gruesome vision of an East End set ablaze by angry mobs, as well as our recent encounter with Mr. Rubenstein. Were we gazing at the match?

"I believe it was composed with little thought," Bell mused aloud. "A bauble to distract us, and perhaps to incite further mayhem by others. Part of his nature seems to be that of a spoiled child crying out for attention, deliberately breaking things to be noticed."

"A very cruel and deadly child," Margaret added.

We turned to the debate raging among the senior officers. Abberline was all for erasing the graffito immediately, fearing the effect it would have should it become public. Officers of the City of London Police argued this graffito was an important clue in a murder within their jurisdiction, and should be preserved until morning when it could be properly photographed.

One inspector suggested erasing only the top line, "The Jewes," and conserving the rest until morning, but Abberline believed no one would be fooled by such a simple maneuver. It seemed the impasse was about to lead to blows when Sir Charles Warren, commissioner of the Metropolitan Police, arrived. We three faded quietly into the back of the crowd and listened attentively as the two sides presented their case to him.

As the senior authority on the scene, and with the graffito within his jurisdiction, the commissioner had the ultimate say in the matter. After hearing both sides, he ordered the writing be erased immediately.

Much has been written by those in comfortable chairs about what a grievous error this was. I challenge any among them to have the fate of hundreds of innocents weighing upon their choice at such a moment and have them discover how heavy a burden that can be. A decision had to be made on the spot without consultation or survey.

Sir Charles put the public welfare over his police responsibilities and had this possible provocation erased. A police constable produced a rag soaked in water, and soon the mysterious message was erased from the wall, though the image shall always linger in my memory.

CHAPTER TWENTY-TWO
DIPLOMACY

Sunday, September 30, cont.

The commissioner received a muffled report from Abberline of what he knew of the two murders, nodded his head, and left. The City of London police inspectors, having nothing to protect or photograph, departed together in a huff.

Abberline remembered his two consultants and approached us slowly, his shoulders sagging with fatigue. "Well gentlemen," he began, "I trust you enjoyed this evening's entertainment. But never fear, we aren't done yet. You have access to our morgue to review the findings of the first victim. The second one lies within the City of London's morgue. Major Henry Smith is their acting commissioner, and it will require his authority for you to enter there."

Abberline looked from Bell to me and back again, before emphasizing, "If you are to be of any use to me, I need you to convince the City police to share information with us."

Bell answered for both of us. "We will do our best, Inspector."

Abberline paused to wipe his face with a handkerchief, then sighed. "I understand the injuries of the Mitre Square victim were far more extensive, so her examination will likely prove more useful. I am willing to exchange any information we have from tonight's and previous victims in exchange for whatever you can learn from theirs. But it is best that this come from you. A moment . . ."

Abberline scribbled a note saying the Professor and I were empowered to speak on his behalf regarding the exchange of postmortem findings between the two police forces, and passed the note to Bell.

"I discussed this with Sir Charles, and he agreed. He advised we not use his name, as it is likely even more unpopular with our colleagues than mine. I suggest you go there right away. Major Smith's office is near the Bank of England. Your Mr. Pennyworth there," he said, nodding toward Margaret, "should be able to take you to it quick enough."

"Aye," said Margaret, in her best Pennyworth tenor. "Straight west from here, a little over a mile."

Abberline nodded and managed a slight smile. "I see now the value of his guidance and shall speak no more of him, though I shall hold you, Professor, accountable for his discretion."

Bell nodded agreement as the inspector continued. "Once you are done there gentlemen, return to my office and I can tell you what we learned from witnesses and a search of Dutfield's Yard in daylight. In return, you can enlighten me with your conclusions from the City morgue. Agreed?"

Bell nodded. "Done and done, Inspector."

"Very well then. Good luck, gentlemen!" And with that, the burly inspector rushed off to lead the hunt for any further clues the killer may have left behind.

Bell chuckled after the inspector departed, and when he saw my puzzled look replied, "We seem to have risen considerably in Inspector Abberline's esteem. We have evolved from annoyances to emissaries venturing into a hostile camp."

I had to smile at his analogy, and I admired his ability to see the humor in our situation when it had quite escaped me.

"While I," said Margaret, "have evolved to a full-blown conspirator in our little enterprise." She turned to me. "Thank you, Doyle, for coming after me this morning. I cannot adequately express my gratitude for turning away from the hunt to fetch me. I will not fail you. Either of you. Follow me now, gentlemen. The City of London police headquarters is insultingly close to the site of the last murder, so put one foot in front of the other and before you know it, we'll be there!"

Margaret's thanks did much to brighten my mood, but little to strengthen my step. Still, there was nothing else to do but proceed. The sooner we examined the corpse, if allowed, the less chance crucial evidence might be tossed casually into the rubbish bin or washed down a gutter. I consoled myself with one thought, however, as the jurisdiction of the City of London Police was smaller, the population of its morgue would be reduced accordingly.

Thankfully it was but a fifteen-minute walk before we arrived at the office of Acting Commissioner Major Henry Smith; my pocket watch read seven o'clock when we entered the station.

I believe somewhere in England there resides a factory that manufactures desk sergeants, for they all seem composed of the same attitude and greet arrivals with the identical air of long-suffering dejection.

Professor Bell presented himself to this specimen, and the faithful guardian inquired resignedly as to our purpose.

"My colleagues and I are consultants to the Metropolitan Police Department. I wish to speak with your acting commissioner to request permission to examine the body from this morning."

The sergeant gave a grimace when Bell mentioned the Metropolitan Police, then shrugged and said, "We're not on the best of terms at the moment with our esteemed colleagues on that force, gentlemen, but I'll ask if Major Smith will see you. As you might expect, he's having a busier Sunday morning than usual. I won't promise nothing."

The sergeant left the room, passing through a door that opened onto a long hallway behind him. He returned but a minute later, which indicated Major Smith was not a man who labored over his decisions, and stated, "Follow me, gents."

We were taken to a door marked Commissioner, and after the sergeant's knock was answered by a muffled "Enter," we did. The sergeant returned wearily to his post, and we were left alone with the office's sole occupant.

Major Smith appeared to be a gentleman more accustomed to the salons of power than the back alleys of the East End. He was slender, approaching sixty, and although it was early Sunday morning, he was meticulously dressed in a dark silk waistcoat and white cravat. His well-tailored coat hung from a tree stand behind him; his white mustache and full head of hair were neatly groomed.

He looked up from a report on his desk. "Good morning, gentlemen," he said in a mild tone, "I do not wish to be rude, but, as you can well imagine, I have a full schedule this morning. Please introduce yourselves and state your purpose."

The tension between the two police departments was telling as Major Smith did not rise to greet us, nor did he invite us to sit. He was making it obvious he was in control of the situation, and we, as agents of the Metropolitan Police, were in disfavor.

"Professor Joseph Bell, sir," began my companion, "Professor of Surgery at Edinburgh. With me is my colleague, Doctor Doyle, and our guide, Mr. Pennyworth. Doctor Doyle and I are acting on behalf of this gentleman's employer." At this, he presented Major Smith with Wilkins's calling card, and it had the desired effect.

Smith's eyebrows rose, he nodded, then slowly returned the card to Bell.

"What has he to do with this sordid affair? I had no idea Gladstone had any interest in this matter."

"He would prefer his interest not become common knowledge," replied Bell. "He has always shown Christian charity in improving the lot of the women this creature is slaying. We have been contracted to advise the Metropolitan Police by using scientific methods my colleague Doctor Doyle has championed. Inspector Abberline apparently feels our assistance merits his confidence."

Major Smith made a face at the mention of Inspector Abberline, but held his tongue and allowed the professor to continue uninterrupted.

"I have a note from him authorizing full disclosure of everything learned from the postmortems of the previous murder victims, as well as what we might gain from the woman found in Dutfield's Yard this morning. In exchange, I request permission to examine the body from Mitre Square with your police surgeon. If I may say, sir, you risk little and stand to gain much."

Major Smith pondered our peculiar contract for a moment, and then, nodding, grabbed his pen and a sheet of paper. "This note states that you and your companions are granted access to the morgue—but only in the presence of our police surgeon, Doctor Brown. He was at the scene this morning shortly after the dead woman was found, so he can also share the position of the body and the reports of the police constables who discovered her. Is that acceptable, gentlemen?"

"Quite, and thank you, Commissioner," replied Bell. "We'll be off."

Smith nodded and then, with narrowed eyes, replied, "I look forward to reading your written report in payment. Tomorrow morning would be most convenient."

Bell grimaced slightly at this, then nodded and said, "As you wish, Commissioner. Tomorrow morning it is."

We saw ourselves out, and at the entrance showed the note to the morose desk sergeant. He nodded and detailed a police constable to show us to the morgue.

"I don't know if Doctor Brown's still about, but if you hurry you might yet catch him. No promises, mind!"

The dour constable accompanying us sighed that "We've a bit of a walk" north to the morgue on Golden Lane. My legs ached at the thought of another forced march without breakfast. Noting my look of woe, Bell kindly asked the constable the address, and we dismissed the officer in favor of hiring a growler that delivered us to the charnel house within fifteen minutes.

Our confrontation with the local Cerberus, that fierce but loyal Guardian to the Underworld, was greatly facilitated by the message from Major Smith. After reading the note, the senior clerk informed us the police surgeon had gone home after the delivery of the body, to have something to eat and return to bed. He would return at two o'clock for the postmortem. I thought Doctor Brown to be a gentleman of praiseworthy wisdom.

"I propose we do likewise," I said, pleading to my companions, given that it was now approaching nine o'clock. "We have had a short night and an overlong morning with nothing to eat or drink. I confess to being quite done in."

Both agreed readily, to my relief. Margaret said she could return to the morgue on her own, and play the role of Bell's personal secretary. We let Margaret off at her address, and then on we went to the Marlborough. I dined ravenously, bathed, and crept gratefully into my bed with instructions to be roused in three hours' time at one o'clock.

I slept deeply, though far too briefly. The last image I recall was of the poor woman in Dutfield's Yard. She was lying on her back in a pool of blood. Suddenly, her eyes opened, and she raised the hand holding the cachous. Her index finger extended, indicating that I look behind me. As I turned my head to see what was there, the doorman gently shook me awake.

As we rode back to the city morgue, I posed a question to the professor (one that had been very much on my mind these past few days). "I have always wondered . . ." I began, "how is it you see things that are obvious to you yet invisible to those around you?"

He sat back for a moment and rubbed his chin. "How would you describe the doorman at the Marlborough?"

I pondered this question, puzzled as to its relevance, but after some thought, answered, "Tall, nearly six feet, sandy-colored hair, and neatly trimmed walrus mustache. Perhaps sixty years old; uniform spotless. He has a deep voice and a Welsh accent."

"Not bad, Doyle," replied Bell. "But would it surprise you to know that he is a former boxer, reformed alcoholic, and was a sailor in his youth? Also, he is perhaps five foot nine inches tall, in his early fifties, and recently widowed."

"How could you know all that?" I asked. "You have spent less time with him than I have, and never without myself present. I recall no such revelations."

"Indeed. Revelations . . ." replied my companion. "Have you observed that the knuckles of both hands are enlarged? The fifth metacarpal bone of the right hand is misshapen, denoting an old and poorly mended fracture commonly known as a 'boxer's fracture.' The thickening of the pinna of his left ear due to one or several hard blows unsuccessfully avoided further supports my deduction of his former avocation. Above the wrist of the right hand is the tip of a dragon's tail tattoo, such as one commonly sees in sailors who have visited Hong Kong. Your misperception of his height is due to your conversations with him with you predominantly seated, while he is standing and wearing his top hat. You misjudged his age due to wrinkles formed from squinting into the sun's reflections off the ocean."

"And his being recently widowed, how on earth did you deduce that?"

"I have noted a certain air of melancholy about him. He will sigh, then unconsciously rub his left thumb over his ring finger, yet there is no ring there. He is thinking of his departed wife, and the thought of her absence makes him touch that space formerly occupied by his marriage ring."

I nodded. Now that the professor had mentioned it, I had noticed the distinct lack of gaiety in the man. I had simply put that down to the nature of his duties and mundane existence.

"But how could you possibly know he was an alcoholic?" I queried. "He lacks jaundice, his gait is steady, and his uniform is always clean and pressed."

"As to his former enslavement to drink," Bell answered, leaning back in his seat and steepling his hands, "there are several enlarged blood vessels on his nose, a hallmark of alcoholics; yet his eyes are clear, his uniform, as you say, is impeccable, and his step stable. Once those blood vessels enlarge they never return to their previous size; but the absence of any other characteristics of the alcoholic, plus the fact that he is now the doorman of this venerable club, leads me to conclude that this weakness has been overcome, despite the recent loss of his beloved wife."

I bowed my head in admiration. "Your deductions ring true, Professor. I must, therefore, ask again, how is it that you see these things while others do not?"

"There's the rub, Doyle. When you look at this man, what do you 'see'? You see a doorman. A functionary. Someone available to do your bidding, and his uniform defines him in your eyes. You do not see more because you do not need to see more. This does not mean that you are an evil or callous man, merely a comfortable one. I think much of the evil we are confronting in this 'Jack the Ripper' is the result of too many comfortable people seeing only the surface of their fellow man, and woman."

Bell's words regarding how the better-off disregarded their fellow man stung because I would have to admit I was often guilty of this. I had but a moment to ponder my shortcomings, however, when the professor concluded our conversation as we approached our destination.

"But this morning, our Jack committed a fatal error. As long as he preyed upon the unfortunates within the East End, the well-to-do could look on with pity. This latest victim, within the confines of the City of London, however, has crossed a boundary that extends into the realm of the most influential within this great city. He was hunted before partly for sport by the mighty. But he has frightened them, and now they will pursue him out of fear, and an anger fueled by fear."

We arrived at the morgue as Bell concluded. Time to visit one of the Ripper's most recent acquaintances, and see what she could tell us of this man who held the East End, and now the City of London, hostage at knifepoint.

CHAPTER TWENTY-THREE
A PROPHESY FULFILLED

Sunday, September 30, cont.

The morgue was situated on the aptly named Golden Lane, as the surrounding buildings were of a much higher standard than those adjacent to the morgue of the Metropolitan Police. It seemed even in death the citizens of the City of London fared better than their poorer neighbors to the east. We found Margaret nattily attired in a dark coat and cravat. Rather overdressed for the occasion, I thought, but if she wanted to play the part of a "dandy" from the West End, she looked it. We all seemed much the better for our rest, and with a renewed vigor we entered the morgue.

With our note from Major Smith in hand, we were granted entrance to the examination room, where we found Doctor Brown awaiting us.

Brown was a slight man in his early thirties, with light brown, thinning hair and tortoise-shell glasses. He was at his desk going over some documents, but stood to straighten his attire and welcome us as we entered.

"Ah, Professor Bell and company. I was told you would be coming. Welcome to our small enterprise." He spread his arms to indicate the morgue in its entirety. "Not as impressive, perhaps, as what the Metropolitan Police can offer, yet we get few complaints. I know of you, Professor, by your well-earned reputation, but your companions have the advantage of me."

Bell introduced me properly, then Margaret as Mr. Pennyworth, his personal secretary.

"Welcome, gentlemen," Brown said. "You should understand that, although we are now at the end of September, this is the first murder to occur in the City of London this year. I am quite accustomed to examining those who expire by violent means, but those have been, for the most part, industrial accidents, overturned carriages, and suicides. Homicide is an unusual cause of death in the financial capital of the world. Our citizens are more apt to terminate their own life than seek retribution against another."

The morgue was roughly half the size of the one used by the Metropolitan Police, appropriate for the population it served. Still, the pale-green tile walls, concrete floors, and the smell of carbolic acid were the same as any other morgue one might visit throughout Europe. Though the neighborhood surrounding the building was of a higher standard, the rooms where the dead yield their final secrets are all the same.

"Given the rarity of homicide in our jurisdiction, gentlemen," Brown continued, "I ask that you bear with me as I examine this poor woman in minute detail. Feel free to ask questions at any time, and you are of course free to depart whenever your curiosity is satisfied. I wanted to be well rested for this trial, and will not rush through for the sake of completion."

"Excellent!" replied Bell. "I am weary of evidence being carelessly lost or washed away. I am happy to assist, but should you find my presence a bother, please say so."

"Nonsense, Professor," replied Brown, "I would be grateful for your help."

Brown motioned to an assistant whom I had failed to notice previously, a short and pale older man with thinning, gray hair and a sallow complexion. I wondered if my previous disregard of him confirmed Bell's conclusion that I saw those beneath my station only when they could be of service to me. I had a pang of guilt at the thought, then thrust it from my mind. I had more pressing matters.

The body awaited us upon the autopsy table, and although the genitals and face were covered with blood-soaked cheesecloth, they did not hide the fact the woman had been eviscerated much as a hunter might gut a stag. Margaret paled and squeezed her eyes shut briefly as we approached the table, and for a moment I feared she would faint.

Then she straightened her shoulders and continued forward. Playing her part of personal secretary, she stood adjacent to Doctor Brown's assistant in the furthest corner of the room and made notes as the examination proceeded. We began with the assistant handing the police surgeon notes he had made at the murder scene.

Brown cleared his throat and addressed us in a manner that reminded me of my days in medical school. "Let me read you my observations from Mitre Square first, and then we can proceed to the postmortem.

"The body is of a middle-aged Caucasian female, thin, well formed; the body was on its back, the head turned to the left shoulder. The arms by the side, both palms upward, fingers slightly bent. The abdomen was exposed. The throat cut across."

Brown paused to lift the cheesecloth over the face and throat, exposing a single deep incision that traveled from one side of the neck to the other, and extended to the spinal column. The powerful precision of the wound made my hands turn cold when I pondered the fury and cunning required to make such a lethal stroke—without hesitation and in a public space.

"The intestines were drawn out to a considerable extent," Brown continued, "and placed over the right shoulder. A piece of about two feet was detached from the body and placed between the body and the left arm, apparently by design."

"You mean to say the murderer was decorating the corpse with her own body parts? Placing them for effect?" I blurted out.

Brown looked up from his notes, surprised by my outburst, then said, "Precisely, Doctor. I believe he was arranging the body to make the maximum effect upon whoever discovered it."

Then, looking down, he read aloud, "The body was quite warm. No death stiffening had taken place. She must have been dead most likely within the half hour.

"There was little blood on the bricks or pavement around. There were no traces of recent sexual intercourse. As the clothes were taken off carefully from the body in preparation for examination, a piece of the deceased's ear dropped from the clothing."

"The small amount of surrounding blood tells us she died instantly," Bell mused. "Your description of the state of the body at discovery is most thorough. I can envision the scene vividly."

"Well then," said Brown, obviously pleased with Bell's remarks, "let's see what we shall see."

Doctor Brown began dictating as his assistant and Margaret took notes. I should mention that in the postmortem suite the assistant is called a Diener, or servant. This title stems from the tradition in Germany, where the examination of the deceased to study disease and its effects began. This practice became known as pathology, the study of pathos, or suffering. The Germans also coined a term for the postmortem I found quite accurate: "autopsy," or "to see for oneself."

Brown pulled back his sleeves and began. "Rigor mortis is well marked, although the body is not quite cold."

"The onset of rigor mortis so soon after death denotes strenuous muscular activity just before death," noted Bell. "Although she was unable to cry out, there was a struggle of some kind."

"Excellent insight, Professor," agreed Brown.

I positioned myself behind Bell and to his left so that Margaret was on the opposite side of the room and I could keep a watchful eye on her. I noted her taking a sharp breath when the face was uncovered, taking one step back, and losing her façade of clinical detachment for a moment. I raised my eyebrows and nodded my head toward the exit, silently asking if she needed to leave. She shook her head, then looked back at her notebook and resumed capturing the two surgeons' observations.

Professor Bell and Doctor Brown, however, were so intent as to take no notice of her, for they were now fully in their element. Bell often bent over to inspect items of interest as Brown pointed them out, and their smooth synchrony around the corpse reminded me of a long-married couple dancing together.

It was apparent that the killer had labored meticulously to make her disfigurement as complete as possible. Imagining him bent over her body in a dark corner of a public square, risking detection at any moment, spoke both of his skill with a knife and the overpowering need he had to mutilate his victims.

"The fatal wound was the severing of the left common carotid artery. Death was immediate, and the mutilations inflicted after death."

Brown went on to describe the neck wound, her disembowelment, the removal of the womb and left kidney, stating that whoever removed the organs appeared to know what they were doing.

In his summary he pronounced, "I believe the wound in the throat was first inflicted, and she must have been lying on the ground. The wounds on the face and abdomen prove they were inflicted by a sharp, pointed knife, and those in the abdomen by one six inches or longer. The throat was severed instantly, thus no noise could have been emitted. I should not expect much blood to have been found on the person who inflicted these wounds. The wounds could not have been self-inflicted."

Despite her initial squeamishness, Margaret slowly became entranced with the blend of art and science that a proper postmortem required. I was relieved to see that, as we progressed, she looked up more frequently, her color returning, and by the end, she was nodding vigorously in agreement as Brown and Bell voiced their observations.

Although Doctor Brown had not previously performed many homicide investigations, this one could serve as a model for any surgeon pursuing a forensic career. Good habits in one field of endeavor tend to carry over into others.

As Brown was washing up, he turned to Bell and asked, "Well, sir, what do you make of all this?"

"I agree with your assessment that the killer has more than a rudimentary knowledge of anatomy, specifically female anatomy" he replied. "To be able to remove the uterus intact without nicking the bladder denotes more than a beginner's skill, especially when you consider he did it in a poorly lit square—and quickly to escape detection. The cuts of the liver appear random, since no portions of that organ were removed. Perhaps he is gradually expanding his knowledge, for this time he has removed a kidney. He has not done so before, while he has previously removed a uterus."

"Interesting, Professor." Brown nodded gratefully. "You are more familiar with his work than I, and I look forward to reading what my colleagues have discovered from his previous victims. I am grateful for the collaboration you have forged between our two agencies."

"As am I, Doctor," Bell agreed. "From what I have learned from the other postmortems, I believe he asphyxiated at least two of his victims before severing their throats. I cannot prove he did so this time; however, his subtlety in technique may have improved so it is no longer detectable. He apparently occludes the airway just firmly enough and long enough for the victim to lose consciousness, then severs their neck once they are supine and the neck stable. This would explain how he can make such a forceful incision in one go, as the neck is supported by the ground, and he can put his weight into the killing stroke."

Brown was entranced by Bell's vivid description of the killer's modus operandi. "Brilliant, Professor! That explains my findings perfectly. Your insight is greatly appreciated."

Bell smiled, savoring Brown's sincere praise. "It appears our murderer has found a technique in which he is comfortable and proficient, and I should be able to identify another of his victims unfailingly. One thing I would like to point out to my colleagues, if you will . . ." Turning, he indicated Margaret and I were to approach, then he rotated the victim's head, first to the right, then to the left, while lifting her hair to expose the scalp. Only a short remnant of the ear lobe remained on each side.

We nodded grimly, recalling the letter in red ink signed "Jack the Ripper." Somehow, giving the Ripper a voice made him even more terrifying.

"Well," Bell continued, "it has been a short night for all of us. I owe Major Smith a report in the morning, so I'd best be off. Thank you greatly for your cooperation, Doctor Brown. Should you ever come to Edinburgh, I would be grateful if you would visit me and find time to lecture my residents on the art of forensic examination."

Doctor Brown glowed at these kinds words and mumbled an acceptance. As a police surgeon, he was unused to notice of any sort, much less high praise from such a distinguished member of the medical profession. I doubt I have ever seen anyone so happy at the conclusion of a postmortem.

CHAPTER TWENTY-FOUR
A LIFE SPARED

Sunday, September 30, cont.

Once outside we had a brief conference regarding our next steps. Bell had to write a report in duplicate of his findings and conclusions of the examinations of the two bodies. Margaret offered her notes, and Bell accepted them gratefully. One thing above all else stood out regarding this latest victim. Her ears had, as had been predicted in the "Dear Boss" letter, been "clipped." This supported the supposition that the letter was a direct challenge from the murderer.

"Are you all right, Margaret?" I asked. "Did you know the victim?"

"Not personally," she replied. "But that doesn't matter, does it? As Master Donne so eloquently stated, 'Ask not for whom the bell tolls, it tolls for thee.' If I had been walking along Mitre Square at that hour, it could as easily have been me."

She shivered at this, then she fixed me with a fierce expression. "I have cared for accident victims as disfigured as she was, but this was not accidental. It was intentional, performed with great malice and, I assume, delight by the man who did it. We live our lives with certain assumptions; the sun will rise, rain will fall, and, yes, sometimes misfortune befalls us. But we go about this great city assuming that, if others do not wish us well, they at least do not intend us evil."

She clenched her jaw and shook her head slowly. "To know there is a man out there, lurking in the shadows, who takes pleasure in our cruel murder, is like introducing a shark into a public bathing area.

It changes the reality for all—not only the victims but the potential victims, of which I am one. So no, Doyle, in one way I did not know her; in another way, I am her."

I touched her arm for a moment, without speaking, for there was nothing to say. We had a murderer to catch. That mattered more than words.

As the only wound to the first victim was to the throat, Bell believed further examination of her body would be fruitless, so a return to the Metropolitan Police morgue was unnecessary. He also had to compose a summary of the findings from the previous two victims for Acting Commissioner Smith if we were to maintain the peace between the two departments.

After viewing the wanton mutilation of a fellow human being at first hand, I was more convinced than ever that forsaking the crime-story genre was a wise decision on my part. Surely there was enough cruelty and injustice in the world without the fictional adventures of my consulting detective to add to them. If people wanted to read of gore and destruction, they could easily turn to any newspaper. I vowed to have no further part in such titillation, and to never pen another tale involving my phlegmatic Mr. Holmes. I was ashamed I had written even one.

Returning to the real world, I was anxious to hear what Abberline had learned from his night's work, but I was reluctant to visit the inspector without Bell's keen mind to make sense of it, so we decided to part for the remainder of the day. Though I had benefitted from my three hours of sleep that morning, I was quite willing to spend the afternoon dozing in a comfortable leather chair at the Marlborough, while Bell labored over his reports.

Margaret agreed to a ride back to her flat. While hailing a cab, I glanced back and saw my two fellow Musketeers in an earnest conversation. Suddenly, Margaret clasped the professor's right hand warmly with both of hers, then dabbed at her eyes as though to wipe away tears. I received a nod from a driver, summoned my colleagues, and made no remark regarding what I had just seen.

We were silent during our trip to Margaret's tenement, each buried in our own thoughts. Margaret's eyes were still moist from whatever had transpired, while Bell appeared to be mentally composing his report. I confess I was jealous of the professor for the heartfelt exchange I had just seen pass between the two of them. I acknowledge such childlike emotions now with great shame, for when we arrived at Margaret's flat, she said to Bell, "You must come in and tell her. I refuse to do it alone!"

Bell smiled warmly and agreed. "Come, Doyle," he said. "We have a brief deviation. I promise to get you to the comforts of the Marlborough within the hour."

I disembarked with my comrades, for so I thought of them now, and paid the driver before filling in the expense in my now well-worn accounts ledger.

We trudged up the stairs, and after Margaret let us in she went straight to Miss Jones.

"Molly, Professor Bell has something to ask you."

Miss Jones had been knitting, and as her hands had been occupied, her habitual rag had been laid aside. She seemed embarrassed to be caught unawares without it, but as she had difficulty being understood speaking through it, left it where it lay.

"Miss Jones," asked Bell, "have you ever been to Edinburgh?"

"No sir," she replied, shaking her head, clearly puzzled.

"I have a proposition for you then," continued the professor. "I would like you to accompany me back to Edinburgh when I return. Phossy jaw is unknown in Scotland, as we have no match factories. You would make an excellent teaching case for my medical students and surgery residents. If you do not mind being examined by a group of cold-handed apprentice healers, I will pay for your trip to Edinburgh and back, and have you admitted to the Royal Infirmary of Edinburgh. Furthermore, I will perform the surgery myself. I will not be able to replace the bone you have lost, but I can restore your appetite, stop the drainage, and clear your mind. You will live, Miss Jones. What say you to that?"

The woman sat completely still for perhaps three heartbeats, then began to sob uncontrollably.

"Y-yes," she managed to whisper. "Dear God, yes!"

Molly stood, and Margaret embraced her for a long time, while we two men stood there, embarrassed at this outpouring of female emotion.

Mine was surely the heavier burden, however, due to the added shame of my unworthy thoughts moments ago about my friends. I had no doubt at that moment; Professor Joseph Bell was a far better man than me.

Once decorum was reestablished, Bell asked if he could show me the hallmarks of her case.

Miss Jones seemed confused by this, but Margaret nodded and reassured her. "He wants to show Doctor Doyle your jaw."

Molly agreed readily enough, and then Margaret, without any coaching from Bell, closed the drapes.

Bell took me by the hand and led me to her. I could tell by the stench of the necrotic bone I was drawing nearer. Then in the darkness, I saw something that both repelled and fascinated me. As a surgeon on a whaling vessel I had seen the Northern Lights glimmering majestically in the Arctic sky. Here I saw the green-and-yellow glowing of phosphorous embedded within her dead and dying bone, slowly leaching out and poisoning her.

I had seen much pain, suffering, and evil this past week. Here was another example, though one with a crucial difference; this evil could be rectified. Perhaps I was so deeply affected by the sight because I saw it as a metaphor for our efforts to catch this wanton killer of the helpless. We could not replace what was lost, but we could prevent further damage. Though an imperfect solution, it was still something.

We said our goodbyes to the ladies of Vine Street, and during our trip back to the club, Bell confessed the idea of taking Miss Jones as a teaching case had occurred to him at the conclusion of the post-mortem. "After I invited Doctor Brown to lecture at Edinburgh, her case suddenly occurred to me as an instructive opportunity. I have no hospital privileges in London, and while we are engaged in this matter I could not give her case the attention it requires. I must return to Scotland by the end of the week due to Her Majesty's pending travel to Balmoral. There are many things I can alter, but the itinerary of a Royal Personage is not one of them. Miss Jones can accompany me, I can assure her prompt admission to hospital, present her case, and perform her surgery."

"How will she return to London, Professor?" I asked. "You may be returning in a month, or not for some time later."

"Once she can travel," Bell explained, "I shall purchase her return ticket and place her on the train. Since it is a direct journey to London, Margaret can meet her at the railway station. My students will get an excellent clinical presentation, and Miss Jones is spared from a slow and painful death."

"Thank you, Professor," I said sincerely. "Both for her sake and for Margaret's."

Bell did not reply in words; his small smile of satisfaction told me everything. As befits a gentleman.

I was still ashamed at my previous jealousy toward Bell regarding Margaret's brief display of affection toward him. To lighten my mood, I attempted a small demonstration for Professor Bell, to show him his lessons on observation had not been wasted.

"Regarding our colleague, Doctor Brown," I ventured. "I deduce that he suffered from rickets as a child, is a life-long bachelor, and studied medicine in France."

Bell looked at me in silent amazement for a moment. I was starting to swell with pride when he suddenly burst out laughing. After maybe twenty seconds of hilarity, he paused to wipe the tears from his eyes. He asked then, not unkindly, "Ah, and upon what grounds do ye make ye'r deductions, lad?" This time I interpreted his Scottish brogue as signifying that he was amused.

"Well, to start . . ." I began defensively, "there is his gait. He has a wide stance and walks with his legs rather farther apart. Someone with rickets has bowing of the femur, which can cause such a gait in adulthood when the bones are fully grown yet still bent."

"And his bachelorhood?" Bell inquired mildly.

"He wasn't wearing a wedding ring," I declared, proud of my new-found powers of observation.

"And his studies in France?" Bell persisted.

"Surely, Professor, you saw the medical degree on his wall in French," I replied, increasingly uneasy about my accuracy, since Bell's expression continued to show his amusement.

Bell shook his head; I hoped in admiration at my conclusions. Then he thoroughly shattered my illusions.

"The stance, Doyle, is due to his early days as an avid polo player. There was a well-scuffed ball resting on the corner of his desk. Those who spend long hours astride a horse develop the same gait you correctly describe. Also, besides bowing of the legs, rickets causes thickening of the wrists and ankles. I didn't see his ankles, but his wrists appeared entirely normal."

My ears were burning, but I felt obliged to defend my remaining conclusions. "And the absence of a wedding ring?" I asked.

"Taken off prior to the autopsy, my friend," Bell said. "I saw him place it in his pocket when he stood. Also, there was a crude drawing on the wall of his office, apparently from a loving child. Only a devoted father would display the work of a budding artist of around five years of age in their workplace."

Now I was like a chess player playing for a stalemate. "And the French medical diploma?" I said, employing my final gambit.

"The diploma is indeed in French," Bell agreed. "But the seal was from the Université de Montréal in Canada. I fear, my friend, that your deductions are wide of the mark. But I am pleased to see you exercising your powers of observation. Do not despair; it will come."

I was saved from further embarrassment as, at that moment, we arrived at the club.

"Ah, here we are!" Bell said with satisfaction. "I have a report to compose for what appears to be a very strict headmaster. I trust you can find some means to entertain yourself while I labor in the vineyards?"

After my less-than-sterling performance at playing detective, I was ready to retreat to the library, sulk, and, of course, nap. I knew my companion would have no difficulty meeting Major Smith's expectations, and the report would not take overly long to produce. My learned companion was as sure with his pen as his knife.

I also knew there would yet be tough sledding ahead. Having once fallen through the ice four times in three days while seal hunting (prompting the captain to inquire if I was trying to swim back to England), that saying holds a special significance for me.

CHAPTER TWENTY-FIVE
THE RIPPER IS BORN

Monday, October 1

The next morning Bell and I dined at six so he could deliver his report by seven o'clock to Major Smith. We arrived on the hour and were promptly ushered into the acting commissioner's office by the gloomy desk sergeant, who greeted us only with a nod and "He's expecting you."

Major Smith was as meticulously groomed as before, and although he did not smile, he did nod approvingly when Bell presented him with the summation of the postmortem examinations for the four victims.

"It's refreshing to deal with a man who keeps his end of a bargain," he said. "Based upon your cooperation, I have decided to liaise regularly with Inspector Swanson, Commissioner Warren's lead man on the murders. It is best for all concerned to put our jurisdictional squabbles aside to bring this cur to heel. Is there anything else you would ask of my office?"

"Thank you, Major," replied Bell. "Might we speak with one of your inspectors to get an accounting of how the body was found, and what you have learned of the victim's movements the last few hours before her discovery?"

"Certainly, Professor, though I doubt you will learn much more than what is in today's papers. I fear some of my men are over fond of speaking with journalists. Superintendent James McWilliam is the man heading our investigation. Let me compose a brief note to him authorizing disclosure of information to you and Inspector Swanson."

The note was written quickly, and, bearing our latest in a series of passports, we returned to the desk sergeant. He nodded wordlessly toward an adjacent hall, which led to the office of Superintendent McWilliam.

We found a slender, pale man immersed in a cloud of cigarette smoke, actively consuming the latest of apparently many vile-smelling specimens. He was in his early forties and, like his superior, was immaculately groomed, and dressed in a suit more in keeping with a successful banker than a police officer.

I recalled Abberline's disparaging remarks about his colleagues in the City of London Police, and inwardly smiled when we presented ourselves to this nervous gentleman who greeted us cautiously through thick horn-rimmed spectacles.

Bell explained our purpose and asked the inspector if he could give us any details regarding the discovery of the body in Mitre Square.

"I can only spare you a moment," he responded, with the raspy voice common in tobacco fiends. "If brevity does not offend, I will spare what time I can."

"Most generous and much appreciated," replied the professor. "Then I shall be brief as well. I have four questions: What can you tell me about the victim? How was she discovered? What did your investigation of the scene reveal? And, finally, what do you know of her activities during her final day?"

McWilliam smiled briefly, revealing the yellowed teeth of the habitual smoker, and nodded. "Her name and movements I can tell you readily enough. Her name was Catherine Eddowes, a middle-aged married woman with no known history as a streetwalker, but she was well-known for frequent public drunkenness. From approximately nine o'clock Saturday night until one Sunday morning she was a guest at the Bishopsgate police station—for public intoxication after collapsing during a performance of fire engine impersonations for an appreciative audience. Mitre Square, where the body was found, is about eight minutes' walk from the station.

"At a quarter before two, Police Constable Watkins discovered the body of a woman lying on her back with her throat slit and her dress thrown up over her waist. Watkins was most affected by what he saw, especially the wounds to the face, which I understand have not been a feature of previous attacks."

Having recently seen her facial disfigurement in daylight in the city morgue, I could well imagine the effect they could have on a nonmedical person when viewed without warning by the light of a bull's-eye lantern.

McWilliam continued. "Watkins summoned a night watchman at a nearby warehouse, then dispatched him to gather reinforcements from other constables patrolling nearby. The watchman soon returned with two others. One fetched Doctor Sequira, who arrived just before two o'clock and, after a very brief examination, pronounced her dead. I got there shortly after two thirty with a robust contingent of detectives, and took command of the ongoing search of the area and the questioning of all found wandering about."

"And no one saw or heard anything?" I asked. "How is that possible?"

The superintendent's brows knitted together in frustration. "I confess I am baffled as to how such a gruesome crime could be committed with so many people nearby. One of our force, Police Constable Pearse, resides at 3 Mitre Square, and his bedroom window looks out upon the murder site scant yards away. And the night watchman summoned by PC Watkins guards the premises of a warehouse directly across the square from where the body was found. The man was awake and on duty when Watkins arrived, claiming to have heard the constable's footsteps as he walked his beat, yet says he heard nothing unusual."

"What of the graffito?" Bell asked. "What route would the killer take to reach the site where the apron fragment and message were found?"

"Well, Professor, after the killer finished with Mrs. Eddowes, the most likely route from Mitre Square to the site of the message is via St. James's Place. This required him to pass by a metropolitan fire station, yet the firemen on duty claim not to have seen or heard anything out of the ordinary. More puzzling to me, however, is that at one thirty City detectives were organizing plainclothes patrols on the eastern border of our jurisdiction, so it appears the murderer passed right through our screen undetected."

He stared down at his hands, which were resting on the desk for a moment, perhaps contemplating how the killer had slipped through his grasp. So close. So painfully close.

He shook himself out of his reverie, and concluded emphatically, "I do not believe in the supernatural, gentlemen, but I cannot explain how someone could perpetrate such a horrendous crime, which must have taken several minutes to perform, in a public square, then float unnoticed through a gauntlet of alert and experienced police officers."

Bell listened intently to McWilliam's recitation. I noticed his body tense when the superintendent related his frustration at the killer slipping through the contingent of plainclothes officers. This madman's skills in murder and evasion did invoke the unsettling vision of a creature from another realm. I shivered at the image.

"Thank you, Superintendent," Bell replied. "You have been brief but most informative. The need for brevity forces us to sift the essential from the chaff. We'll leave you to it, but should we have questions in future, I hope we may call upon you again."

McWilliam nodded, responding amiably to Bell's praise and professional bearing. Often afterward, when confronted with an obstructive individual, I have thought back to how the professor would respond in such instances and have found his example worthy of imitation. He never compromised his dignity; yet never did he detract from another's. His assumption that all men saw themselves as honorable allowed him to enlist their sympathies to whatever cause he was championing. Sadly, his skill in winning people's collaboration, like his observational and deductive skills, was something to admire but difficult to emulate.

The fact that Bell, Margaret, and I were not agents of any official body meant that while we had to negotiate our way into the investigation, we were not encumbered with the animosities that permeated the police hierarchies within London. In retrospect, I shake my head in admiration at the way my old mentor exploited the situation.

It was scarcely nine o'clock when we found ourselves outside. "What now?" I asked.

"I want to learn what Inspector Abberline has discovered since yesterday. Let's add Pennyworth to our party and return to Spitalfields. I would also like to speak with Doctor Phillips to see if his postmortem revealed anything of interest from the other victim. That should take the rest of the day."

Bell was a dynamo, fueled with purpose. I believe after seeing the handiwork of the killer in the morgue the day before, the importance of our mission was impressed upon him, as my conversation with Margaret after the postmortem had done to me.

"Tomorrow I'll compose a report for Wilkins," Bell said. "I'll need to delay my departure until Thursday, so I recommend arranging a meeting with him on Wednesday at the club, preferably in the morning. Then I need to return to Edinburgh, Miss Jones in tow, to fulfill my obligations. Her Majesty's household expects her to remain at Balmoral for one month before affairs of state require her return to London. I shall of course be available for consultation via the post or telegram. What of you, Doyle? Will you remain here as my correspondent, or go back to Portsmouth?"

"I should return to my practice soon, so my patients recall who their physician is, as well as spend time with my wife, who is pregnant with our first child."

I am ashamed to admit that, as engrossed as I was in the investigation, I had forgotten to mention Louise's pregnancy. Bell gave me a celebratory clap on the shoulder and wished Louise and me well. I believe when I was in Bell's presence, I tended to assume the role of medical student once more and forget at times we were now colleagues. To his credit, Bell never treated me as anything but a fellow healer from the moment he arrived in London.

"Like you," I continued after warm handshakes were exchanged, "I can return to London at need. I am confident Miss Harkness can keep us abreast of any new developments while we're gone."

This phase of our hunt was drawing to a close, and we had nothing to show for it. We could only prepare ourselves to follow a fresh trail, when it inevitably came.

CHAPTER TWENTY-SIX
THE DEATH OF LEATHER APRON

Monday, October 1, cont.

When we arrived at Margaret's flat, Miss Jones was still beaming at the prospect of her pending surgery. When Bell advised her to be prepared to travel in three days' time, her glow became even more pronounced.

"I shall tidy up my affairs here on Wednesday," Bell told her, "then take the first available train to Edinburgh on Thursday. We will go directly to the Royal Infirmary from the station and admit you to my service. Expect one week of clinical presentations to our medical students and surgical residents, then surgery."

Bell touched Molly lightly on the jaw. "The blood supply to the head and neck is robust, so healing should be brisk. One week of post-operative care and additional presentations, then you should be fit to travel home."

Molly nodded. Her gaze told me everything. She trusted him completely.

"I shall inform Miss Harkness three days before your release," Bell said, "so she may receive you at the station. If I am not required to return to London in a month's time, then I shall correspond with one of my colleagues here to evaluate you to see if you need further care, and to inform me of the result. Is that satisfactory?"

"Anything you say, sir!" Miss Jones said, carefully but enthusiastically enunciating each syllable, while nodding vigorously and taking Bell's right hand in both of hers.

Bell blushed slightly, surprised and gratified by her reaction. He nodded kindly and carefully extracted his hand from hers.

Much of my practice consisted of reassuring patients with minor ailments, thus I envied Bell his opportunity to make a real difference in the life of his patient through his surgical skill and generous heart. I had recently become interested in studying eye surgery, and Molly's case made this career path look all the more appealing. My writing up until then had had only middling success; thus the opportunity to earn a supportable income while making a vast improvement in a person's life held a strong appeal.

Miss Jones made us tea while Bell shared with Margaret the essence of our conversation with Superintendent McWilliam.

"What do you deduce from all this?" Margaret asked at the conclusion. "Surely you give no credence to McWilliam's suggestion that we are dealing with some murdering specter?"

"My philosophy does not allow for such phenomena," replied Bell. "We are dealing with an unspeakable evil, to be sure, but one composed of flesh and blood. As to his ability to move about the East End through a network of experienced police officers seeking him, I have some thoughts. His method of execution, we now know, is one of suffocation followed by slitting the throat once the victim is supine. He could continue to suffocate them, but I think his anger is so intense toward women he needs to finish his foul work with the knife."

Margaret shivered, and I felt as though a cold hand had been placed on my heart as I imagined Margaret walking the dark streets of the East End, alone.

"Recall his random stabbing of the liver of his last victim," Bell continued. "Yet, he took nothing from it. The liver would be congested with blood, and ooze freely—but not spurt. In the same way, the throat wound would bleed briskly, yet with the heart slowed and the victim upon her back, he could have easily leaned back and avoided becoming blood splattered. If he pulled his sleeves back," whereupon Bell pulled back his own sleeves and held his hands up, as though gowning for surgery, "he could prevent any blood contaminating his clothing altogether.

"As to his evasion of the police, I once holidayed at Penzance and was amazed at the lifeguards' ability to monitor some three hundred bathers simultaneously. I asked one how he was able to safeguard so many at the same time, to which he replied he rarely focused on any particular person but monitored movements; those moving smoothly were in no distress. He was looking for abnormal, jerky motion, and with his mind searching for that pattern, he could efficiently overlook hundreds of individuals yet immediately find the one swimmer who needed assistance."

"How is that relevant, Professor?" Margaret asked, furrowing her brow.

Bell smiled. "I believe our policemen are looking for someone moving furtively with blood-splattered clothing. A man walking slowly and confidently in pristine apparel would easily escape their notice; his appearance does not fit their image of the murderer."

Bell assumed the tone of voice I recalled so well from his lectures in medical school. "Our killer is mad—of that, I have no doubt—but he has a ruthless cunning and nerve that scoffs at consequences. I suspect he does not fear punishment—not even hanging—but dodges detection for the joy of the chase and to prolong his game. Once captured, I wager that rather than plead for mercy in the dock he shall boast of his cleverness and the horrid nature of his crimes. He feels the need to degrade his victims, even after death, to demonstrate his superiority."

Bell's description of the killer fit perfectly with what I had seen but had been unable to express so aptly. We think in words, for language is how we make sense of the world. Until this experience could be articulated, it was unformed. My vision of our foe was made clearer by my teacher's deductions.

"Miss Harkness's supposition that our killer is meek in appearance, one which I strongly support," Bell said, while nodding toward her, "further explains both the viciousness of his attacks and his ability to escape detection. He has probably been humiliated by women, and chose this macabre means to demonstrate his masculinity. Then he uses his unassuming aspect as a disguise to slip through the clutches of his pursuers, thereby proving to himself he is also exceedingly clever. Unless he makes a mistake or we are fortunate enough to catch him en flagrante, he will probably have quite a run before being brought to justice."

"I fear you're right, Professor," said Margaret, "though it brings me no comfort. We have three days before you two depart. How should we spend our remaining time together, and what would you have me do once you're gone?"

"I should look in on Doctor Phillips to learn if the postmortem showed anything unexpected, as well as update Abberline with our findings from the second victim, while asking him to share whatever his efforts have uncovered. I would not plan anything beyond those two meetings yet. Let us see what our colleagues have discovered and go from there."

Margaret nodded agreement with our itinerary, but said nothing, her downward gaze informing me she was busy digesting the professor's lecture on the personality of the killer.

Bell elected to see Doctor Phillips first, explaining Phillips's examination was complete while Abberline's was ongoing. Therefore, the later in the day we visited the inspector, the more he would have to tell us.

The chief clerk merely nodded to us when we arrived and confirmed that Doctor Phillips was in. Thankfully, he had a small office upstairs and I, for one, gratefully redirected my footsteps to the more mundane world of bureaucracy.

The police surgeon was writing his report on the victim and seemed grateful for the pause in his labors.

"I come bearing gifts," began Bell. "Here," he said, placing a document into Phillips's hands, "is a copy of the postmortem of the second victim we now know was named Catherine Eddowes, an intemperate woman apparently, but with no known history as a streetwalker. Frugal Scotsman that I am, I trust you have some new intelligence for me regarding the other lady as means of payment?"

Phillips eagerly scanned the postmortem summary, and seemed pleased with what he found there. Looking up, he shook his head in mock sadness. "Alas Professor, I have nothing of like value, though I do have some small crumbs which will hopefully make your visit worthwhile. The papers are full of what transpired early Sunday morning, and I have been told to expect a visit this afternoon from a woman who believes our guest is her sister. That would at least give a name to the first victim of the night."

"Having a name would prove useful, no doubt," I remarked. "That will allow the police to be able to recreate her movements more accurately."

Doctor Phillips shook his head. "So far, this information has brought us no closer to catching the killer, but at least it gives the appearance the police are doing something worthwhile."

I smiled in sympathy. "There is no way to tell how your efforts may bear fruit, before the harvest. Console yourself that at least your patients do not return with fresh maladies."

Phillips smiled at my attempt at levity, "If I do my job properly, Doctor Doyle, they don't come back at all!" There is always some professional rivalry between surgeons and physicians; it is a constant source of jokes between us.

"As to my findings at the postmortem," he said, "I found bruises of varying vintage signifying repeated trauma. Apparently, she was a woman who knew hardship and violence all her life, who met a violent, if speedy, end. It appears the killer was interrupted before he could complete whatever bloody rites his madness requires."

Phillips grimaced, "At least this woman was spared the degradation of mutilation. Small comfort perhaps, as the denial likely spurred our killer, now aroused by the frustration of the first murder, to seek and strike down the next woman he encountered."

"I agree," Bell concurred. "The second victim was not even a streetwalker, and was killed in a public square, with apparently no attempt to lure her into a secluded alley. He must have been compelled to kill and desecrate the victim as soon as he saw her, and was unable to wait long enough to take any precautions. When he attacked Mrs. Eddowes, I believe any woman would have served."

Margaret shivered the slightest bit at this, but otherwise kept her manly composure. The thought of being viciously assaulted by this lunatic without warning or provocation must have been a terrifying one. When he only killed prostitutes, other female residents of the East End could comfort themselves that as long as they did not agree to liaisons in dark places, they could feign safety from the killer. Now this illusion had been shattered, and nighttime for the women of Whitechapel had just become even more terrifying.

"Thank you again, Professor, for this," Phillips said, indicating the postmortem of Mrs. Eddowes. "I regret I cannot repay you in like coin now. Sadly, however, I am sure there shall be future opportunities to make good my debt to you. Good day!"

"I am now more anxious than ever to learn what Inspector Abberline's inquiries have turned up," Bell said, once we'd stepped outside. "The great disparity in injuries between the two victims is striking. From what we have deduced of the killer's character, we can be sure it was no gesture of either mercy or respect for the woman he had just slain. Perhaps we have a witness who interrupted him? Anything we might learn to distinguish him physically from the crowd would greatly aid us."

"Do you think he is now targeting all women?" asked Margaret. "Or was this second attack an aberration due to his failure with the first?"

"I should rather think the latter, Miss Harkness," replied Bell. "And I believe your use of the word 'failure' is exactly how he perceived the murder. He does not kill merely to rob a woman of her life. No. He failed to desecrate her body, so he was unfulfilled by her murder and, having become aroused, had to kill again. And quickly. That would explain both his wanton selection of his victim and the public space he chose to kill her. It was our best chance to date to capture him, yet he slipped away once more despite a robust police presence, including one slumbering scant yards away, and the nearby watchman. His bold disregard for the odds of discovery speaks of an overpowering compulsion to perform his beastly rituals. Well, let us visit Inspector Abberline to see what he can tell us."

As we sought transport to Spitalfields, a newsboy hawking papers happened by. I overheard him use the term "Jack the Ripper."

I purchased a copy of the *Star*, and learned Commissioner Warren had decided to release the contents of the letter addressed to the Central News Agency we had studied in Inspector Abberline's office. From that moment on, "Leather Apron" was no more. The legend of "Jack the Ripper" was born.

CHAPTER TWENTY-SEVEN
HOMICIDE, INTERRUPTED

Monday, October 1, cont.

Inspector Abberline looked as though he hadn't slept since last we saw him. I have noticed over the years that the more people disparage public servants, the less time they have spent in their company. Before me was a man who had the weight of an entire community on his shoulders, confronting danger and criticism at every quarter from people he would never meet and who were, for the most part, ungrateful.

I have never doubted that one of the strengths of the British Empire lies in its capable and dedicated functionaries. May we never lack for men, and now increasingly women, who undertake the necessary and unpleasant tasks that keep us safe, the streets clean, the byways intact, and the mail delivered. Inspector Frederick George Abberline was, to my mind, an exemplar of those who take the title of public servant literally and with considerable pride.

The poor man was sitting in his chair dressed in the same clothes we had last seen him in two days before. His muddied boots were resting on his desk, and a report was balanced precariously upon his paunch as he attempted to read it while keeping both bloodshot eyes open.

He started so violently when we walked in that he nearly fell out of his chair, and I suspect he had just begun to doze off when we entered. It was now eleven thirty in the morning, thirty-four hours since he had roused us from our sleep. Bell and I had made up for that short night's slumber, but the inspector was obviously in arrears.

Bell smiled sympathetically at him as he offered a copy of the post-mortem on Mrs. Eddowes. "Here you go, Inspector, as promised. I think you'll find the City of London police more willing to share information going forward. They have neither forgotten nor forgiven Commissioner Warren's order to erase the graffito, but they have decided to be pragmatic. I can see you are quite played out and I urge you to get some rest. I cannot praise the comfort of the cots in your conference room, but in your current state they will serve well enough. If any should ask, you can say it was doctor's orders. Four hours minimum, starting now!"

Abberline looked at him for a long moment, pondering Bell's words, then sighed and agreed. "Aye. I'm no good to anyone right now. Go to the desk sergeant and ask for Sergeant Thicke. You may recall he led the constables who responded to your brawl with Tommy and his lot. He can tell you as well or better than I how goes our investigation into the murder in Dutfield's Yard. Until later, gentlemen."

With that, the exhausted man rose from his chair and tottered off to the relative bliss of the cots that awaited him down the hall.

We were soon in the presence of the indomitable Sergeant Thicke. I later learned that he was known in Spitalfields as "Johnny Upright." His appearance was remarkable for his almost rigid posture, thick blond mustache, and loud checked suit. I had noticed his name often when reading of the previous murders as being at the scene shortly after the body's discovery and, after reading the news article and seeing him in action, understood why he was known to the local criminals as someone to be avoided.

It was evident "Johnny Upright" had little use for private consultants, but when Bell told him that Inspector Abberline had referred us, he sighed and responded to our questions dutifully.

"I can spare ye twenty minutes, and then I need to return to the streets. There's some folk I've yet to speak with. There's plenty more to learn yet, but I'll tell ye what I know. If ye don't mind me stuffing me gob while we talk, then ask away!"

Having little choice, we agreed.

"Tell me how the body was discovered," Bell opened.

"Ah, now that is an interesting story, to be sure," began the sergeant. "At one o'clock in the morning, a Jewish gentleman named Diemschutz was returning to the International Working Men's Educational Club to fetch his wife.

"The pony pulling his cart shied left as he entered the court and refused to go further. Looking down, he saw a dark shape on the ground and prodded it with the end of his whip. When he was unable to stir it, he got out of the driver's seat and, striking a match, saw a woman lying on the ground before the wind blew the fire out."

Sergeant Thicke took a generous bite from his ploughman's lunch and, after a moment of vigorous chewing, resumed his story. "Fearing the woman was his wife, Mr. Diemschutz ran into the club and found 'er quite safe. He then announced loudly there was a woman lying outside in the yard, but he didn't know if she were alive or dead. He returned to the yard with a candle, accompanied by several club members. With the improved light he saw the body lying in a pool of blood and the woman's throat cut. Immediately everyone there rushed off in all directions screaming 'murder' and 'police' at the top of their lungs!"

Despite his initial reluctance, Johnny Upright was now thoroughly enjoying his tale of midnight murder. He leaned closer to us as he continued his story.

"As dark as it was within the yard that night, our Mr. Ripper could have been right there on the other side of the cart when Diemschutz struck his match. It's a wonder we didn't have a third murder."

Thicke reapplied himself to his meal, and Bell asked, "And what of the victim? Any leads on who she might be?"

He shook his head. "Nothing for sure," he mumbled while chewing. "Luckily I don't need to know 'er name to ask folks if they might have seen 'er about before one o'clock. On that point, we've some leads. There's two gentlemen that think they may 'ave seen 'er around eleven in a doorway of the Bricklayer's Arms on Settles Street. It was raining pretty heavy, so she was biding 'er time to let the rain pass in the company of a man about five foot five with a black mustache, dressed in a black morning suit and billycock hat." Sergeant Thicke smirked as he informed us, "They say the couple seemed in no hurry to go out into the weather, and that the gentleman was hugging and a kissing on 'er pretty heavy."

"Strange," Margaret remarked. "If that man were our killer, I wouldn't expect him to linger in the open so long, nor to draw attention to himself. If it was him, his nerve is even greater than we thought."

"Aye," agreed Thicke appreciatively. "Our two gents said it was odd how a gentleman so respectably dressed should go on so in public; and they chaffed at them a bit, saying, 'Watch out! That's Leather Apron getting round you!' Well, they was off like a shot after that, and our witnesses say they headed off together toward Commercial Street."

"A useful description," I said, feeling encouraged by the details the witnesses had provided. Surely this had gotten us a step closer to catching him! "Any other sightings after that?"

"At eleven forty-five, a Mr. Marshall, residing at 64 Berner Street, says he saw a man and a woman kissing outside No. 63. He overheard the man say to the woman, 'You would say anything but your prayers.' The couple then headed off toward Dutfield's Yard. Mr. Williams describes the man as about five foot six, stout, middle aged, cleanshaven, and respectfully dressed in a small black cutaway coat, dark trousers, and a round cap."

I was keenly disappointed at the differences in the description of the victim's male companion. In a fictional tale there would be an unbreakable chain of sightings with various witnesses giving identical details. I was learning a crime story and the real world were as different as chalk and cheese. How frustrating it must be, to labor in an environment where two people could view the same event or person in a similar light, yet produce very different statements. Did either of these accounts describe our murderer? Neither? Both? Any of these possibilities seemed equally likely. It defied reason to believe our killer could solicit a woman and escort her to Dutfield's Yard unnoticed; yet his ability to pass through the streets and alleyways at will made anything likely.

"We have a new system for making sketches of criminals," Thicke mumbled while chewing. "It's called a 'Portrait Parle,' so named by the Frog who designed it. Means 'speaking picture.' We tried it with the witnesses, but it was so dark when they saw him they couldn't give us anything useful. Pity. Jack's got to make a mistake sooner or later. We'll be ready when he does!"

We thanked the good sergeant for the information, and left him contentedly picking his teeth.

"I think it's time for Doyle and me to return to the club," Bell said to Margaret. "The papers will have additional information, given the number of journalists prowling the East End. What of you, Miss Harkness? Aren't your editors clamoring for some insight from the East End?"

Margaret scowled. "Given my pledge of silence during the investigation, I can't report on that." She sighed. "I suppose I could interview some of the residents, but I am currently not in the good graces of my male 'colleagues' after berating them for slipshod reporting. They shrug and reply they are newspapermen, not historians. So no, I am unlikely to be summoned to report on anything related to the murders."

Her acid reply made it clear Bell's simple question had touched a very raw nerve.

I changed the subject as quickly as I could. "Well then, let's get you back to Vine Street and Miss Jones before we two return to the Marlborough. An afternoon reading the papers and learning what others have discovered is a luxury I am quite ready to enjoy."

"I wish there were clubs for women!" Margaret fumed. "A leisurely afternoon reading the paper sounds like paradise. I don't suppose I could come along?" the last said with a wicked grin, knowing full well the havoc her presence would cause among the staid gentlemen roosting in their male sanctuary.

Bell smiled broadly, no doubt imagining middle-aged barristers flapping their arms in horror at her approach, before he returned to the business at hand. "I need to complete my report to Wilkins," he said. "I heartily agree our Mr. Pennyworth can ably fill us in once we are gone." He bowed to Margaret in mock seriousness before continuing,

"Nothing I have learned over the past twenty-four hours leads me to believe we are any closer to capturing the man. I intend to return once my duties in Edinburgh are complete, but Miss Harkness can keep the trail warm until then. She has been seen in our company regularly and can make a convincing case as Mr. Pennyworth that 'he' is acting as our agent pending our return. Are you agreeable, Miss Harkness?"

Margaret smiled, revealing a lovely set of dimples I had not previously noticed. "You may depend upon me, Professor. My research for my next novel and the investigation into the murders dovetail nicely. I shall correspond with both of you as the situation warrants. Shall I see you before Thursday morning when you depart with Molly?"

"Only if necessary, in which case we'll send a courier beforehand," Bell replied. "I'll have the doorman get me a timetable and send word to you tomorrow as to what time to have Miss Jones meet me at the rail station on Thursday."

Margaret nodded, and off we went. There was little conversation during our journey to Margaret's flat, each of us deep in thought.

As she disembarked she remarked, "Very well, gentlemen." Margaret repaid Bell and me with her own mock-serious bow. "Until Thursday morn . . . or the next disaster."

Mr. Pennyworth disappeared into the dark entryway, while Bell and I exchanged a nod of respect for this unorthodox woman.

Upon our arrival at the Marlborough, I dashed off a note to Wilkins informing him of our need to delay our departure until Thursday, and requesting that we meet Wednesday at our usual time of nine o'clock. The doorman at the Marlborough quickly dispatched the message via one of his waiting street Arabs, and the boy returned with an affirmative reply within the hour. The doorman was not required to gather newspapers for us this time, however, as the club was full of all the latest reports of the murders. I needed only to gather them up and sift through the harvest, then bring to Bell's attention anything I thought worth his notice. In the meanwhile, he jotted down his thoughts by way of a first draft for Wilkins.

While I was dissatisfied by returning home without the fiend's head as a trophy, I would not miss having to report to someone or otherwise account for my time and efforts. In Portsmouth I was solely responsible for my practice and head of my soon-to-be growing household, and, frankly, that was how I liked it. Mr. Wilkins was not an unreasonable employer, but employer he was. I was looking forward to being shed of him, if only for a while.

I had no shortage of news to share with my companion, so I decided rather than constantly interrupting him, I would provide a summary once I had learned all there was from what lay before me. After I had underlined the last article of interest, I looked up to see him sipping tea and looking at me expectedly.

"What have you to report, my friend?" he enquired. "By the look on your face, you have a great deal to share."

"First, there is the matter of a reward. You recall how Sir Warren of the Metropolitan Police has consistently refused to offer one? Well, the mayor of the City of London has authorized a payment of five hundred pounds to anyone who can provide information leading to the Ripper's apprehension. It appears that taking a life within the Financial Square Mile is a more serious matter than within the East End."

I recalled our conversation en route to the City of London morgue, and Bell's prediction that now that the killer had crossed into the realm of the great and powerful, the resources to catch him would be redoubled. It saddened me to think I lived in a society that put varying values on human life, but this reward was ample proof it was so.

Bell shook his head. "I agree with Abberline in this, as well as in many other matters. The reward will only hinder the investigation, for now every charlatan or soothsayer with a crystal ball will come forth with a vision, rumor, or something a friend of a friend may have thought they heard or saw. The police will find themselves chasing so many false leads any effort at real police work shall be nearly impossible. Is there any good news amongst all the ink you've scanned this afternoon?"

"The letter we examined in Abberline's office has, as you know, been released by the police in hopes someone may recognize the writer."

Bell sighed. "Which I suspect will incite everyone who has a grudge against their neighbor to accuse them of being the Ripper. Folly heaped upon folly. I am starting to think we three may soon be the only ones left doing any serious work in this matter. Any other good news?"

Before I could respond, we were interrupted by a much-revived Inspector Abberline, who had another letter from the man who wrote in red.

CHAPTER TWENTY-EIGHT
JACKY SPEAKS AGAIN

Monday, October 1, cont.

Bell rose to greet him. "Inspector! We weren't expecting you. Nonetheless, welcome." He bade the inspector take a seat and offered him refreshment.

I was again impressed by how my colleague treated this good public servant not only as an equal, which he of course was—in every way and more—but almost as a friend.

Abberline shuffled about a little, not entirely comfortable in our posh surroundings, and refused a seat.

"I'm to home as quick as I can," he explained. "But I have something I wanted your thoughts on before I call it a day. It was faster I come here direct."

He reached into a leather valise and produced an envelope marked with today's date and addressed to "Central News Agency."

"What do you make of this?"

Bell took the envelope and opened it. Inside was a plain postcard with a postal mark of October first from the London E postal station. Having risen, I stood beside the professor's armchair, and so I could clearly notice what appeared to be a bloodstain and writing in the now familiar red ink with the following message:

I was not coddling dear old Boss when I gave you the tip, you'll hear about Saucy Jacky's work tomorrow double event this time number one squealed a bit couldn't finish straight off. Had not the time to get ears for police. Thanks for keeping last letter back till I got to work again.

Jack the Ripper

Bell scrutinized this latest message, leaning back in his chair to remove his shadow from the letter. After a full minute, one that seemed like an eternity to me, and probably as well to the exhausted inspector, Bell returned it to him and spoke slowly. "The postmark tells us this was written and sent after the first letter was published in the newspapers. Given the style and use of red ink, I am confident this is the work of the same individual who wrote the previous message. This 'double event' is not confirmatory evidence that this note is from the killer, however, as news of the double homicides was carried in the evening papers that day."

Abberline glared at Bell. "All well and good, Professor, but how does this help us?" He spoke with the impatience of a tired man. Even my good Doctor Watson would have perceived that.

"Given what we know," Bell replied patiently, "I see one of two possible conclusions: that this is a genuine communication from the killer, or it is a hoax perpetrated by a newspaperman from the Central News Agency."

"How can you be so specific as to who might have forged it?" Abberline asked, his fatigue and puzzlement showing in equal measure.

"Consider, Inspector," Bell answered. "The role of the Central News Agency is to gather information and write articles to be picked up by newspapers to be published under that paper's byline. Only someone in the newspaper business would know this agency exists, as they print nothing under their own name. How would someone who isn't a journalist know they exist, much less know their address?"

Abberline nodded his head wearily, showing he was following Bell's explanation so far.

"Given the competition in the journalism trade, I cannot believe a newspaperman from one enterprise would send such a lucrative story to another."

"Is there anything here that leads you to conclude it is from the killer?" I asked, trying to expedite Bell's explanation to speed Abberline's much-needed journey to bed.

Bell was pensive in his reply. "The only factor for the murderer being the author is the mention in the previous message of 'nicking' the ears of the next victim. Whatever the case may be, Inspector, now that the first letter has been released to the public I predict the practice of forging letters to newspapers, members of parliament, and reverend clergy, all purporting to be from Jack the Ripper, shall soon become the pastime of many a literate person of weak character. I wish you a well-earned night's rest, sir, for I fear on the morrow you will find your troubles will have only multiplied."

The long-suffering man sighed as he contemplated the image of his desk overflowing with false letters, and with a long face he bade us good evening before he shuffled off.

"I think that is the cruelest act I have ever seen you perform, Professor," I protested. "Surely the inspector deserved better than you painting such a dire picture as to what awaits him tomorrow. The man was exhausted, and rather than give him some hope we might be drawing nearer to a conclusion of this affair, you heap ashes upon his head as though he were Job himself."

"What would be crueler then?" Bell replied, calm as ever. "To give him a false vision only to have it snatched away by the reality he shall surely confront tomorrow? At least now when the letters pour in— and they shall—he will not waste resources treating each as though it were from the killer. We are facing a sly and heartless enemy and we will not profit by chasing shadows. I will add this postcard to my report to Wilkins and complete my draft. Tomorrow we will peruse the papers, pay our respects to Abberline and Major Smith, and request Pennyworth be accepted as our representative. Wednesday I'll give my report to Wilkins, then we can make preparations for our departure on Thursday."

It was an odd turn of events how Margaret's false persona of Pennyworth had become a distinct individual in his own right. When she put on masculine attire, she also adopted manly mannerisms, as well as a deeper voice, and I at times briefly forgot there was a woman beneath the façade. Her observations and comments when alone with us, however, remained distinctly her own. Yes, Pennyworth would represent us ably.

"I am in no humor to go out tonight to dine," Bell sighed. "A simple meal here at the club and an early turn-in suits me to my bones. I may need to be at my most persuasive tomorrow, especially with the stern major. He is a politician, not a policeman, and I need to convince him it is in his best interests to allow our 'man' to remain in contact with his superintendent. Well, one shadow at a time; I'm to dinner and bed. Care to join me in the dining room, Doyle?"

It was odd at one moment to be discussing the horrible actions of a madman, the next to be comparing the qualities of various wines, but such is the world we inhabit. One must learn to compartmentalize, or the madness of the whole may overwhelm us.

We retired to our beds early, already preparing in our minds for the pending separation of our hardy band of Musketeers.

CHAPTER TWENTY-NINE
MY SHADOW'S REFLECTION

Tuesday, October 2

W e woke to a blustery day announcing summer was over and autumn had commenced in earnest. I wrote a quick letter to Louise informing her of my imminent return, and prepared for my departure.

Bell emerged from his chambers, his shoulders sagging from the effort of writing his summation and ready to catch some fresh air. He had dutifully produced two copies of his report, one for Wilkins and another for Abberline, and we were soon on our way to Spitalfields.

As we journeyed I noticed how many men were wearing checked suits. Bell gave me a quizzical look when I sighed, but I merely shook my head, and we continued in a companionable silence as I doubted my suspicions that someone with a poor taste in fashion was stalking us.

Inspector Abberline was in a surprisingly good mood when we arrived at his office, and he greeted us warmly.

I quickly learned the source of his merriment was the intelligence that the City of London Police Headquarters was overrun with those who were convinced their mysterious neighbor or some churlish publican was Jack the Ripper. Each supplicant was clamoring loudly for an inspector to accompany them to arrest the accused, then to expedite their collection of the reward.

He proudly told us he had instructed his desk sergeant to direct all those inquiring about the reward to Major Smith at the City of London headquarters.

I tried to feign disapproval of his actions, but failed utterly. The image of the impeccably groomed man besieged by a horde of loud, unwashed, and ill-mannered East Enders was enough to make a Yogi laugh out loud. Were I an observant Catholic, I would be in sore need of confession.

It was a rare moment of much-needed levity. Bell let loose with a deep laugh, and I felt privileged to be allowed in on the joke.

After our laughter subsided, Abberline's smile faded as he returned to business. Questioning of the staff of nearby lodging houses revealed the woman found in Dutfield's Yard was called Elizabeth Stride, or "Long Liz," a play, no doubt, on the name Stride. She earned her "doss" money by cleaning rooms at a lodging house on 32 Flower and Dean Street, where she had resided on and off for the past six years. In addition to her bed, she earned sixpence a day.

I remarked. "With her pay at the lodging house and free lodging, she had no need to walk the streets."

"As to that," remarked Abberline, "I'll let you be the judge. At half-past six, her chores done and sixpence in her pocket, she went to the Queen's Head pub. She was back at seven and dressed to go out, departing at half-past seven. Sergeant Thicke has already told you what witnesses reported of her movements. Her actions appear to be those of a woman who, if not a regular streetwalker, was not above it from time to time."

"Thank you, Inspector," said Bell. "By the by, I should tell you Doyle and I are departing on Thursday the fourth. Until our return, we hope to stay in contact with you via Mr. Pennyworth. Is that acceptable?"

"Well, he's kept his mouth shut and stayed out of the way. As long as he behaves himself, we'll keep him up to date. Sergeant Thicke knows everything as soon as I do. If he's available, I'd prefer Pennyworth deal with him. Written reports to my superiors are no longer enough, it seems. I am increasingly called to Whitehall to update Swanson and the commissioner on our progress."

"I'll inform Pennyworth," I promised.

"We thank you, Inspector," Bell said. "I do not envy you your burden."

Abberline nodded amiably, our laughter together apparently still lightening his mood, and we left.

Once outside, I asked Bell if another visit to the City of London police was in order to request Pennyworth represent us.

Bell nodded. "Perhaps it's best I go alone," he said. "The station will be teeming with those seeking the reward, and journalists seeking stories. While I may pass as one more treasure hunter, the two of us are more likely to stand out and draw the attention of Mr. Collier or another of his kind. The note signed by Major Smith doesn't state how long our access is allowed, nor does it mention Pennyworth at all. A brief conversation with Superintendent McWilliam will update me on Mrs. Eddowes's murder, and hopefully I can persuade him to accept Pennyworth as our surrogate."

We parted ways, and with Bell off to the City police station, I went back to the club, but I had too much nervous energy to loiter there for long. Needing the release of a brisk walk, I donned my overcoat and strolled about the neighborhood. I stopped off for a pint at a respectable public-house where I had the strangest feeling I was being watched, and once, while pausing before a store window, I noticed the reflection of a man in a checked suit and bowler hat looking at me intently from across the street. I turned slowly so as not to startle him and to get a better look, but when I faced the street once more he was gone.

Puzzled and a bit uneasy, I headed unhurried but direct to the club to inform the professor when he returned that we had attracted the notice of someone, or "ones," given the ubiquity of checked suits in London. I knew not what this meant, but I very much wanted him to know that I, at least, was being watched.

CHAPTER THIRTY
THE BRASS RING

Tuesday, October 2, to Sunday, October 7

Bell frowned worriedly when I shared my suspicion, but he paid me the compliment of not asking if I was sure. He understood I would not bring this to his attention otherwise. We agreed there were too many possibilities to know what this meant.

"It could be the journalist Doctor Phillips warned us of," said Bell, "a plainclothes detective, either public or private, who is trying to determine what our role in this matter is, or it could be the killer. All we can do at present is to be aware of the possibilities and to warn Miss Harkness. It is worrisome, I agree; but there is nothing we can do for the moment."

The final report complete, Bell suggested an early dinner at the club. "Tomorrow I shall render unto Mr. Wilkins, then prepare for my journey home as well as for my patient's. I have tickets to buy and a case summary to prepare for my presentation of Miss Jones to the staff."

I was embarrassed that due to my focus on our investigation, I had completely forgotten the task awaiting him upon his return to Edinburgh. Soon my days would be filled with the routine practice of a GP; my nights turned to my novel *Micah Clarke*, now nearing completion, and my pregnant wife.

Bell would resume the demanding life of professor and surgeon at a teaching hospital, treating the most desperate and destitute within Scotland. At the same time, he needed to be ready to respond at a moment's notice to attend to our Most Sovereign Monarch should she require him, scarcely washing his hands before leaving the bedside of the humblest of her subjects to lay those same hands upon Her Majesty.

I suddenly appreciated the full spectrum of the world my mentor and colleague inhabited, and how he could talk with people from all walks of life. He served them all with the same humility and eagerness, which explained his greatness as a teacher, for each student saw something in him they desired to emulate.

The next morning Wilkins arrived at the club promptly at nine o'clock for our report and to settle accounts. This time Professor Bell did all the talking, giving me the opportunity to observe the interaction from a comfortable distance.

Wilkins listened to Bell's summary with hooded eyes and steepled fingers, his composure only altered when the autopsy findings were presented; then he leaned forward and nodded encouragement, signaling Bell to continue.

By mutual consent, no mention was made of the man I suspected of following me, since I had no proof; nor was there anything to be gained by alarming Wilkins needlessly.

When the report was finished, Wilkins turned to me and asked if I had anything to add.

"Professor Bell speaks for me," I replied. "I could never have gathered such comprehensive findings on my own."

"Indeed," Wilkins replied, the slightest hint of disappointment in his voice. "It was on my recommendation that you two were included in this manhunt. While your findings are interesting, can either of you honestly tell me we are any closer to capturing this 'Ripper' than before you joined the investigation?"

Bell and I shook our heads in unison.

"I thought not," he said dryly. "I understand your mutual desire to return to your normal lives. You Professor, say your duties in Scotland will keep you there for at least a month. I proposed you both thirty days' employment. Should there be further murders or fresh evidence to examine, I would offer you another fortnight, as the time remaining of our initial contract. If I summon you once more, will you come?"

"Aye," Bell responded, without hesitation.

"As will I," I affirmed.

"Very well, gentlemen. How shall we keep in touch?" Wilkins asked.

"We have . . . ." I began, meaning to mention Margaret, when Bell cut me off.

"We shall leave our addresses for both routine post and telegrams. Write as you feel the need to update us. It would be most convenient if you share whatever you have with the two of us at the same time, which will prevent the delay in one of us writing to the other to share the information. How may we contact you?"

Wilkins raised an eyebrow at Bell's interruption. "The doorman here has proven to be discrete and reliable," he said. "As I prefer the other staff remain ignorant of our involvement, it is best to send your correspondence here to the club, and the doorman will see I receive it quickly and quietly. Is that satisfactory?"

"Quite," we both answered.

That business concluded, Wilkins settled our accounts at the club, as well as my incidentals and an additional three pounds to each of us for an extra day's service, and then, bidding us a safe and speedy journey, he departed.

"I say," I complained to Bell, "that was rather blunt the way you interrupted me when I started to mention that Margaret would act on our behalf while we are gone."

"I apologize, Doyle, but you know his feelings on her involvement. As long as her fees do not come directly from his, or rather his employer's purse, I see no reason to share our methods with him."

"Any additional insights on Mr. Wilkins?" I asked, changing the topic to soothe my irritation. "As for me, I deduce he studied to become an accountant, will always be a bachelor, and can tell you precisely how many pairs of shoes he has and how soon the oldest will need a fresh sole."

"He doesn't lack for precision in his habits," replied my companion, smiling. "And, although you make those comments in jest regarding his footwear and marital status, I suspect you are entirely correct. He is very much what some would call a 'cold fish,' and although I do not hold myself out as an expert on the feminine mind, I doubt many would find him an appealing life mate. He can also tell you to the penny how much money he has on his person as well as the amount to the farthing in his accounts.

"Disorder is abhorrent to him, which is why I believe he recommended you to Gladstone. Your detective is logical, scientific. Cause follows effect as surely as night follows day. Such a worldview would appeal to him."

It was still short of noon when we perused the train schedules for the next day's departures, and the ever-faithful doorman quickly procured our tickets plus the one for Miss Jones after we made our selections.

Bell sent a message to Margaret via one of the street Arabs, stating the platform and the time once we had our tickets in hand. He asked that she and Miss Jones meet him at the station.

I admired the efficiency of the courier service these urchins provided, as well as the opportunity it gave them to earn some means by which to sustain themselves. I smiled at the resemblance his street couriers bore to the "Baker Street Irregulars" I had contrived in *Scarlet*.

I felt awkward as I contemplated my departure. I had not had such close male camaraderie since my days as a ship's surgeon. This man whom I had always admired had become something more than a teacher and mentor, someone I now considered a close friend.

Margaret was also much on my mind. In the twentieth century, friendships between men and women are nothing unusual, but in those days a man of my station rarely became overly familiar with a woman other than his wife or an immediate family member. I had enjoyed getting to know her as the intelligent, brave, and inquisitive person she was. I savored our conversations and had grown to rely on her common sense, and I knew life back in Portsmouth would appear dull by comparison.

There was also unease on my part regarding my growing affection for her, but I shoved those concerns aside, telling myself ours was an intense friendship forged through shared adversity and nothing more.

I fully expected my return to Portsmouth would soon drive her from my mind.

Knowing Margaret would be preparing Miss Jones for her journey, Bell and I left the ladies in peace. As I would not see Margaret before my departure, I wrote a brief note and entrusted it to Professor Bell to give her at the station. I have no copy but recall the contents clearly.

> Dear Margaret,
>
> I regret not having the opportunity to say farewell to you in person. I eagerly await the next chance to join forces with you and the good professor. If we may in some way help bring this monster to justice, I shall consider my life to have been well spent.
>
> I should warn you I have recently become aware of a man in a checked suit following me. I do not know his identity or his purpose, so beg you to "take precautions" until his intent becomes clear.
>
> Sincerely yours,
> Porthos

My journey home went smoothly. Louise was starting to show the growing life within her, and my sister Lottie was proving a capable and patient helpmate. Louise's mother had returned home by the time I arrived, and I suspect my sister had something to do with that, but I never inquired. The adage regarding the dental health of a gift horse seemed to apply, and I gratefully accepted the resulting peace and quiet without question.

I removed the sign from the entrance to my practice announcing my absence, and considered placing a notice in the local paper of my return but decided against it. Portsmouth was, and continues to be, a small town, so I stopped in at a nearby pub to have an ale, knowing my presence there would serve as well as any three-inch advertisement in the back of the paper to let my patients learn of my return.

I had the strange ennui old soldiers often experience after surviving great battles. I was like one who had lain down his sword, but without the satisfaction of having won a victory of any kind. Still, life goes on, although it was not until the third day back, on the seventh, when I girded myself for confronting the stack of correspondence awaiting me on my desk.

I worked methodically through it, looking at the oldest first. As I drew to the end, I came upon an envelope from London without a return address. It was marked only to "Doctor Arthur Conan Doyle, Portsmouth." The stamp was from the fifth of October, the day after my departure from London. The heft of the envelope told me it contained something in addition to a letter.

Thinking it from Margaret, I slit it open eagerly, and as I did so a well-worn brass ring fell out. The letter was written in a familiar red ink, and the contents froze me to my chair.

> My Dear Doctor Doyle,
> I trust the cheap trinket I took from the whore on Hanbury Street suffices as a means of introduction . . .

CHAPTER THIRTY-ONE
A SUMMONS
TO EDINBURGH

Sunday, October 7,
to Saturday, October 13

When I learned of you joining our merry dance I took the time to read your absurd little tale. Words cannot express my joy after reading it to know I was being tested by the creator of this all too perfect and orderly Detective. You would make the world think there is a balance to the Universe; that everything has a reason, and all actions follow a predictable pattern.

Well Sir, you are correct, but not in the neat and orderly way you suppose.

The very Science you hold out as a source of Wisdom declares Chaos is the true nature of Reality. Consider Professor Darwin's *On the Origin of Species* from which the term 'Survival of the Fittest' has 'evolved'. (Forgive me my little jokes, but it is only through humor we make life bearable at times, don't you agree?). The panther hunts the deer. Over time, the deer become smarter and faster as the less intelligent and slower are culled from the herd. The panther, in response, must become stronger so that he is capable of hunting these evolved deer. The panther improves the deer, and they in time strengthen the panther. And so it goes and has gone for Millennia. So yes, there is an Order to our Universe, but it is written in blood and with great cruelty. I am merely an agent of this immutable reality. The strong feed on the weak, and no theorem or act of Parliament will ever change that.

As I read of your Mr. Holmes, who seems capable of deducing a man's motives from thin air, I felt the need to demonstrate how impotent his Science of Deductive Reasoning must be in the face of Chaos. I kill at will, and none can mark me. I defeat you as well as an army of Detectives, Inspectors, and Superintendents at every turn. But I am a sporting man. I know you and your Companions have labored hard and are in need of rest. I will sharpen my blades, bide my time, and strike again when I know you are fit to rejoin the game. My prey thus far shows no evidence of evolution. Thus, my work is far from done.

Derisively Yours,

JTR

I sat unmoving for perhaps ten minutes as I absorbed this ghoulish taunt. I was uncertain if it was truly from this Jack the Ripper, but I knew that whoever the author was, he was not someone I should care to meet in person. Obviously, I would forward this to Bell right away, and I cursed my laziness for taking so long to read my mail. I decided to copy it as exactly as possible first, and then send the original with the brass ring to him.

As I copied the phrase "you and your Companions," the use of the plural form of the word "Companion" suddenly struck me. This must mean the fiend knew of Margaret as well as Professor Bell! Whether he knew her as Pennyworth or by her real identity was not revealed, but the thought of the killer stalking her in the shadows or, worse, coming to her door now that Miss Jones was in Scotland, chilled my marrow. Could this letter be from my shadow in the checked suit?

I was torn between sending her a warning telegram or rushing back to London immediately. Finally I had to admit, grudgingly, returning to London would be pointless. I had no idea who the author was, nor was I sure what he knew about Margaret; I could not protect her from a phantom. My original impulse to forward this to Bell remained the best course of action, and I would ask his advice regarding what we should tell Margaret of the letter. I had already warned her of the man following me, and I was unsure what more I could say, except that the tone of this letter conveyed the malevolent intelligence I envisioned in the Ripper.

It being Sunday, I posted the letter with the battered brass ring within as soon as the post office opened the next morning, and then turned my steps toward my practice like one sentenced to the gallows. I knew I would have no peace until I received my friend's reply.

That night I dreamt again of the murdered woman in Dutfield's Yard. As before, the dead woman opened her eyes and gestured to look behind me. As I began to turn, I felt a hand on my left shoulder and in the bright moonlight I saw a flash of steel, and then I awoke violently, soaked in sweat.

I recall the next three days poorly. My old patients began to trickle in, and more than once I had to justify why my treatment for their ailments differed from those prescribed by my colleagues during my absence. I learned how difficult it is to earn a patient's trust, and how quickly it can be eroded, but I was at best only half there.

Finally, on Thursday the eleventh of October, four days after I posted my macabre correspondence to Professor Bell, I received his reply.

Doyle,

Forgive the delay, but I have pondered the significance of the unusual letter you forwarded me long enough to miss the last collection of the day. I agree we cannot verify the authenticity of the author, but we would be foolish to disregard it out of hand. The brass ring strengthens the possibility it is genuine, however. It is a touch I believe the casual crackpot would not have contrived.

I also agree the use of "companions" was deliberate and was a veiled threat toward Miss Harkness. I have already written to her and requested she travel to Edinburgh to help Miss Jones withstand the surgery, and then accompany her back to London. Miss Harkness trained as a nurse as you recall, and having her present will aid Miss Jones considerably. Fortunately there is a dormitory for nurses adjacent to the infirmary where she can lodge.

While we cannot forever hover over our comrade, perhaps her temporary absence will put the writer off her trail, and he will turn his ill intentions elsewhere. It is certainly better for both her and Miss Jones that Miss Harkness reside here for the present.

As for the letter and the ring, although we must share them with the authorities, the police in Edinburgh are not engaged in the affair. A message to Abberline might be misrouted due to the many letters doubtless sent his way by those seeking the reward. Therefore, I suggest we wait until our return to London to share the letter and ring in person.

I have presented Miss Jones to our medical students and will have my surgical residents examine her Monday next, with her surgery scheduled the following day, the sixteenth of October. Assuming there are no complications, she and Miss Harkness should be back in London in a little over a week's time after, around the twenty-fourth.

I shall not reveal the letter you received to Miss Harkness until she is preparing to return to London. I believe it is better for her to act normally, in case she is under observation by your correspondent. A sudden change in her activities might provoke him into rash action. Once he has lost the scent and she prepares to return, she can take the necessary actions to safeguard herself and her companion.

I will write further once the surgery is complete and I have a date certain for their journey back.

Sincerely,

J. Bell

I was greatly relieved at Bell's elegant method of removing Margaret from immediate harm. Knowing Margaret would soon be safe, I had my best night's sleep since returning from London. I received a letter from her the next day, written shortly before she departed for Edinburgh, and my mood improved even further.

Dear Porthos,

Before I begin I should inform you I will be in Edinburgh for the next fortnight to care for Molly. Professor Bell has requested me to assist, and I feel guilty it took his summons to remind me of my duty to a dear friend. In recompense, I shall make this letter as informative as possible.

The papers are full of the adventures of two Private Detectives in the employ of *The Evening News* named Grand and Batchelor. They questioned a greengrocer named Matthew Packer, who lives two doors from Dutfield's Yard. During their interview, he recalled selling grapes to a man and a woman around eleven forty-five the night of the murder.

He described the man as around thirty-five years of age, five feet seven inches tall, and a little on the stout side. Mr. Packer was quoted in the papers: "I am certain he wasn't what I would call a working man, or anything like us people that live around here."

Mr. Packer was taken to the morgue by the two Private Detectives, and he identified the body of the Dutfield's Yard victim as the grape buyer.

The image of a well-dressed stranger dangling a bunch of grapes before a woman to lure her to her death recalls the Serpent and the Apple in Genesis, and is sure to have much play in the papers. Given my new acquaintance with the Science of Postmortem examination, I will withhold judgment until Doctor Phillips reveals the contents of Miss Stride's stomach.

Meanwhile, I had a surprise visit yesterday from the Reverend Robert Harkness, my father. I may have told you how displeased he is with my career path. To his credit, he expressed sincere concern for my safety. To his discredit, he informed me he had selected an agreeable and well-to-do young man as my husband, and I was to accompany him back home to Worcestershire immediately, where I could be "safe." I have found, however, that safe and bored are much the same. My half-sister, Hope, was with him to help me pack, and his confidence I would follow him provoked a stronger response than I am sure he was expecting.

Needless to say, my father returned home without me, though Hope spent the night. I had not seen her in some time, and while he told Hope to "talk some sense" into me, I fear she is even less content at home now after seeing how I live, than she was before.

To placate my father I have agreed to acquire a dog for my safety.

If I told him what other precautions I take, he might require time in hospital, especially if I had been dressed as Pennyworth when he arrived! As rats are a common problem here, I will be seeking a Terrier. I am thinking of buying a bitch but naming her "Johnny," in homage to another female you know who uses that name professionally.

Nothing else of relevance to relate at this time, Dear Porthos. I will convey your warm regards to Molly, knowing you intend them.

Sincerely Yours,

Margaret

Reading the letter, I could hear her voice: forceful, opinionated, and intelligent. I realized how much I delighted in her company, and I worried for her safety. I was surprised her father would believe Margaret would meekly submit to his paternal decree.

I contemplated the image of her father arriving unannounced, expecting her to renounce her life in London and follow him obediently to wed a man she had never met. I began to understand why she fought so fiercely to assert her independence. It must have been a prolonged battle growing up under his roof to develop the strength of will to become her own person. In many ways, that took more courage than facing down a bandit with a razor.

Two days later, Professor Bell and I received identical letters from Wilkins updating us on events back in London. His message reflected his general personality of an efficient, if bloodless, functionary.

Dear Doctor Doyle and Professor Bell,

No new actions to report regarding the Ripper. Inquests for both of his recent victims have been held and would be comic if the subject were not so serious.

A man purporting to have sold grapes to the murdered woman found in Dutfield's Yard has been discredited by the police surgeon who performed the postmortem, stating no grapes were found in the stomach. All in all, it has been a farce of the lowest quality.

At present, the streets of the East End are deserted at night save for vigilant police constables grimly making their rounds.

Although my offer for another fortnight still stands, I cannot in good faith urge your return until there is fresh ground to cover. When that might occur, sadly, only one man knows for sure.

With the inquests concluded, I see no reason for further correspondence pending new developments, so do not look for any more letters from me. When you desire to return to London, please telegraph me as before, and I will arrange for your lodging.

Respectfully,
Wilkins

It appeared all of London was holding its breath after the "double event." No one dared believe this ordeal was over, but for now the increased vigilance seemed to keep the beast in his lair. Police constables walked their beats while neighbors kept watch over each other. The unfortunates huddled wherever they could in groups, and avoided the dark alleys of Whitechapel at night; yet we all knew it was only a matter of time before the police whistles would sound and the cry of "murder!" ring out once more.

CHAPTER THIRTY-TWO
A MERITED REBUKE

Friday, October 19,
to Monday, October 22

I continued in this dark mood until Friday the nineteenth of October, when I found a letter from Edinburgh in my mailbox. I tore it open with great eagerness and was prepared to feast hungrily on all it contained. I was even more enthused when I recognized Margaret's delicate hand, though her words were not as gentle as I had hoped.

> Doctor Doyle,
>
> First, I am pleased to inform you Molly has undergone surgery and did well. Anesthesia was a challenge. Ether could not be used since the oral cavity was the site of surgery, and a large amount of the gas would have been expressed directly into Professor Bell's face, rendering him unconscious in the course of the procedure. An injection of Morphine was used both pre- and post-operatively, and Miss Jones did not suffer unduly.
>
> Her right mandible will be forever weakened, and she will never be able to fit artificial teeth to it as the professor fears the stress of chewing might cause the jawbone to fracture. Nevertheless, the removal of the necrotic bone and the poisonous phosphorus lodged within it should restore her health to a remarkable extent. I will be forever grateful to Professor Bell for the restoration of my dear friend who can never repay him.
>
> Thus my anger and feelings of betrayal by those whom I had

come to consider my comrades runs deeper than they otherwise might. You know precisely the betrayal of which I speak: not revealing to me immediately the vague threat upon my person by this anonymous writer. I understand you two chivalrous gentlemen wanting to protect me and to do what was best for me. I thought however that by now I had made it Quite Clear I am the only person qualified to make that determination. I have been struggling my entire life against limitations upon my independence, no matter how well-intended, due to what I see as a random event of Nature: my gender.

Neither of you has the right to withhold information which concerns me "for my own good." If you cannot treat me as an adult, we shall have to part ways. I think I have expressed myself very clearly on this matter and will not speak of it further unless either of you give me cause. I suspect Professor Bell envies you the time it has taken me to temper my anger since he informed me, as well as the relative safety you have, given the distance currently separating us. Putting my ire aside for the moment, I do think bringing me here to care for Miss Jones was the correct course of action. I would have much preferred, however, that it had been my decision with all the information at hand.

I will update you once Miss Jones and I return to London. The little the Scottish papers contain on the matter convinces me we have, by chance or design, selected the best time to be absent.

Be well, Porthos. I am STILL a loyal Musketeer.

Respectfully Yours,

M. Harkness

I placed the letter down. My first reaction was anger. I had been in agony, fearing the anonymous writer with the brass ring was stalking Margaret while I was helpless to protect her. Although Bell devised the stratagem to get her out of London, I had fully supported it and had only wished I had thought of it first. I could not believe how ungrateful this woman could be to friends who had done all they could to remove her from harm.

I opened the top drawer from my desk, grabbed some stationery, and, scribbling furiously, began to articulate how wronged I felt, explaining we had acted only out of deep affection for her. The letter was therapeutic, for as I began to articulate why she should be thanking us for taking care of her, I thought of her character.

I recalled Margaret standing between me and a straight razor, squarely confronting danger and asking no quarter. This was not a woman who asked men to protect her, but one who sought to make her own way in the world. Her grit, intelligence, and readiness to break with tradition were the very things that attracted me to her. I sadly conceded that, by her lights, I had betrayed her friendship and trust.

I began to understand how frustrating it must be for her to possess such spirit and intellect, only to have it so lightly disregarded due to her gender. Shakespeare appeared to have the right of it when he had Hamlet inform his companion, "There are more things in heaven and earth, Horatio, than are dreamt of in your philosophy." The world is vast, and my understanding of at least half of it was most incomplete.

I took a long walk and, after some reflection, felt the need to express my remorse at our well-intended subterfuge. When I returned home, I sat down and, though it was difficult, penned the following.

Dear Margaret,

I have taken your admonition to heart and sincerely apologize for not being entirely honest with you. Good intentions count for little when they are used as an excuse to treat a competent person such as yourself with anything less than the respect they deserve.

I cannot guarantee I can undo a lifetime of customary thought and behavior overnight, but I do promise to accept your reminders should I lapse in future. I appreciate your contributions to our enterprise and your friendship, and I look forward to continuing our mutual struggle against this great evil.

My best wishes to Miss Jones and for your safe return to London.

Sincerely,

Doyle

Meanwhile, my medical practice and efforts on my novel, *Micah Clarke*, were going well. My hiatus from writing and my growing powers of observation, due to Bell's example, allowed me to deepen my descriptions of my characters, much like an artist who has added a new tint to his palette.

Three days later, on Monday the twenty-second, Margaret's subsequent correspondence arrived, accompanied by one from Professor Bell. I cowardly read the professor's letter first in the chance I would receive a warning from him before reading hers.

Dear Doyle,

I gather you received a diluted version of the lecture I had from Miss Harkness regarding her ability—nay, her right—to make her own decisions, and how our well-meaning patronizing efforts were most devoutly not wanted. Then, of course, she wholeheartedly supported our plan to have her leave London to tend to Miss Jones. Something about "means and ends," I think. No matter. I regret having angered her, but I must compliment her on one skill few seem to have mastered. Once she has made her point, she does not belabor it, and we have gotten along swimmingly since my upbraiding over our deception.

Miss Jones has progressed remarkably well, and though I am proud of the surgical result, her recovery is no doubt due in large part to the skilled care she has received from Miss Harkness.

I have given my patient leave to return to London on the twenty-third. She will require thrice daily saline rinses for the next two weeks which Margaret can easily oversee. I cannot justify her continued stay, knowing the excellent care she will receive back in London.

Miss Harkness has assured me she will continue to "take precautions" once the two of them are home. While I am sure you will join me in my concern for her safety, there is nothing either of us can do until we return ourselves.

All news from London continues to be quiet for the moment. The Ripper's handiwork bespeaks the fierce pleasure he takes in these murders, however, and I do not doubt there is more blood to be spilled. We can only hope for a clearer trail in the aftermath.

No news from Balmoral, by the way. Her Majesty will probably outlive us both. I will be more than satisfied if she returns to London shortly with no need of my services save those required of any loyal subject.

Best wishes,

J. Bell

Reassured by Bell's letter, I opened Margaret's fearlessly.

Dear Porthos,

I trust all is well in rustic Portsmouth. No doubt Professor Bell has informed you Molly and I will soon be back in London.

Professor Bell kindly lent me his copy of your detective story, *A Study in Scarlet*. I see the resemblance between your Detective, Mister Holmes, and our mutual friend in regards to his powers of observation. I do agree with Bell's assessment, however, that he is far more congenial than Sherlock. (Wherever did you get that name?) I find your tale to be a tad dramatic in part, but when Holmes takes the stage and gathers evidence to catch the killer, it shines. I can see now why Mister Gladstone would ask Holmes's creator to look into the Ripper murders.

Be of good cheer, my friend. Knowing someone may intend me ill grants me a great advantage. They shall not catch me unprepared.

I shall write again once I am back within the warm, if aromatic, embrace of the East End.

Sincerely,

Margaret

Despite Margaret's cheerful tone, I knew I would not rest peacefully until the three of us were together again. Milton famously wrote, "They also serve, who only stand and wait." Truly, that was the most challenging task I have ever undertaken in my life. But I had no choice. I could only bide my time until, to paraphrase Shakespeare, I could go into the breech once more.

CHAPTER THIRTY-THREE
ODDS AND ENDS

Thursday, October 25, to Saturday, November 3

Finally, my patience was rewarded with another letter, postmarked from London this time, and bearing Margaret's distinctive script. I tore it open with zeal, and read it quickly once, then more slowly a second time.

> Dear Comrades,
>
> Molly and I are back in our familiar haunts. Her appetite has returned with a vengeance and, although Professor Bell was apologetic that she can now only chew on her left side, this has been her condition for some time. The difference is chewing is no longer painful, and her food doesn't taste of rotting flesh. Hippocrates once wrote: "If the nutrition is good and the wound is clean, the wound will heal," so I am stuffing her like a Christmas goose and rinsing her wound regularly.
>
> Currently I only go out during the day and, be assured, take precautions when I do. I have not noticed any suspicious characters in checked suits lounging about, but it would be foolish to conclude your shadow owns only one suit of clothes.
>
> Making the rounds this morning I started with my new friend Sergeant Thicke. He told me it would serve no purpose to go round to the City of London Police. Their force is inundated with false leads submitted by all those desirous of the five-hundred-pound reward, and they have little time for anything else.

Sergeant Thicke suggested I speak with Mr. Lusk, Chairman of the Mile End Vigilance Committee, who we met on the twenty-ninth of September when you were shown the first Ripper letter. He has received some threatening letters, and suspicious-looking strangers have been asking about him within his neighborhood.

Thankfully, Mr. Lusk remembered me being with you that day, for when I knocked at his door, he had to unbolt two locks and then peered suspiciously through a crack secured by a very robust chain. Once allowed entry, he told me he had recently reinforced the door and doubled the locks. He was a shaken man and easily startled.

He had received two threatening letters addressed as "Dear Boss," and on the sixteenth of October, he received a small package wrapped in brown paper with a smeared London postmark. Inside the package was a poorly preserved piece of kidney and a brief message:

> From hell
> Mr Lusk
> Sor
> I send you half of the Kidne I took from one women prasarved it for you tother piece I fried and ate it was very nise I may send you the bloody knif that took it out if you only wate a whil longer
> Signed Catch me when you Can
> Mishter Lusk

Mr. Lusk is now considerably in fear of his life, and I cannot fault him. One crackpot attempting to emulate the Ripper may, in some ways, be more dangerous than the original, as his "admirers," if I may use such a term, may be less selective in their victims and therefore even more destructive. It is a sad state of affairs when a man who puts himself forward to help his neighbors should become the target of such cruelty.

There are increasing incidents of Jews being attacked on the streets. Recently a police inspector had to barricade himself into a house with a Jewish tradesman to protect the poor man from a mob.

It was a very near thing before constables arrived to drive the crowd away. Sergeant Thicke says everyone on the force is on edge, fearing mass violence if the Ripper strikes again.

There is much evil stirring within the East End, my friends. We must act quickly, to extinguish the spark to the firestorm Abberline so rightly fears.

Come when you can,

MH

I was greatly concerned by the events Margaret related at the end of her letter. I had seen a small example in the case of the cobbler, Mister Rubenstein. To imagine an open insurrection within the confines of London was beyond my imagination. It seemed the Ripper could now go on extended holiday, as many others were willing to spill blood in his stead.

Given the deluge of Ripper imitators, however, I was becoming increasingly doubtful that my letter with the brass ring was authentic, though two things still nagged at me. How had the writer known to contact me? And what did they know of my "companions"? Was it the mysterious man in the checked suit I had glimpsed briefly in the store window, or was it someone within the police force?

The thought of a police constable as the Ripper gave me pause. Sergeant Thicke was well known for his checked suits, though the pattern tended to be far louder than that of my unknown shadow. "Johnny Upright" seemed to delight in announcing his presence, perhaps to intimidate the felons he dealt with on a regular basis.

I did notice reports of the murders often mentioned Sergeant Thicke arriving at the scene shortly after the discovery of the victim. He was well known in the area, and it would be an easy matter for him to murder someone and "arrive" on the scene soon after, so he had the means. If assisting in the murder investigation increased his chances of promotion, he would also have a motive.

Was it the newspaperman, Mr. Collier, whom Doctor Phillips had warned us about in the pub? The murders were certainly selling a lot of papers. His nude drawing of a woman that I noticed protruding from his jacket demonstrated an excellent knowledge of female anatomy. His fondness for drink, however, would not make for the steady hand required to murder as quickly and precisely as the Ripper.

Could it be Wilkins? He certainly had plenty of disdain for the Ripper's victims. I recalled Bell's comments about his need for order, however, and could not conjure the image of this fastidious little man rummaging through a freshly disemboweled body. I believed he would faint at the sight of a bloodstain on his shirt cuff.

Finally, I considered the mysterious Mister Charrington, who had apparently made it his life's work to force all the prostitutes of the East End out onto the street. Whether he was truly the Ripper or not, the killer could certainly count Mister Charrington among his allies.

My head began to ache as I tried to solve this riddle with insufficient information. I could only keep all these possibilities in the back of my mind and plow on. More than likely the Ripper was someone I had never met.

Meanwhile, my dear Louise had developed that glow often seen in women great with child, though both my sister and I despaired at times of her variable dietary demands as her pregnancy advanced. Fortunately she was never a woman who tended toward jealousy, for it was but five days later, on the thirtieth, when I received another letter from Margaret.

My Dear Friends,

Molly continues on the mend. I have no doubt our Surgeon will be quite pleased.

The Metropolitan Police have shown no dint in their activity to catch our killer. The East End has been further reinforced with constables conscripted from outlying districts, as much to control the increasing anti-Semitic tone of the region as to assist in the Ripper's capture.

They just concluded a house-to-house search in an area comprising several neighborhoods. There were even trials this past week of bloodhounds in a couple of public parks, which were sufficiently encouraging, and Commissioner Warren has ordered the body of any new murder victim not be touched until the hounds can be brought to the scene and put on the scent.

There are already grumblings from the areas which have had their constabulary decreased, and while the East End is increasingly resembling an armed camp, I doubt Police Commissioner Warren will be able to sustain the criticism for long.

Meanwhile, speculation as to the identity of the Ripper continues to run rampant. I have even heard rumors mentioning Joseph Merrick, "The Elephant Man," who resides in the Royal London Hospital on Whitechapel Road. The logic goes that due to the hideous mutilations performed by the killer, only a person as deformed as Mr. Merrick could be capable of such atrocities. No one can explain how a man with his well-documented lameness and physical deformities could traverse the streets of London unnoticed, but fear of those different from ourselves can defeat reason at every turn.

I hesitate to mention it, as it may be due to the apprehension your warning gave me, but I have had the odd feeling of being observed the past two days while "dressed." I am only slightly exaggerating when I say there seems to be a man in a checked suit on every street in London.

Hopefully, the time is drawing near when I may see you two again and we drive this madman to ground. The first frost is not far away, and the ladies of the street will be hard-pressed to survive if they cannot soon return to their usual livelihoods. Write me when you know your itinerary.

Sincerely yours,

Margaret

I had to face the painful reality that, while in Portsmouth, there was nothing I could do to safeguard Margaret from her possible mysterious follower, and I had no obvious reason to return to London. My sleep was troubled anew, and I was in a foul mood, when on Saturday the third of November another large envelope arrived postmarked London E, and lacking a return address. My hands shook as I opened it.

A brass ring tumbled out.

I laid the letter aside, went to the liquor cabinet, and poured myself a generous portion of Scotch. I have no shame in admitting I downed a healthy dose, then unfolded the cheap stationery, knowing before reading it that it was a summons.

Dear Doctor Doyle,

Your presence is kindly requested to rejoin our little Danse Macabre in London. I have been patient, but winter is approaching, and my little pigeons are starting once more to leave their roosts at night. It is time to remind them, and the bumbling Police, to whom the night truly belongs. I give you three days, that is until the sixth, to tidy up your affairs in that little rural practice of yours, and then I will unsheathe my blades once more and seek my prey. Time for Nature to reassert herself.

I was very disappointed in your performance last time, but have charitably ascribed it to a lack of motivation. I have decided therefore to select someone you know as my next victim, hoping this may bring out the best in you. I want to give you every opportunity to test your view of reality versus mine before I demand you acknowledge your defeat. But I am getting ahead of myself. Another Pas de Deux, I think, before we get to that discussion. I look forward to speaking with you then. As the Good Book says, "Now I see into a mirror darkly." Soon all shall be revealed. Will that give you any comfort, I wonder?

Until

JTR

I laid the letter down, and then sank my head into my hands. I had telegrams to send, but for just a moment I needed to sit still and repress my need to scream.

CHAPTER THIRTY-FOUR
THE HUNT RESUMES

Monday, November 5

Wilkins readily agreed to reserve our lodgings, and soon we were back at the Marlborough Club. It was as though no time had passed. He apologized that he would be unable to meet us upon arrival, so we agreed to meet at nine o'clock the following day. Bell and I arrived late on the afternoon of the fifth, within half an hour of one another, and as soon as we had unpacked, set off together for Vine Street. The door opened on the second knock, and a small black-and-brown terrier ran happily to the door to greet us.

"Johnny?" I asked Margaret.

"Johnny," she affirmed. "More useful than a husband, wouldn't you agree?" she asked with an arched eyebrow.

I noticed, as promised, this Johnny was female.

Despite the momentary distraction of Johnny's enthusiastic greeting, my pulse quickened at the sight of Margaret, and her smile told me she was happy, in some measure, to see me as well.

I was angry with myself for my foolish infatuation with her, reminding myself of my pregnant wife awaiting me in Portsmouth. Despite my best intentions, however, the time spent apart had done nothing to lessen my attraction to her. The quiet joy I had in her presence, and my concern for her well-being, was undeniable. I eased my guilty conscience by telling myself that, while I could not master my heart, I could restrain my actions. That would have to suffice.

Bell performed a quick exam of Miss Jones and pronounced her released from his service. He praised Margaret for her excellent nursing care.

I was impressed by the transformation. Molly had gained at least five pounds, her odor was normal, and there was no drainage nor accompanying rag to cover her mouth. I noted a well-healing fresh surgical scar on the skin overlying her right jaw, and a slight droop to her mouth on that side, indicating damage to the facial nerve. Her outward appearance otherwise was unremarkable. Miracles do happen; it seemed I was in the presence of one now.

"Please, do join us for tea," she offered happily. "I just put on a fresh pot!" An unremarkable statement from anyone else; in Molly's case, it was a proclamation that her life was renewed. Johnny trotted happily after her as she went to fetch the tea, and I could tell the two had already become fast friends.

We seemed quite a happy family as we sat sipping tea, scratching Johnny's ears, and catching up with one another.

"Anything new about your possible shadow?" I asked Margaret.

"Perhaps," she said, with an odd smile. "I had the same feeling yesterday, so entered a pub and ordered an ale. Shortly after, two men, both dressed in checked suits, walked in together and avoided my gaze when I looked at them. Nothing conclusive, but I doubt the Ripper has an accomplice, so the presence of two men is somehow reassuring. If they continue, I am sure between the three of us we can corner one of them."

Once the teapot was stored, I shared the full details of the last message from my mysterious correspondent. I hadn't had time before our reunion to describe the contents due to the three-day deadline given me and the brevity required of a telegram.

The unveiling of the brass ring quieted the room, and when I read the letter a chill came over us all. Looks were exchanged when I read aloud the section making threats against someone I knew.

Margaret nodded, looking grim. I was certain she was the least anxious person in the room.

When I finished, a moment of total silence followed before Professor Bell paused from petting Johnny and asked to see the letter for himself.

After a minute's perusal, he spoke thoughtfully, "The writer demonstrates an obsession with you, Doyle. Your fictional detective represents a rationality he utterly rejects, and he is using these poor women's murders to taunt you. He will not stop until he is captured or killed, and I fear he may make an attempt on your life. I believe we have our work cut out for us."

Until now I had been primarily concerned for Margaret's safety. The depth of ill will this person had toward me had not occurred to me before. Suddenly I knew the fear of dark places and movements within the shadows; I did not want to be the deer in this madman's object lesson in evolution, but I felt most unpantherlike.

We decided to go out briefly to celebrate our reunion, and to bring Molly along, Johnny in tow, as Molly would not leave the flat without her. It was nothing elegant, just sandwiches at a small coffee shop by Fenchurch Street Station, but Molly acted as though we were taking her to the Tea Room at Harrods.

Margaret excused herself for a moment, and when she left, Molly turned to me and asked, "Did Miss Margaret tell you about her father's visit?"

"Yes, she did," I answered. "She said she was touched he was concerned about her."

Molly snorted at this, and the sudden fire in her eyes set me aback. Up until now, I had thought of her as a rather meek and self-effacing woman.

"Oh, he was concerned all right!" she said forcefully. "Concerned what his parish thought. You never 'eard how she and I came to live together, 'ave you? It'll only take a moment."

The writer in me sensed a story, and I nodded for her to continue before Margaret's return.

"I was working in the match factory. Me jaw was festering pretty bad, and me and the other girls refused to work anymore until the white phosphorus was gone. The girls could see 'ow I was getting on, and they didn't want to turn out like me."

"Couldn't the management just bring in other workers?" I asked.

"Yes, they could. But we stood in front of the door, not letting anyone in. Miss Margaret was there at the gates to write about it when the bosses sent in the strike breakers. They were men with large clubs, there to force us back. Miss Margaret stood up to one who was about to hit me pretty 'ard, so when he grabbed 'er and threw 'er to the ground, I 'it him with a paving stone."

"Good God!" I cried. "And the police did nothing?"

"They weren't there. Why would they be? What were we to them? Well, as soon as I laid the man out, Miss Margaret grabbed me and got me out of there. She decided to live 'ere so she could tell our story. To make others understand what we go through, just to stay alive. When her articles in the paper started coming out, the bosses sent a couple of men around to find 'er, and that's when she began carrying a gun and dressing like a man."

I could easily envision Margaret taking on a hired thug to protect a friend, and had to smile at the image I had previously had of her as a helpless "lady of letters." I have rarely been more wrong.

"And another thing," Molly said quickly, watching for Margaret's return. "Don't mention 'er father. At first, she thought 'e came here because he cared for 'er. T'was 'er half-sister, Hope, who told 'er the real reason. 'E was afraid if she were murdered by the Ripper, 'is congregation would think she'd become a streetwalker. It was all done to protect his reputation. Nothing more."

Bell shook his head. "No wonder she wants to make her own way. I see now why asking her to come to Edinburgh without telling her of the threat made her so angry. She has probably been betrayed or ignored by her father all her life. We are fortunate she didn't resign when she found out."

Margaret reappeared at that moment and, by our sudden silence, knew we had been talking about her. She looked at Molly, who shrugged back at her, and we left the shop to return to the flat. Margaret seemed thoughtful, so to distract her I mentioned once more how well Molly appeared, and how happy she was to be out of doors.

Margaret looked at her, smiled, and said this was the first time Molly had eaten in public in the past two years. I envied Bell his power to improve someone's life so profoundly, thus strengthening my growing interest in eye surgery.

Later, while Bell and I were boarding our cab by the train station, I thought for a second a figure in a checked suit stepped out of the shadows of a nearby alley. He stood there barely long enough for me to see him, then stepped back into the darkness and disappeared. I wasn't certain, but his actions made me wonder if he deliberately wanted me to notice him. I wondered who else had noticed our return.

CHAPTER THIRTY-FIVE
ABBERLINE RELENTS

Tuesday, November 6

When Wilkins arrived the next morning he seemed to have aged at least five years. He appeared genuinely happy to see us, though his German accent had returned, denoting the duress he was suffering. When I asked about his worn appearance, he grimaced and said that Mr. Gladstone was becoming impatient with him and, by extension, us, due to the lack of demonstrable progress in our investigation.

I had not explained my reason for our sudden need to return to London, but thanked him for his trust in us and for expediting the necessary arrangements.

He nodded and said he awaited my explanation now.

I produced the copy of the first letter and the original of the second, as well as the second ring, Bell having kept the first.

Wilkins assumed his favorite pose of steepled fingers and half-closed eyes. "Well, Professor. Doctor Doyle is apparently impressed with the authenticity of these letters. What is your opinion?"

"I am uncertain if the author is the Ripper," he replied. "But there is no doubt this person means Doctor Doyle ill. Our murderer has been idle for nearly a month. If he has not left London, each night which passes without another victim increases the likelihood of a killing the next. It was time for us to return, regardless. If we cannot fulfill Mr. Gladstone's expectations within the next fortnight, I am willing to forgo my stipend save for the cost of lodging."

"As am I," I vowed.

Wilkins smiled for the first time in our acquaintance, then laughed agreeably. "I admire your sense of honor, gentlemen, but the Bible clearly states a workman is worthy of his hire. Besides, Mr. Gladstone has given me very strict instructions. Therefore, I have no discretion regarding your payments."

Wilkins brought out his bulging wallet, then began to thumb through its contents. "Here are twenty-seven pounds for you both for the day you have been here already and the next eight days, as other matters shall require my attention until the fourteenth. If nothing further develops by the seventeenth, I will request a summary, and you will be free to return to your usual occupations. Is that satisfactory?"

We both nodded assent, and Wilkins bade us good day.

We met with Pennyworth as arranged at one o'clock outside Spitalfields Station. The desk sergeant seemed not to have noticed our absence, or at the very least not to have mourned it, and he gestured wordlessly for us to go back before we even asked if Inspector Abberline was in his office.

The inspector, however, appeared pleased at our return, and although he confessed there was currently nothing new for us to review, he was still grateful for the reinforcements.

"Doyle has some items to show you, Inspector."

"I do. Since our only means of getting these to you, other than by post, was in person, the delay was necessary. Here they are."

Abberline's expression changed once I revealed the contents of the two letters allegedly from the killer. He shook his head. "You were certainly right about one thing," he said. "The postal service will soon have to take on extra hands, what with all the letters flying about, each one claiming to be from the Ripper. I should be cross with you two for not getting these messages to me sooner, but I don't have the manpower to do anything about 'em. It does seem that whoever wrote these notes has you dead in his sights, Doctor, and while I cannot spare a man to provide you protection, your old digs in the conference room are available anytime." This last was said with a wink, knowing how much I suffered from his cots, which were seemingly constructed of iron canvas.

"Thank you, Inspector," I replied. "Regretfully, I believe we are in need of your continued hospitality. If the letters are genuine, he will strike sometime within the next week. I think it best we spend the nights here as before, until either he kills again or a week has passed."

While I had no joy at the prospect of more nights at the station, we had returned to London with the expectation of a pending attack. We would be best positioned to respond if we were immediately available.

But what of Margaret's safety? If the murderer intended her as the next target, how could I, in good conscience, leave her alone? The recent appearance of two men following her, for reasons known only to themselves, increased my fear tenfold. Recalling how disappointed Margaret had been at being excluded from our vigils before, I decided to try my best to reverse Abberline's prior decision. As Margaret had correctly pointed out, she deserved better. The fact that I would know she was safe when she was with us would be a bonus.

"I say, Inspector," I added. "Would it be acceptable if our assistant, Mr. Pennyworth, stayed here with us? If we do get called out, he could guide us once we were ready to leave the scene." I sensed Margaret tense beside me while Abberline looked at her thoughtfully, then nodded.

"I'm so desperate to get this over with, I'll pretty much give you carte blanche." Speaking to Margaret, he remarked, "You've kept your own counsel so far as I know, and not caused us any grief." Returning to me, he continued, "Bring him along then, but he gets the last cot. I've no more to spare. You want to invite anyone else, you'll have to throw him overboard."

Bell looked at me and winked, while Margaret "manfully" did her best to suppress a smile. I knew she would be grateful—at least until she experienced the professor's snores.

"As for me," Abberline said, "I'm in sore need of some nights in my own bed, or the Ripper will be able to number me among his victims just due to fatigue. Ten o'clock, as usual, gents?"

We agreed, though my concurrence was the least enthusiastic. I considered buying a candle so that I could place wax into my ears, much as Ulysses's crew was fabled to have done prior to braving the sirens.

Once outside the station, Margaret touched my arm for a moment and quietly said, "Thank you."

I have heard many speeches of over an hour's duration that conveyed far less import than those two simple words from someone who had come to mean so much to me. I nodded, unable for the moment to respond.

Bell smiled and asked, "And what of Miss Jones? Will she be all right?"

"She never goes out at night," Margaret replied. "You may not have noticed, but I have made good use of my new acquaintance with the builder, Mr. Lusk. He had one of his men fortify our door and install a stronger lock. Miss Jones has a police whistle, and I shall also leave her my derringer. And Johnny would raise quite a fuss if Molly were threatened. She may be small, but she has already proven her worth with four-legged rats. I don't doubt she'd leave a mark or two on the Ripper, given a chance. Molly will probably be the safest resident of the East End while we traipse along dark alleys in the London fog. If you are overly concerned about her, you might ask her to take you in," she said with a smile.

While reassured about Molly's safety, I regretted the loss of Margaret's firearm by our side. I had been much impressed by its effect on the hooligans we encountered with Mister Rubenstein, and on the man with the straight razor, and I'd come to rely upon it to lessen my concerns about our safety.

We agreed to part ways for the next few hours until we picked Margaret up on our way to the station. Bell said he had some colleagues with whom he wished to confer while in the city, so he and I also went separate ways, and I returned alone to the club.

As I alighted, I saw a man across the street, about five foot six, in a checked suit and wearing a brown bowler hat. He seemed to have no purpose but to stand there while reading a paper. My fear for Margaret's safety, my anger at the way I had been taunted in the letters with the brass rings, together with the mutilations of the victims I had seen firsthand . . . all of it boiled over in one primal moment.

At that instant, the only thing I could see was this man, as though he were standing at the end of a long, dimly lit hallway, and he alone was in the light. I bore straight toward him, and when I was about ten feet away, he lowered his paper to peer over it, and, seeing me, dropped it and ran.

CHAPTER THIRTY-SIX
THE GOALKEEPER

Tuesday, November 6, cont.

I am a large man, but I was still an active sportsman at the time and could move quickly for short distances. I put my head down like a bull and took off after him. His small size allowed him to dodge others on the sidewalk far better than I, so I took to the street, preferring to weave amongst the cabs and wagons.

I was giving it my all, startling horses and enduring their driver's oaths, and once or twice stepping into horse residue at full speed, nearly falling over as a result, but it was quickly obvious he was pulling away. I was losing heart when I saw the sidewalk ahead blocked by some construction work, thus causing the passersby to become tightly packed.

My quarry paused, looked back at me, and I felt a surge of power as I gained on him.

He turned and ran into an alley to his left. I followed at my top speed, just in time to see him run through a shadowed doorway on the left side at the end of the back street.

My breath was becoming more labored now, and I was forced to slow down, coming to a complete stop at the doorway, both to catch my wind and to avoid an ambush.

Entering with caution, I was at first blinded by the darkness after leaving the sunlight behind. My sight temporarily useless, I relied upon my other senses. Listening carefully, I heard heavy breathing nearby but was unable to locate it. I found myself in a dark, narrow passage. As my eyes adjusted, I realized the walls on each side of me were large barrels, stacked three high, such that I could not look over them. I smelled beer. A brewery.

I knew it was foolish to hunt a possible killer in the dark and unarmed, but my anger was only made hotter by the chase. I had two choices: go forward down the beer-lined path, or leave. I went forward.

The passage ran for about twenty feet before opening out into a large central area. I was approaching the end when the final column suddenly toppled over in front of me, and I leapt back just in time to avoid it landing on top of me. The top barrel burst open, covering the floor with its contents.

The man in the checked suit ran toward a door on the far side. I resumed my pursuit, but when I jumped over the barrels in my path I slipped and fell hard on the beer-slimed floor.

I scrambled up as fast as I could, and saw my man fling the door open and run out. I was careful not to slip again, but by the time I made it outside I had lost sight of him. Then I saw a man in a checked suit with a brown bowler hat walking away from me about one-hundred feet to my right. As I braced myself for another sprint, I noticed another man, in a similar suit and hat, walking away to my left at roughly the same distance.

Paralyzed with doubt, I looked down and saw wet footprints, which probably smelled of beer, going to my right.

My quarry was being coy as he walked along the sidewalk at a normal pace, doing his best not to draw attention to himself, and I used that to my advantage as I trotted along the street behind a passing hansom, shielding me from his view.

It was only when I pulled up alongside him that he noticed me, and the chase was on again. I was flagging and began to despair when we both saw a bobby in a small park ahead, passing the time with a governess pushing a pram. The young bobby appeared quite intent on "comforting the comfortable," to use Abberline's phrase, and was so distracted he did not notice the two of us playing hares and hounds down the street. I was too short of breath to muster a decent hail, and I feared the time it would take me to reach him would allow my shadow to escape. My quarry turned right, away from the constable, and I labored on in breathless pursuit.

Fortune finally favored the bold, however, for he veered into a narrow alley, only to find the large warehouse doors on either side locked. I stood there at the alley's entrance, blocking it, while he stood at the far end leaning against a soot-stained brick wall, and we both caught our breath.

I approached him slowly, still heaving as I recovered from my prolonged exercise, and assessing the area for danger. He appeared unarmed, but that could change quickly, as the East End had already taught me.

I have played goalie on various football teams, and this experience served me well, for he suddenly made a rush at me, in hopes of either bowling me over or slipping through my grasp. I had the better of it, however, and was soon grasping the man by his lapels. I was about to give him a "Glasgow Kiss," or head butt, when he raised his hands in surrender.

"Who are you?" I demanded. "What do you want of me?" As I am just over six feet tall, I towered over him. His face turned pale as I partially lifted him by his coat.

"Be-be-begging your pardon, sir!" he stammered. "I don't know what you're about!"

"I know you've been following me." I insisted, still angry, though I was already starting to doubt the wisdom of my action. I had tossed the dice; no backing out now.

My captive's eyes betrayed him. He looked away for a moment before replying. I have treated women whose injuries were explained by their husbands as "falling down the stairs." A liar needs to recall his story, while a truthful man can speak straightaway.

"I'll call a bobby if you don't let me go this instant!" the man demanded.

I released my grip on his lapels, to avoid a charge of assault, but held onto his coat sleeve. "Go ahead. I would like to hear your explanation to a policeman if not to me."

"For standing on a street corner?" he sneered.

"I have seen you at least twice before," I said. "Who are you? If you don't tell me this instant, I will be the one to call the police."

As I suspected, when I called his bluff about summoning a bobby, he changed his tune.

"No need for that, sir," he said. "A simple misunderstanding. My card will explain everything."

He handed me a simple plain business card with the names Grand and Batchelor, Private Detectives. I recalled Margaret's letter about the detectives under contract to the *Star* newspaper who had interviewed the greengrocer next to Dutfield's Yard.

"Ah, yes. The grape detectives," I sneered back.

He bristled at this. "Laugh if you like; we found a grape stalk in a drain in Dutfield's Yard."

"Proving beyond doubt," I countered, "that some residents of the East End eat grapes. Well done. I also have reason to believe that you and your associate have been following a Miss Margaret Harkness. For what purpose? I am in an ill temper, and concerned for her safety. Explain yourself!"

The man sniffed in an attempt to look dignified. "That's privileged information, between us and our clients!"

My left hand was reaching for his lapel when he realized the two of us were alone in the alley. I am not ashamed to say I was quite prepared to give him reason to reconsider, when my captive relented.

"All right, sir! No need for violence." The detective straightened himself to regain his dignity and said, "Me and my mate were just following anyone who seemed involved in the investigation. We noticed you and another man frequenting the police station. Then this woman with you. Honest. We get paid good money for any stories we bring in. We thought you and your friends might have something to do with the investigation."

"If you had nothing to hide," I replied, "why did you run?"

At this, the detective snorted. "The way you were coming at me, I thought you were about to kill me on the spot. Any sane man would run if a man nearly twice his size went after him with the look you had in your eyes!"

"And why did you avoid the constable?"

He shrugged, "Private detectives aren't too popular with the police. They see us as one short step above criminals. He'd as like arrest me on general principles, just to have it all sorted out at the station. Besides, I was giving you the slip until I made a wrong turn. Now, if you are finished attacking me, Doctor, what is your role in all this?"

Recalling Abberline's and Wilkins's insistence that we remain out of the press, I was momentarily at a loss for words. I have ever been a poor liar but have found a half-truth is often a better subterfuge than a complete lie.

I answered that my companion and I were physicians from Scotland, and were in London to observe how the findings from the victims' postmortems benefitted the hunt for the killer. We had no official standing, but planned to share our observations with our colleagues once we returned home.

The man scratched his chin, disappointed by my answer. "Well then, if you have no further plans to assault me, sir, I'd best be off."

"Before I let you go, I have two pieces of advice."

The man sighed in relief as I released my grip on him, "First, you are to stop following Miss Harkness and myself. Immediately! If I see you again or hear that she is still being followed, I will risk the gaol to stop you."

He nodded as he brushed imaginary lint where my hand had just been, "And the second piece of advice?"

"Either buy another suit or join the circus. You look ridiculous."

I nodded permission for him to depart, and after a cautious bow he turned on his heel and walked away. It was only after he left that I realized I had failed to ask which of the two detectives he was. It was much later before it occurred to me that I hadn't asked if he was only in the employ of the newspaper when he referred to his "clients." But something else was pulling at my sleeve, trying to get my attention.

The doorman at the Marlborough sniffed as I passed him in the entrance way, and he informed me with great dignity that laundry service was still available that day should I require it, my beer-splattered and sweat-soaked clothes not escaping his attention. I will leave it to your imagination to visualize the state of my boots.

I mumbled my thanks, chagrined to be seen in such a condition inside that venerable establishment, and went directly to my room to bathe and change clothes. It was only once I was soaking contentedly in the bath that I understood what else was bothering me: the detective had addressed me as "Doctor" before I told him my profession.

CHAPTER THIRTY-SEVEN
STANDING WATCH

Tuesday, November 6,
to Friday, November 9

Even partially solving the Adventure of The Ill-Dressed Detective should have given me some sense of accomplishment; yet it only deepened the underlying question as to who knew about Margaret, and therefore was able to refer to "my companions." I sadly concluded I was none the wiser for the confrontation with my shadow.

I fell asleep in the quiet refuge of the reading room and did not stir until five o'clock when Bell roused me. When I informed Bell of my afternoon's exercise, he laughed heartily at my description of my pursuit of the detective.

"A fine bit of derring-do, my friend," Bell said, his eyes shining with amusement.

To my surprise, he was complimentary at my explanation of our presence to Mr. Grand/Batchelor.

"Your idea of a series of talks about how medical inquiry may assist police investigations is an excellent one, Doyle. I shall give the matter some thought, and perhaps your efforts at deception may prove truer than you intended."

"We should inform Margaret that her suspicions about being followed were correct," I said, "though I doubt either of these two fools is clever enough to be the Ripper."

We dined from the buffet board within the club around seven

o'clock; then I packed what little I would require for the night, and we were off.

We collected Margaret on the way and bade Miss Jones goodnight. Margaret's "undress" was her usual East Ender Pennyworth ensemble, with the addition of a gray wool workingman's cap. She explained that her hair fit snugly underneath, and therefore would not come loose in her sleep. She feared the wig she sometimes wore would fall off in the night, so she'd braided her shoulder-length hair to prevent any strands from coming loose. Should someone come in to awaken us, her head would be sufficiently covered to avoid raising suspicion.

I told Margaret of my encounter with the detective, Bell adding to my encounter with dramatic embellishments, and my companions had a good laugh at my expense as I felt my ears burn.

"Dear Porthos," Margaret gasped out finally, "I didn't know our adventure would require a baptism of beer. I can only imagine the look the doorman gave you!"

Then, catching her breath, "At least we know who our shadows are. I hope they do not take your advice, about buying a new suit of clothes I mean, it makes it easier to notice them, though joining the circus was not a bad thought at all. I predict they'd have a great future."

We arrived at the station, and I led Margaret to the conference room where our unwelcoming pallets awaited. I pointed out the loo at the end of the hall, and assured her stalls were available. I also counseled her about the importance of falling asleep before the professor, but she assured me that after a year's residence in the East End she could sleep through nearly any disturbance. I merely smiled and said nothing more.

The next three days blurred into a succession of long nights and short days. I slept poorly, no doubt due in part to the unyielding nature of the cots, but also to the volcanic rumblings that regularly issued from Bell's corner of the room. To my surprise, though not amusement, his bass was joined by an alto accompaniment from Margaret, and I was the doomed audience for this recurring nocturnal concert.

I suffered greatly from their competing cacophony, only dozing intermittently in the station, then augmenting my meager sleep with afternoon naps. I would judge their contest a draw, by the way. Although Bell had the greater volume, Margaret had a high-pitched wheeze at the start of every exhalation that could cut one's nerves as sharply as a surgeon's blade. Trust me, dear reader, this judge's decision was made only after endless hours of meticulous contemplation and comparison.

It was the morning of the ninth of November when we parted company with Margaret after our third uneventful night. I was beginning to doubt the value of our vigil. Once we were back at the club and had dined, Bell joined me in the reading room, where I had laid aside some articles I wished to discuss with him.

We were well into our second pot of tea when a police constable, very much out of breath, consulted with the doorman, who promptly pointed in our direction.

He came straight to us and without preamble gasped out, "I was told to fetch you straight away! There's been another murder!"

There was a police wagon waiting outside for us, and we were soon speeding along, accompanied by the young constable.

"Are we headed for the station?" I asked him.

"No," was his terse reply, "but not far off. I can tell you this, gentlemen, it's the worst yet!"

That answer cast a chill on me, one unrelated to the weather. Bell and I looked at one another; his concern mirrored my own: by wagon, Margaret's flat was "not far off."

CHAPTER THIRTY-EIGHT
AN ACQUAINTANCE, REVISITED

Friday, November 9, cont.

The journey inside the closed police wagon was terrifying. We could not look outside due to the crowding of additional constables within, and my knowledge of London geography was not sufficient to inform me which direction we were headed, much less the streets we traveled. I listened in fear for the sound of a train, which one could often hear close to Margaret's tenement. If a train had been nearby, however, I doubt I would have heard it over the pounding in my chest. The nausea from my last trip inside a police wagon returned in full force, probably more due to the spinning of my head then the rocking of the coach.

Finally, mercifully, the wagon stopped. I could hear the voices of a crowd outside. The doors opened and, taking a deep breath, I looked out. A line of constables was holding back a throng of onlookers gazing at a dark, brick-lined archway, with the words "Miller's Court" written above it.

It was approximately one o'clock when we arrived. The constable who accompanied us led us through the archway into the court itself. There were several additional police constables, a couple of inspectors we had not met before, and our old acquaintances Doctor Phillips and Inspector Abberline. The constables had formed a half-circle around a door at the far end of the freshly whitewashed courtyard, thus keeping the occupants at a distance while the inspectors took turns looking through a window around the corner from the door into the room. The window was broken and partially blocked by newspapers and an old coat.

I gasped! I so clearly remembered the young laundress Mary standing in that door waving goodbye, then cheekily blowing me a kiss. I was relieved beyond measure it wasn't Margaret's flat we were visiting, but recalling the bold woman who had lived here I had a surge of guilt at my own relief. By wishing for Margaret's salvation I was condemning another.

CHAPTER THIRTY-NINE
THIS PLACE OF WRATH AND TEARS

Friday, November 9, cont.

Surprisingly, the door was still closed. Bell went straight to Abberline to ask, "What's the situation, Inspector, and why is everyone outside?"

Inspector Abberline was flushed, apparently laboring to maintain his composure. "It's the damned hounds, Professor! We're waiting for the bloodhounds to arrive per Commissioner Warren's directive. No one is to enter the room until they are here and get the scent. If you'd like a peek to see what all the tumult is about, you're free to look into the window over there, though I doubt you'll thank me for the sight."

Bell and I exchanged grim glances. I took a deep breath and walked resolutely to the window. I peered within . . .

In my medical training, I thought that I had seen the worst that could happen to a human being.

I was wrong.

Even now, these many years later, I struggle to express the horror of what lay before me, reminiscent of the paintings of hell by that insane Dutch artist Hieronymus Bosch. A body lay on the bed, head turned toward the window. Note that I did not say "face," for there was little remaining save the eyes, which were open and staring back at me in eternal terror.

There was blood everywhere inside the room. Everywhere. The abdominal cavity had been opened, its contents entirely removed, with mounds of raw flesh resting upon the table beside the bed. There was more to see, and the eye is naturally inclined to roam, but while we see with our eyes, as Professor Bell has often said, we observe with our mind. Mine could absorb no more.

I staggered back and, am ashamed to say, vomited promptly.

Bell placed his hand on my shoulder to console me, then went to stand next at the window. I heard his sharp intake of breath, but that was his only outward evidence of the impression the scene inside made upon him. After perhaps a full minute at the window, he stood back, satisfied for now, and turned sadly to me.

"Under no circumstances should we summon Mr. Pennyworth here," he said, careful to use Margaret's alias so as not to arouse suspicion from any of the police all about us. "I will withstand a hundred lectures before I curse him for the rest of his life with the memory of this scene," he continued in a lowered voice. "He can accompany us to the morgue later if desired, but I do not want our friend to see how cruelly this poor woman was slaughtered in the one place she felt safe." Bell's shoulders slumped. "Such a brave little soul." He sighed, "Snuffed out merely for the sake of some cruel sport." He looked at the ground and murmured "The man who could do this is beyond my comprehension."

Abberline came up to us, and through clenched teeth said, "We bleed the other districts of London to flood the East End, and what do we accomplish? We merely drive the Ripper indoors to do his handiwork." He ran his hand over his face, then his usual stoic nature reasserted itself, and he asked if there was anything we could deduce from what we had seen.

"It took no great skill to perform the mutilations and evisceration I observed, Inspector," Bell answered. "Any butcher or abattoir worker who possessed a complete disregard for the cruelty of the act itself would have the necessary skills. What can you tell me of her discovery?"

"Simple enough," responded the inspector. "She was in arrears for her room, so the landlord, Mr. McCarthy, sent his assistant Bowyer around to collect at about ten forty-five this morning. Bowyer knocked on the door but got no answer. He reckoned she hadn't the rent and was laying low, so he looked in the window here to see if she was hiding inside."

Abberline pointed to the window, and I noticed his hand was trembling. Even this old veteran was shaken by what he had seen, and I was less ashamed at my reaction. "When he pulled aside a curtain that was helping to block that broken window he . . . well, you saw what he saw. He hotfooted it back to Mr. McCarthy and could scarcely speak, but was able to say there was a lot of blood. Mr. McCarthy came here straight away and, after looking inside, sent Bowyer to us.

"Inspectors Dew and Beck were on duty when Bowyer arrived. Dew told me the poor man was so frightened that at first he just yammered away until finally he said, 'Another one. Jack the Ripper. Jack McCarthy sent me.' The inspectors followed Bowyer back here. They tried the door but were unable to open it, so Bowyer took them to the window and both looked inside."

Abberline shook his head sadly. "We believe the body is that of the resident, a Miss Mary Kelly, a well-known streetwalker in this area. We won't know for sure, of course, until we can have a close acquaintance identify her. She was keeping company with a Joseph Barnett, according to the neighbors. I've sent a constable round to fetch him from the lodging house he lives in now. I tell you, gentlemen, I don't envy him the task that awaits, both because of how it may affect him and the little he'll have to go on."

Abberline scratched his chin in thought. "I hear from the neighbors that her man Barnett left after quite a row a couple of weeks back. He didn't like her bringing customers to their bed; she was angry with him for not helping with the rent. This looks like Jack's work, but I shouldn't forget to ask Mr. Barnett about his whereabouts last night as well. There's no sign of forced entry. As the door is locked from outside, if we find Mary's key inside that would mean the killer already had his own.

"From what I can tell through the window, our killer was here for some time. I would think the longer he stays in one place, the more likely he would be to leave something behind that may help us identify him. Perhaps in his frenzy he got careless and left us a clue. I promise you that if he did I'll follow it to the gates of hell if I have to!" This last bit was said with a fierce determination that transformed his usually calm and thoughtful appearance into a determined warrior's. I was glad we had a man of Inspector Abberline's caliber in charge.

It was half-past one in the afternoon when an inspector arrived and announced the bloodhounds were not coming. I can only surmise this was due to the curse of bureaucracy that infects every human undertaking. Abberline, furious at the needless delay, ordered his men to break down the door.

The landlord fetched a pickax, then tore the door open himself. Perhaps this was to minimize damage to his property, but in fairness he did so with a will and was as sickened by the scene inside as any of us.

I remained outside, having seen quite enough already, while Professor Bell entered with Doctor Phillips. Neither of them touched anything, however, until Doctor Thomas Bond, another police surgeon, arrived. Sadly, the use of fingerprints, now standard procedure in criminal investigations, was not available then. I cannot help but wonder how things might have turned out had the police access to such techniques.

When the examination was complete, the professor came out and said in quiet tones that there was no need for further inspection of the body back at the morgue, as the killer had essentially done the postmortem for us. Nothing of interest remained of the body itself—that could be opened or otherwise viewed—that had not been made visible at the scene or been removed by the killer.

"Her body parts were arranged about the body," Bell said, morosely, "just as they were for the Mitre Square victim. Only . . . more so. No doubt because the killer had more time due to the seclusion of her room." Bell clenched his fist and whispered hoarsely, "He arranged her, Doyle . . . like flowers in a vase . . . for some bizarre artistic effect! I cannot fathom this man. Perhaps . . . perhaps it's better I cannot."

I merely nodded. What words could have offered him the slightest comfort?

Bell was somber and silent for a moment more, then straightened and looked me keenly in the eyes. "I'll find him. Wherever he goes, I'll find him. I'll see to it he pays."

I extended my hand. "No, Professor," I said, returning his gaze. "*We'll* find him."

Bell grasped my hand and, at that moment, each knew the other's heart. An oath had been sworn.

There had been a fire in Mary Kelly's grate hot enough to melt the handle and spout of a tea kettle, and the ashes contained the wire rim of a woman's hat. A woman named Maria Harvey later told police she had stayed with Miss Kelly two nights earlier that week, and she'd left some clothes behind. The police speculated that her clothes must have been the source of the fire, as Mary Kelly's garments were found hanging neatly on a chair at the foot of the bed. Inspector Abberline surmised that the clothes were set alight to provide the Ripper with light for his gruesome labor.

The examination of the body was completed at three forty-five, and shortly afterward it was removed to the city morgue. A large crowd had gathered outside the entrance of the courtyard as news of the newest murder victim had spread, while the Lord Mayor's Procession was underway less than half a mile away. This ancient ceremony presenting the new Lord Mayor to the people of London had drawn a considerable number to enjoy the spectacle. As the news of the latest atrocity moved through the crowd, however, many left before its conclusion to partake of other, less formal, entertainment.

I imagined the pomp and circumstance celebrating the new Lord Mayor, attired in his ermine-trimmed robe and his chain of office, contrasted with the subdued removal of Mary Kelly's body.

"No eulogy for Mary," I said.

Bell cleared his throat, bowed his head, and, in a voice uneven with emotion, began to recite a recently published poem by William Henley, his pronounced brogue attesting to his emotion:

"Out of the night that covers me,
Black as the pit from pole to pole,
I thank whatever gods may be
For my unconquerable soul."

A multitude rushed out of their apartments and bore silent witness as Mary made her final journey out of Miller's Court. I heard a distant band playing processional music.

"In the fell clutch of circumstance
I have not winced nor cried aloud.
Under the bludgeonings of chance
My head is bloodied, but unbowed."

Women openly wept and men of every class doffed their caps as she passed by in the battered and often used "shell," a large coffin-shaped wheeled box covered by a ragged and filthy cloth, while Bell continued:

"Beyond this place of wrath and tears
Looms but the Horror of the shade
And yet the menace of the years
Finds, and shall find me, unafraid."

I watched the most wretched of Her Majesty's subjects render their honors upon one who had lived gamely among them and so cruelly been taken from their midst, as Bell concluded, choking on the final line:

"It matters not how strait the gate,
How charged with punishments the scroll,
I am the master of my fate:
I am the captain of my soul."

The sound of a distant crowd cheering marked the end of the Lord Mayor's ceremony; here in Miller's Court, no one spoke a word.

We were released for the moment, Abberline asking us to visit him the next morning in his office. We two Musketeers knew that our duty lay now in sharing our unexpected day's activities with the third, and to tell her we would not be spending the night in Spitalfields station; the calamity we had been awaiting had happened.

We sat in silence during the ride to Vine Street, Bell looking out of the hansom, deep in thought, while I had the feeling once more of something pulling at my sleeve, trying to get my attention.

Margaret had heard of the recent murder already while out buying food, and she'd gone to Miller's Court, but as she had not been in her Pennyworth attire she'd not been allowed to enter.

I shared Bell's eulogy with her, and she, like me, was deeply affected by his tribute to Mary. His nobility of spirit had impressed me ever since I served as the clerk of his surgical service not so many years before. This entire adventure had only strengthened my respect for the character of my old mentor.

"I'm sorry we weren't able to include you, Margaret, but Abberline sent a wagon for us, and we had no control over our movements until we arrived," I said, lying as convincingly as I knew how. In truth, I was not sorry at all, sharing Bell's desire to spare Margaret the visions of Mary Kelly's butchery.

Margaret brushed that aside, for her fury was directed elsewhere. "The bastard!" she snarled. "To think this brute who kills women for sport is at this very moment laughing at the terror he's inspired. The second letter was correct, Doyle. I know you and the professor assumed the writer intended me as his next victim . . . I feel guilty that he chose poor Mary instead. He couldn't have been following us the entire time; how would he know we met with her? How would he even know about us?"

Suddenly I feared I would vomit again. The answer to Margaret's question had stopped pulling on my sleeve and now stared me in the face.

"The answer has been right in front of me the entire time, but I lacked the wit to see it!" I declared, furious. My friends stared at me with blank faces.

"Unless the killer has been shadowing us continuously, how could he possibly have known of our meeting with Mary Kelly? Who else besides we three could have known?"

Margaret looked at me blankly, while Bell began nodding his head as comprehension dawned.

"Think, Margaret! Who is the one man to whom I gave a list of all our activities and contacts?"

Margaret's face turned pale, and her knees almost betrayed her when the realization struck. With a voice husky with emotion, she whispered, "Wilkins."

CHAPTER FORTY
HANNIBAL'S SON

Friday, November 9, cont.

"Exactly!" roared Bell. "Wilkins! It was he who supposedly convinced Mr. Gladstone to contact you. We have kept him abreast of the investigation, yet we never verified his identity. A simple cardboard card with gold lettering and an impressive address, and we gave him our complete trust. The bah-stard!"

Margaret began to tremble. "Mary! Poor Mary! He wanted to kill someone you knew, remember? That's why he wanted you to meet with a streetwalker . . . and I led you straight to her! I'm the reason she's dead!"

I took both her hands in mine, looked into her eyes, and said firmly, "Nonsense, Margaret. *He* is the reason she is dead. I was taken in by his deception. If anyone else is to blame, it's me, for accepting this man's identity at face value. Please. The burden is mine, if not Wilkins's, or whatever his name is. We cannot bring her back. But I swear to do all I can to make him face justice."

"But what proof do we have?" she asked plaintively. "We don't even know where he lives. Your only means of contact is through the doorman. Could he be an accomplice?"

"No," Bell replied with conviction. "The doorman is accustomed to carrying out the random requests of powerful men all the time. To send a message to one address though addressed to another would be in a day's work for someone in his position."

"So how can we track him down?" Margaret wanted to know, still seething.

"Simple enough," I said. Anger of my own was now replacing the shock, and it was serving as a powerful tonic to clear my mind. "Send Wilkins a message and follow the messenger."

"Perfect," said Bell, nodding, his eyes cold with fury. "Track the beast to his lair using the very means he has used to keep a watch on us."

It was nearing sunset when we arrived back at the Marlborough Club. Margaret, in her Pennyworth persona, was loitering across the street with her derringer in her coat pocket, while I handed a message to the doorman for Wilkins marked URGENT. The note requested a meeting as soon as possible regarding the murder that had happened that day. Margaret would follow the messenger, while Bell would follow her at a discrete distance. The professor argued the courier could have been warned about either of us attempting to track him, so Margaret, in male attire, should be able to pass along unnoticed behind him until the message reached its true destination.

The doorman merely nodded when I placed the message and a one-pound note into his hand. Bell was already outside, hidden in the shadows but in view of Margaret. As we could not be sure of the doorman's innocence, I agreed to remain behind and within easy sight of him. Thus, he would be reassured there was nothing unusual regarding the message, and I could observe him as well.

I spent an anxious ninety minutes before the response to my message arrived, just before my friends' return.

Dear Doctor Doyle,

I regret other concerns prevent me from meeting with you at this time. I can well imagine the reason for your sudden summons. Perhaps you, or at least Professor Bell, are not entirely incompetent, although you must admit I have provided you with ample opportunity to discern my true role in this affair. As I can only assume you had the messenger followed, we can dispense with the charade. Now is the time to see what effect motivation has upon your performance. I desire to meet with you, and very soon. I will not deny myself the pleasure of seeing the look of abject defeat upon your smug face. The little whore I butchered this morning whimpered as I sliced her. Well, at least until I sliced her some more. I look forward to giving you a personal demonstration.

I will make this as easy as I possibly can then. My next victim will be Hannibal's Son. Stop me if you can.

Until we meet again,

Wilkins no more

My two companions returned shortly afterward, looking more tired than I had seen either of them before.

"What happened?" I asked, trying to keep my voice as normal as possible. Where did the messenger go?"

They looked at one another, then Margaret answered. "The German Embassy."

I digested this thunderbolt while I wordlessly handed over the written reply to Margaret, which she and Bell silently pored over together.

I do not know who was more surprised: I, by the destination of the message, or my comrades, by the reply.

"He is canny, this Jack," said Margaret, finally. "We cannot touch him while he is inside the embassy. Even if we could convince Abberline this man is our killer, he would not be able to get a judge to issue a search warrant for his private residence. If we confront him on the street, he can claim diplomatic immunity that only the ambassador could waive. Even if a search of his quarters were agreed to, the embassy staff would most likely remove all incriminating evidence before the search to avoid a scandal. The only way we can stop him is to catch him in the act."

"Our best chance is to find this Hannibal's Son," said Bell. "Who today can claim to be a son of that extinct dynasty?"

I had a flash of inspiration, "Hannibal does not refer to a person exactly, but a place. Specifically, to Hannibal, Missouri, in America. Jack intends to murder Mark Twain!"

CHAPTER FORTY-ONE
THE TERRIER

Friday, November 9, to Saturday, November 10

There was a long silence as Bell and Margaret digested my out-burst, then each began to nod slowly, recalling the announcement outside the Old Vic when we had attended the poetry reading together.

"Twain is here for a three-night run, as I remember," said the professor.

"Starting tomorrow night," I replied. "So, all we must do is convince Abberline of our suspicions and have sufficient forces discretely on hand so that when Wilkins, or whatever his name is, makes his move we can catch him in the act and take him into custody."

"Let's break down your proposal into each of its parts," replied Bell. "First, without any proof save an easily forged letter, we convince an inspector of Scotland Yard that Jack the Ripper is a diplomat of the German Embassy. Second, we assume the police are sufficiently cunning to protect Mr. Clemens from an attack while not alerting the killer to their presence. Third, we catch the killer in an act so obviously malevolent it will pass the strictest legal review as proof of murderous intent, allowing the police to bring him into custody. Finally, the foreign secretary can convince the German ambassador it is in the best interest of relations between our countries to waive diplomatic immunity. All four of those conditions will have to be met if he is ever to stand trial for his crimes."

"Then what do you propose?" I asked, feeling suffocated by our apparent helplessness. "Do nothing?"

"Not at all, my friend," Bell replied. "But we should realize the hurdles we must overcome. I suggest we start with the police in the morning. Inspector Abberline would not be found in his office at this late hour, but he is expecting us tomorrow morning. We can rehearse our arguments and see how we do with the first challenge."

Bell was right, of course. My feeling of triumph for having solved the riddle of the next victim left me. It seemed the Ripper was as elusive as ever. I could only hope the trust and respect Bell had earned with Abberline would cause him to believe that our wild story contained an element of truth.

"Odd, don't you think?" Margaret asked. "Up until now, he has only attacked women. It is quite extraordinary for him to threaten to attack a man, especially one as prominent as Mr. Clemens."

"I agree, Miss Harkness," said Bell. "But if we are confident this man is the Ripper, we have to take him at his word. We can do no less."

I agreed. If we disregarded this threat out of hand and Mr. Clemens were to die we would have to bear the burden the rest of our lives.

We decided to pick Margaret up at nine o'clock on our way to the station the next morning. I walked with her in silence to the nearest cab, asked the driver to take her directly home, and gave him a one-pound note to ensure he did so.

I passed a fitful night, furious at the man who could butcher an innocent woman then dance away, unscathed, to mock us. I finally arose before six and took the opportunity to read the latest about the investigation of Miss Kelly's murder. What I read was not encouraging. An editorial from the *Times* caught my eye.

> As long as this murderer . . . is cool enough to leave no clue behind him . . . his crimes may continue. Unless there were a policeman, not merely in every street, but in every house in Whitechapel, it is impossible to secure the safety against this "monster" of such women as yesterday's victim . . . as long as these Whitechapel women offer

themselves to the slaughterer, and the slaughterer does not lose his head, it is unjust to blame the police for failing to protect them.

The truth in the article frightened me. There would never be enough policemen. If Jack the Ripper were to be stopped, one way or another, it was up to us.

The statement by a Mr. George Hutchinson, an acquaintance of Mary's for over three years, was poignant to me in one particular:

> About two o'clock on the morning of the ninth, I was coming by Thrawl Street, when I met the murdered woman.
>
> A man coming in the opposite direction to Kelly tapped her on the shoulder and said something to her. They both burst out laughing... He then placed his right hand around her shoulder. He also had a kind of small parcel in his left hand with a strap around it.
>
> .... followed them. They stood on the corner of the court for about three minutes. He said something to her. She said: "All right, my dear. Come along. You will be comfortable."

I recalled Mary Kelly telling us how she would try to get a potential customer to laugh before taking him to her room, as a way of assessing the potential danger. If this man described by Hutchinson was indeed the Ripper, it appears he passed the trial quite readily. The image of her taking the monster into her refuge only to realize his true nature when she was powerless to stop him, trusting in his laugh, saddened me in ways I cannot describe. This man did more than take lives. He took hope.

When we entered the station later that morning, the desk sergeant nodded with an odd smile on his face as he gestured for us to proceed to Abberline's office. I quickly learned the source of his merriment, for as we approached I could hear a high-pitched, raspy voice berating the inspector at a remarkable volume.

"How dare you bring his name into this affair, Inspector! If it didn't increase the chances of this getting out, I would have you sacked!"

We entered to see a short, thin gentleman in a double-breasted frock coat and top hat catching his breath, presumably for the next volley. Abberline was sitting at his desk looking at his accuser wearily. When we entered, his eyes turned on us, his glare extinguishing any hope I'd had of persuading him of our story.

"Well, speak of the devil!" he cried, "Or devils, in this case. Professor Bell, Doctor Doyle, and Mr. Pennyworth, allow me to introduce you to my guest, Mr. Jonathan Wilkins, personal secretary to Mr. Gladstone, who by the way, says he has never heard of any of you!"

There was stunned silence as Mr. Wilkins eyed us furiously over his pince-nez glasses, and I suddenly felt weak, having been exposed to Inspector Abberline before we had a chance to explain.

Mr. Wilkins advanced with the ferocity of Margaret's terrier pursuing a rat, while holding a letter aloft in his right hand. "I received this note this morning from an anonymous source advising me that a Doctor Doyle and Professor Bell were misrepresenting themselves as my agents and, by inference, were acting on behalf of Mr. Gladstone. Explain yourselves, sirs. I will brook no evasion!"

"I freely admit we have never met, sir," I began. "I was contacted by courier shortly after the murder in early September by a man who misrepresented himself as you. Professor Bell and I have met with him at the Marlborough Club on Pall Mall, where he lodged us and paid all expenses. The doorman will verify the dates we have lodged there, and the receptionist can describe the man who paid our bills as well as produce copies of the receipts. Here is the card he gave us, as well as the letter he said was signed by Mr. Gladstone, stating we were acting on his behalf."

Wilkins studied the card and letter suspiciously. "The card is not one of mine," he replied cautiously. "The stock is a lighter shade than what I use, but correct in every other detail. The letter is on paper the same quality and tint as Mr. Gladstone's. Whoever," and here he raised his eyebrows to indicate his suspicions of us had not yet fully abated, "wrote this letter has at some time viewed correspondence from his office. Describe this man for me."

"About five foot six, pale, dark hair, and he has a trace of a Prussian accent," I answered. "He is obviously well-to-do, else he would not have been able to fund us so lavishly, though he dresses modestly."

At the mention of a Prussian accent, Wilkins's demeanor changed, his shoulders relaxing as he pondered my words.

"Inspector Abberline," he said. "I am satisfied that Doctor Doyle was duped by a cunning charlatan. As I am anxious this misadventure not be picked up by the papers, and I am sure that these gentlemen do not wish to tarnish Mr. Gladstone's name," at this he looked at me with raised eyebrows over his spectacles, "I will not file suit.

"You may continue to cooperate with them as you see fit, as long as the real nature of their agency is understood. Gentlemen, I would like to speak to you in private. I will await you at the entrance of the station, from whence we can adjourn to a place of your choosing to continue this conversation. Please do not leave me waiting long."

When Mr. Wilkins said, "not file suit," it occurred to me we were liable both for civil and criminal proceedings. A civil suit could be brought against us if he alleged we besmirched his employer's name, and Inspector Abberline would be totally within his rights to charge us for hindering a police investigation. We had narrowly avoided the one, now to confront the other.

The inspector glared at us in silence while considering the situation. Finally, he sighed deeply, his shoulders slumping, "My hands are full as it is, and dealing with you lot is just one more thing that would require a long report that I would have to write and carry to Whitehall.

"I also think you acted in good faith, and I know you had no hand in the murders as you were here in the station house during the 'double event.' But I cannot work with you any further. If word were to get out about how I was taken in, my promotion to Scotland Yard would be in question. You must leave here now, and don't come back."

"But Inspector," I cried, "I have reason to believe we know who the Ripper is, and who his next victim will be! He has threatened to kill the American author Samuel Clemens! You must listen to me!"

"Oh?" said Abberline in a weary tone, "and how would you know that? Told you himself, has he?"

"In a manner of speaking, yes," I replied.

"Then in a manner of speaking, let me tell YOU that you had best leave this station right now, else you'll be spending another night here, further down the hall in a cell!"

"Come, Doyle," said Bell. "There is nothing further to be gained here. The inspector has been most generous with his time and his trust. I regret our parting ways in this manner, but I should have foreseen this. Let's see what the real Mr. Wilkins has to say before we plan our next move."

We trudged wearily out of Abberline's office, defeated for the moment. I was puzzled by the professor's comment that he should have foreseen our current predicament but was hopeful our meeting with Mr. Gladstone's real secretary would bring some light to our present darkness.

Soon we were to learn a new name for our adversary, and an explanation for his fascination with blood.

CHAPTER FORTY-TWO
BLOODLINES

Saturday, November 10, cont.

We adjourned to a nearby pub with private salons in the back, and once the door was closed Mr. Wilkins turned to us and said, "Tell me all you know about my doppelganger."

We related our meetings, his appearance and professed heritage, and finally the message we tracked to the German Embassy, and its ominous reply.

"I believe the man you are dealing with is Herr Graff," the real Wilkins informed us, "though that is not his real name either. As part of my portfolio, I am responsible for advising Mr. Gladstone on foreign affairs. As he is still an influential man, he is often invited to official functions."

The terrier reemerged briefly as Wilkins waved his finger at us sternly, "My employer has no desire to undermine the long-range goals of Her Majesty's government, whatever party may hold the reins for the moment, so I am regularly briefed by staff from the Foreign Office before attending such functions with him. I receive a short biography of all foreign dignitaries and what they may hope to accomplish in their dealings with us."

Wilkins sniffed disdainfully. "I have met Herr Graff on more than one occasion; regarding his heritage, he has lied to you in two instances. His mother is, in fact, English, and his father is not Prussian, either, though I prefer not to specify his exact origins. Suffice to say he is heir to a noble house within Germany. You physicians will surely understand the significance that a brother of his died in childhood after a fall that was complicated by hemophilia."

At that comment he looked at us with raised eyebrows. Hemophilia is a disease of coagulation associated with one particular bloodline: Her Majesty Queen Victoria's. Herr Graff was a grandchild of our monarch.

I swallowed hard at the revelation of the man's heritage; any accusation against him without the most damning evidence would be futile, and liable to place the accuser at considerable risk of prosecution for slander.

"Graff is an alias adopted for his current assignment at the embassy. Officially he was assigned here as a minor functionary to 'learn statecraft' in preparation for his ascension to the throne. Unofficially, I was told he was sent to England to allow a scandal to cool regarding his former nanny. I do not know the details, but if you believe this man to be the Ripper, I can only guess it wasn't pleasant.

"He will be a difficult quarry to bring to justice," Wilkins continued, "for, despite his minor post, due to his nobility he is accountable only to the ambassador, who is currently in Germany for consultations with Herr Bismarck. The police cannot touch him unless apprehended at the scene of a crime. Mr. Gladstone has a great sympathy for these unfortunates, as you well know, so I can assure you he would applaud whatever you can do to stop these killings, but we are unable to help you in any way."

"What you have told us is most helpful," answered Bell. "As we are acting in an unofficial capacity, our freedom of action is greater than that of the police. It is our only advantage, as it appears Herr Graff holds all the other cards. Thank you for your insight, Mr. Wilkins. We shall have to consider our next move carefully."

"Good hunting to you, gentlemen," replied Wilkins. "I wish we still placed the heads of malefactors on the London Bridge. His would make a splendid trophy! Good day."

After the genuine Wilkins left, I turned to Bell and asked, "What did you mean, you should have foreseen this turn of events?"

Bell smiled thinly. "Think, Doyle. Who do you think sent the real Wilkins the anonymous letter that stripped away any assistance from the police?"

"Graff," said Margaret, who had been silent until now. "Of course," she continued. "There was no longer any advantage to him in maintaining the deception. Exposing us in this way destroyed our credibility with Abberline. We knew the man was ruthless. We forget his cunning at great peril."

"Just so," replied the professor. "Knowing he intends to murder Mr. Clemens, do we use him as bait, or do we warn him and provide him with what protection we can?"

"Good God, man!" I answered, "I cannot in good conscience allow the man to be dangled before this fiend like a goat tethered for a tiger. I could never live with myself should he come to harm by such callousness."

"Nor I," replied Margaret. "Many innocents have died already. I want to stop this killing as much as anyone, but we must find another way."

Bell nodded. "I agree. Then we must find a way to warn Mr. Clemens, and protect him to the best of our ability. Our killer is sly, but until now he has had things entirely his way. He is no doubt gloating even now on how he has turned the police against us. I feel our greatest hope is that in his pride he shall grow careless. He wants to confront us, or rather you, Doyle, though on his terms. We must do all we can to change the odds in our favor before that moment arrives."

"He will not find me unwilling," I vowed. "I cannot face him soon enough. I am tired of boxing at shadows."

Bell and Margaret looked at me as though seeing me anew. I had gone into this affair halfheartedly at best. No longer. I was fixed upon my target, and I would bring Graff to justice or know the reason why. We exchanged looks, and I knew the same fire burned within their breasts. Miss Kelly would be avenged. The Three Musketeers would see to it.

"It is now approaching noon," I said. "I propose we find where Mr. Clemens is lodging," then indicating Margaret, "and have you request an interview. If you can achieve an audience, we can use that opportunity to warn him. Neither Bell nor I can provide a plausible excuse to meet with him before his performance tonight; you are our best hope."

"I shall conjure up my most enticing persona." Margaret mimed a coquette, batting her eyes, which I found rather unsettling as she was still in male attire. "But first we must find his hotel, and I must lay the stalwart Mr. Pennyworth aside for the moment. I will need some cosmetics to aid my cause."

Mr. Clemens's performance was scheduled to run from eight o'clock until ten that evening. Assuming he would arrive at least thirty minutes beforehand, and it was now noon, that gave us seven hours to locate and warn him.

I hired a cab to take Margaret directly home, with the understanding we would come for her as soon as we knew where Mr. Clemens was staying. Bell and I hailed a second one to return us to the club, and our indispensable doorkeeper was tasked to gather all the local papers while we dressed for the theater.

Mark Twain was known as an entertaining speaker. I hoped fervently his performance tonight would end in laughter, not tears.

CHAPTER FORTY-THREE
A MUSKETEER, TRANSFORMED

Saturday, November 10, cont.

I soon found a notice of Twain's arrival from America mentioning he was lodging at the Great Western Railway Hotel, part of the Paddington Station complex.

On Vine Street, I had to pay our driver an additional shilling to wait for us, and I remained aboard while Bell brought Margaret down, as I feared the driver would abandon us otherwise. Bell, therefore, was the first to witness her transformation, and with a mischievous grin awaited my reaction when they emerged. Truthfully, I only recognized the woman joining me because she was with the professor.

Margaret's cheeks were rouged, her lips tinted, and she was in a black satin dress that boldly declared her femininity as surely as her Pennyworth attire obscured it. The bodice was tight-fitting, and the neckline extended two inches below the collarbones, the limit of modesty at the time, with a ruby pendant that pointed downward like a signpost toward her breasts. She glowed with an air of confidence I found even more entrancing than her wardrobe as she seated herself opposite and faced me.

"Your mouth is open, Porthos," she remarked, not unkindly, pleased by the effect her appearance had on me. "If this doesn't get me an interview, then I am sustaining a tight corset for no good reason, and I shall be quite cross."

Bell meanwhile continued to smile with obvious enjoyment at my discomfiture. Ignoring Bell's delight for the moment, I gave the driver the hotel's address, and he drove his horses smartly forward.

We arrived just before three o'clock, three hours before Mr. Clemens would commence preparations for his performance.

Margaret produced her card, identifying herself as Margaret Harkness, Independent Journalist and Author, and upon handing it to the concierge requested he send it to Mr. Clemens's room and inquire if he was available for a brief interview.

He snapped his heels like a sergeant-major on parade, then delegated a young bellboy to serve as messenger.

Margaret ensured the young man got a good look at her, and once he had, apparently impressed given his lingering gaze, he reluctantly left for his appointed mission.

"Now we wait," said Margaret, her arched eyebrows hinting at her satisfaction with her effect upon the bellboy.

The bellboy's forehead was moist when he returned. He reported that Mr. Clemens would be unavailable for the next hour, as he was in the midst of a nap and anxious to go back to it as quickly as possible. If Miss Harkness could wait until then, he would see her in one of the private meeting rooms connected to the lobby, and he could give her a half hour of his time.

"Oh, and another thing," the bellboy said in parting, "he'll only meet with you, Miss Harkness. When I mentioned the two gentlemen with you, he said he hadn't time to be charming for three people. They'll have to wait outside."

We had returned to our conversation when I noticed a police constable talking to the concierge, handing him a note, and then departing after glancing in our direction. The concierge nodded and summoned the same young man, who accepted it and slipped it into his pocket.

Something about the constable seemed familiar to me, even from across the expansive lobby, but I had been in the company of so many constables over the past few weeks that it would have been more remarkable if I did not start recognizing some of them. I put it out of my mind and returned my attention to my companions.

When Mr. Clemens entered the lobby, he was dressed in his trademark white linen coat and trousers. His shock of white hair, bushy eyebrows, and thick white mustache made him immediately recognizable. The bellboy pointed Margaret out to him, and Mr. Clemens brightened considerably when he saw her. Before the American could come forward, however, the bellboy handed him the note presumably delivered by the constable. Mr. Clemens read the note, looked puzzled, then shook his head and returned it to the bellboy before advancing.

I was still a relative unknown at the time, and I'm sure Clemens hadn't read anything I'd written, or even heard my name. His renown was, and still is, worldwide. I had devoured all his major works and several of his short stories. I looked at him and saw the epitome of success a writer could ever aspire to. One which seemed unreachable to me.

To be in the presence of the creator of Huckleberry Finn and the Celebrated Jumping Frog was humbling. Fame has a cost, as I was later to learn, and some bear it better than others. It fitted Mr. Clemens as comfortably as his white linen suit, for the deference others paid him he neither expected nor demanded. I could easily see the spark of mischief in his eyes, an adult version of Tom Sawyer, I fancied.

"Good afternoon, lady and gents," he said. "No need for introductions. I read Miss Harkness's card, you all know who I am, and regretfully I shall not have time to speak with you gentlemen."

He bowed to Margaret with a courtly flourish, his abundant eyebrows rising as he viewed her up close. "Miss Harkness, I can give you a half-hour, then I will need to make myself pretty for the unwashed masses. It is always a pleasure to meet with a fellow author, for we belong to a guild of explorers . . . travelers to worlds of whimsy. I look forward to learning where your whimsies have taken you. There is a small meeting room off the lobby where we can speak undisturbed. Shall we?"

He nodded amiably and escorted the now blushing Margaret to

the private conference room as smoothly as a dancer on the stage. The entire time with him may have lasted thirty seconds, yet his presence and the glint in his eyes were not to be forgotten. Without ever raising his voice, he had taken complete command of the situation. I have often wished for his gift in subsequent meetings with the press.

I admit to being jealous of the way Margaret had blithely floated off with Clemens, leaving Bell and me to cool our heels in the lobby, but we had brought her to speak with him, and it appeared we had succeeded. Perhaps too well, my inner voice suggested.

Finally they emerged, and Mr. Clemens bowed slightly, kissed Margaret's hand, and left for his room.

Margaret was plainly taken with the American, for she stood stock still for a moment to watch him depart. Then she stirred herself and turned to us, a slight flush on her cheeks telling us more than perhaps she would have liked.

"I trust the interview went well?" inquired Bell, with a faint smile and twinkle in his eye. "You seem to have rather enjoyed yourself."

"It was marvelous!" she said enthusiastically. "I may, in fact, have enough for the interview to be published under my name in the *Star*. I had wanted to inform him of the threat immediately, but you saw how he manages a conversation. He seemed interested in my work and was very sympathetic to the plight of the matchgirls, whom I have helped organize. I was as much the interviewee as the interviewer. He was never the least bit patronizing, but treated me as an equal despite my femininity and lesser body of work." She sighed. "The time flew by."

"All well and good," I huffed, "but the threat? Did you inform him of the danger?"

"Oh yes," she replied, as though it was of no more import than the weather. "When I told him, he said that during his time as a riverboat pilot on the Mississippi he had come across 'some pretty ornery cusses,' and was not overly concerned.

"We know his verbal skills would prove useless against Herr Graff, but there's nothing to worry about for the moment. The bellboy handed Mr. Clemens a note from Inspector Abberline as he entered the lobby;

the inspector has decided to send a constable here at seven o'clock to escort Mr. Clemens to and from the performance."

"Why didn't you say that at first?" I asked, more forcefully than I had intended.

Margaret gave me a coy smile. "I was getting around to it, Doyle. Don't fret."

I decided there were times when I preferred her as Pennyworth, when her actions were more predictable. Still, in this game of chess with Herr Graff, it seemed we had foiled his latest gambit.

"We should go to the theater tonight to hear him speak," Margaret said. "Just to be sure he's all right."

"Of course, Margaret," I answered. "Just to be sure. Besides, we're already dressed for the theater."

Bell gave me a wink when I had replied, "Just to be sure." Margaret's motives clearly were not only due to her concern for the American's safety, but I admitted to myself I was probably as keen as she was to hear him speak. We dined at a fashionable restaurant and proceeded to the Old Vic.

In a moment of extravagance, I purchased a box for the three of us, off stage left, so we could hear and see without distraction from the audience. As we sat and I gazed out at the crowd below us, I had to wonder if I was gazing at the Ripper, hidden in plain sight. I was reassured that Abberline had sent Mr. Clemens an escort.

Mark Twain was an engaging speaker. I believe no one ever gave a better voice to his words than he did himself, for he had the writer's sensitivity to nuances of words, coupled with the storyteller's love of performance. He gave readings from *Huckleberry Finn* and, one of my favorites, "The Celebrated Jumping Frog of Calaveras County."

We laughed and, from time to time, our eyes misted as he spoke of his life and those of his creations along the mighty Mississippi, a river he could bring forth as fully formed as any of his fictional characters.

Clemens told a ghost story halfway through, of the Lady with the Golden Arm, whose spirit goes looking for the man who cut her arm off after death, asking in a ghost-like lament, "Who stole my Golden

Arm?" The lights were lowered as he spoke in sepulchral tones of the wandering spirit coming closer and closer to her grave-robbing husband's bed, as he cowered beneath his blanket, her precious arm beside him. Just as the ghost turned the doorknob, and her voice was at its loudest, the lights flared up as Twain leaped forward, pointing to the audience and shouting, "You did!"

The audience jumped as one, then laughed in embarrassment. As we recovered, Margaret laid her hand lightly upon my arm. It seemed like the most natural thing in the world. Her hand lifted as the lights came up at the end of his performance, and we applauded vigorously.

Although Twain's reading was remarkable, in hindsight I believe our enthusiastic applause was also an outpouring of thanksgiving for this "golden" moment together.

As I left the theater, I told myself that the day my words could stir emotions the way his did, I would be a writer indeed.

We took Margaret home by cab. I insisted on seeing her to the door, wanting the moment to last as long as possible. Bell waited to ensure our cabbie did not leave without us, but when we arrived at Margaret's door, a little before eleven o'clock, it flew open as she inserted the key into the lock.

A flushed Molly rushed out with an envelope in one hand, Margaret's derringer in the other. Though she was clearly agitated, I noted the hand holding the derringer was steady. The Ripper would not find her easy prey.

"A man came by not ten minutes ago with this for you, Doctor Doyle. I had him slide it under the door, so I can't say what he looked like."

"Good for you, Molly," Margaret said, concerned and relieved at the same time. Johnny came out to greet us, and sensing something was wrong, looked fiercely about for something to attack, growling.

Curious, I examined the envelope. My mind froze when I recognized the handwriting of the man I now knew as Herr Graff. Its very presence told me he had not been idle at all; the final set of our "danse macabre" was about to start.

My Dear Doctor Doyle,

You and your friends seemed to enjoy the performance tonight very much. I admit I have been tasking you rather severely of late, and do not begrudge you a brief entertainment. Our time together is drawing to a close, however, and we'd best conclude our business tonight.

By the way, I nearly came over to say hello this afternoon in the hotel lobby. I thought for a moment you recognized me. I was both irritated and pleased you did not. Irritated, as I thought we had become close enough that you should know me at once, and pleased my costume had deflected your gaze. There are few people more trusted than the British bobby, and I have used my disguise to good effect on more than one occasion after one of my encounters with the working-class women of Whitechapel.

I had to hand the letter over to Margaret to read out loud, as I was suddenly unable to focus my gaze when I realized Mark Twain's escort to the theater this night had been none other than Saucy Jacky!

CHAPTER FORTY-FOUR
ALL FOR ONE

Saturday, November 10, cont.

Margaret cleared her throat, and in a quavering voice read the letter.

The presence of additional constables from outlying districts has allayed their suspicions as I pass amongst them, such as the night of my so-called "Double Event." Oh, what a night that was! A very tricky thing too, and I am still amazed at how neatly I pulled it off.

As an avid devotee of the theater, I saw to Mr. Clemens's safe arrival to the Old Vic this evening. He and I have much in common, as neither of us likes to disappoint our audience. We differ however, to a great extent regarding our opinion of the inferior peoples of the world. His sympathetic portrayal of a Nubian in *Huckleberry Finn* fully merits my blade. Suffice to say there was a deviation in his return to the hotel. If you wish to save his life, you will immediately come to Fenchurch Street Railway Station and proceed eastward on foot along the tracks, where I await you with my hostage.

I will wait no longer than midnight. If you do not arrive by then, my unwilling companion will pay. As you British like to say, "You know I'm good for it!" The clock is ticking, Doctor Doyle. Are you ready for your final lesson? You have been a most inept pupil, and I have the patience for only one more session.

Come if you dare,

JTR

My optimism of scant moments before left me immediately after reading this challenge from Graff. It seemed he had outflanked us once more.

"I shall go alone, of course," I said.

Margaret looked at me. The steel in her eyes told me I was greatly mistaken.

"All for one and one for all!" she whispered hoarsely. "I know I speak for the professor as well."

"You certainly do!" Bell said, as he came up the stairs to see what was delaying me. "Whatever it's about, Miss Harkness, you can speak for me."

Margaret wordlessly handed the letter over to Bell. He whistled low as he grasped the contents.

"Surely, Doyle," Margaret said, "you know neither of us is going to sit idly by and let you face this creature alone." Then, placing her right hand gently upon mine, she said calmly, "Don't protect me. Do me the honor of trusting I can help you. We began this together, and you know we must finish it together. We can walk to the station from here. Professor, release the cabby, while I change into something more suitable for the occasion. Doyle, you can wait in the front room while Molly helps me undergo a rapid transformation."

I hadn't known such loyalty between friends since my days on the SS *Hope* in Arctic waters. It was good to have such "shipmates" at my side, especially in heavy seas such as these.

It took Margaret less than ten minutes to emerge in her working-class Pennyworth attire. She patted her jacket pocket and assured me she was "taking precautions." The professor had his cane, though I was unarmed.

Margaret produced a much-chipped cricket bat, one that she had used on rats before Johnny joined her retinue. "Here, Doyle. Know how to use one of these?"

I bristled at this, for I had always considered myself an excellent batsman. Looking over this much-scarred veteran, it seemed I could scarcely do it more harm, and thus, somewhat stone-faced, I accepted my Excalibur.

In one of my tales I would have the heroes give brave speeches as they marched off to battle, but as we began our walk toward the station we turned silent, each in our thoughts, wondering what test awaited us and how we would measure up.

Time is a slippery thing. An hour in a boring lecture can seem like an eternity, while a month-long holiday can pass as quickly as a day. During our march to the station, time walked in leaden boots, dragging us onward, while fear made my heart rush like a racehorse. My hands were ice-cold. I was grateful my friends had not let me face the Ripper alone.

We found the station deserted when we arrived. The last passenger train for the day had departed before ten o'clock. Fenchurch station was the end of the line before the docks, however, and trains from central London would run throughout the night into the freight yards.

I took a deep breath as we stepped off the station platform, and went forward into the dark to confront Jack the Ripper on his own terms.

CHAPTER FORTY-FIVE
A KNIFE IN THE FOG

Saturday, November 10,
to Sunday, November 11

Although the passenger station was vacant, there were still several wagon cars on side tracks that cast large shadows within which Herr Graff could easily hide.

"We should walk abreast," said Bell. "Margaret, as you have our only firearm, you should walk in the middle, along the track. Doyle and I can walk a few feet on either side; that way, no more than one of us can be overwhelmed by a surprise attack, while Margaret in the center can bring her weapon to bear."

"I suspect you have other motives as well," Margaret said dryly, "but the tactic is sound all the same. Let's go. I have some words I'd like to share with Herr Graff."

I took the right side, Bell the left. The familiar feel of the cricket bat in my hand was reassuring, and I vowed in silence that if I could land one solid blow I would finally turn the tide in our favor.

We walked eastward in this manner, slowly, for when the clouds passed over it was hard to see, while the rough stone of the rail grading made for uneven footing. The damp cold made my breath fog as I breathed in the taste of the moist earth, which oddly reminded me of the lingering after-notes of a good German Riesling. The only sound was our footsteps on the slick stones and our increasingly labored breathing as we struggled to move forward. The mist began to rise slowly from the cold ground, heralding the approach of a thick London fog.

After five minutes we had walked approximately four hundred yards, and the tracks had decreased to two from the eight that departed the station.

Suddenly, Margaret cried out, "Look! Straight ahead!"

The clouds parted a little . . . I could observe a man dressed in white crawling on his hands and knees, headed away from us, trying vainly to stand up, only to resume crawling.

Margaret flew down the tracks, while the professor, hindered by the loose stones, lagged behind. I cast a quick look over my shoulder, expecting Graff to come at us out of the shadows, but not seeing him I joined the chase with a will.

We were about forty yards behind as Margaret reached the man. Abruptly he stood up and, with a constable's cudgel he had shielded beneath him, struck her a severe blow full in the face.

Margaret gave a weak cry, dropping her derringer and crumpling at his feet; her bowler hat fell off, exposing her braided hair.

Bell and I briefly halted, stunned by this turn of events.

The man calmly removed the white coat and threw it away before grasping Margaret by the hair with his right hand and roughly pulling her to her knees.

"My compliments, lady, and gentlemen," said Herr Graff. "Right on time."

Bell and I began to rush forward, but halted when Graff took a long slender knife from beneath his coat with his left hand and placed it against Margaret's throat. "Stop where you are!" he commanded.

Bell and I froze and exchanged glances, unsure how to proceed.

"Step onto the track, gentlemen," Graff instructed. "Now walk slowly forward, side by side, until I tell you to halt. Professor Bell, drop your cane. And is that a cricket bat I see in your hands, Doctor Doyle? Really? I don't know whether to be insulted or amused. In any event, lay it down; but thank you for that touch of the absurd."

We did as instructed, dropping our meager weapons and standing together on the track, for we had no choice. My fists clenched in fury at how he had outwitted us. Again. I have never felt a deeper sense of humiliation, and bile burned the back of my throat.

Margaret's head began to rock slightly from side to side. I took it as a hopeful sign that she was recovering from the blow, though her eyes were still closed.

"Far enough," Graff said, when we had closed the gap to about ten yards, lightly stroking Margaret's face with his knife.

His transformation was striking. Gone was the pale functionary of Wilkins. Before us, there now stood a man glowing with a powerful and seductive self-assurance. I could easily understand why someone would follow him into a dark alley, unquestioning. I shivered at the silky character of his voice.

His actions were in sharp contrast to the bobby's tunic he was wearing, half-unbuttoned and gaping open. His pale face seemed to glow when the moonlight broke through the clouds, which, accompanied with the gathering fog and the dark color of the tunic, gave his face a ghost-like quality, only adding to his menacing appearance.

"Where is Mr. Clemens?" I demanded. "What have you done to him?"

"I did nothing to him, Doctor," Graff replied blandly. "I fear this stalwart constable," he began, and then performed a slight bow to indicate himself, "deserted his post and left Mr. Clemens to find his own way back. By the way, I am grateful you stopped by Clemens's hotel while I was there. It made my little gambit regarding Mr. Twain much more convincing."

"I'm curious," said Bell. "Were any of those letters to the Central News Agency or any of the others to the papers really from you?"

"What an odd question at this moment. Is it because of the ears, Professor? Mrs. Eddowes's missing ears?"

"Exactly," replied Bell grimly.

"I was so taken with the letter you shared with me," answered Graff, pleased at his own cleverness. "I knew if I could add that little touch to my next acquaintance, it would lead you and the police down a very long rabbit hole. You must admit it was a lovely embellishment."

Graff would stop stroking Margaret's face with his knife while he was talking, the conversation distracting him from his captive, so I decided to engage him as much as possible.

"Why do you do this?" I asked, unsure if there could be any answer.

Bell nodded slightly, encouraging me to keep Graff occupied, and I noticed Margaret's eyes were fluttering open, though she still looked quite dazed.

"I did promise you a lesson, didn't I? Very well. The only person who ever mattered to me was my little brother, Ernst. We were both born with hemophilia, a gift from our grandmother, a lady you hold in much higher esteem than do I. Ernst fell from a balcony when he was seven, due to the carelessness of our nanny."

"A fall from a balcony could cause the death of any child, hemophilia or no!" I interjected.

"Once again you speak with authority over things you know nothing about!" seethed Graff. "It was a severe fall, yes, but he would have lived had he not borne our family curse. This defect bestowed by women onto their male children.

"Blood. Fascinating liquid, isn't it, Doctor? It flows and sustains life. Yet, if it flows too freely, it takes life away. I find it ironic when others refer to my 'royal bloodline,' not realizing that to me it is not an endowment of nobility, but a damnation."

Margaret's eyes were now fully open, and her hands came slowly up to her waist, preparing herself for any opportunity. Graff, lost in his story, was oblivious.

"I grappled with the image of an all-powerful and supposedly loving God allowing my brother to die due to a curse bestowed within my mother's womb, and the incompetence of a slack-jawed servant."

Graff paused and looked down at Margaret. He began stroking her face with the knife once more, lovingly. I had a sudden frightful insight; Graff loved his victims. Incapable of normal feelings, the emotions he experienced when he tore a person's life from them was the closest to passion he could achieve. For a brief flicker of time, I got a glimpse of his naked, hungry soul, and beheld the great loneliness that was his burden.

Graff continued, lost in his reverie. "Then I discovered Darwin, and the commentaries of Herbert Spencer, who coined that phrase 'survival of the fittest.' Suddenly my brother's death made sense. He was flawed, so he was removed. I am also flawed but, by using my intellect, I have adapted to a world more dangerous to me than to others. I have become adept at handling swords, knives, and all manner of edged instruments. I would be their master, not their cowering slave."

"And the women's wombs?" I asked. "Removed because that is where the curse is bestowed?"

Graff's face, pale in the moonlight, leered at me. "Well done, Doctor. I'll make a detective of you yet."

"The real Wilkins said there was some incident involving your nanny," I prompted, continuing to play for time. "What became of her?"

Graff smiled, his teeth glowing in the dim moonlight. "Oh, in time I reunited with the bitch who let my brother fall," he said, as though fondly recalling a moonlight cruise. "And I showed her the price of her failure. Afterward, I was sent here to your shores, my second homeland and the source of my affliction. I read your pitiful detective tale, which preached the old lie of 'order.' I could not tolerate your prattle and had to show you how very impotent your vision is; but how to do so?"

Graff laughed deeply; the same laugh, I wondered, that had reassured Mary Kelly?

"Then it came to me: do unto others as I had done unto one, then appeal to your vanity and greed and draw you here so I could watch you scurry about, all the while keeping me abreast of the manhunt. I found Professor Bell's reports quite informative; it was reassuring to know how far afield my pursuers were. Well done, sir!"

Bell bared his teeth at this taunt. "Ye know we won't let ye get away with this!" he declared.

Graff shook his head. "Ah, we'll discuss that in a moment, Professor. You're getting ahead of me."

He cupped Margaret's chin with his knife hand, and tilted her head back to gaze into her eyes. "I would be most ungrateful if I did not also thank you, Margaret, my dear, for fulfilling your role so well. I knew a man of Doyle's station could never sympathize with women of the lower classes. I confess when I discovered *you* are John Law, I was taken aback. Then I saw the possibilities. Fate had been kind to me, at last."

He smiled at her. "I needed you, or someone like you, to make Doyle care what became of my victims. Well done, my dear. Well done indeed!"

Margaret maintained a stone visage, while Graff paused in his soliloquy to gently caress her face with his knife once more before resuming.

He raised his eyes to meet mine. "A woman's purity is her most sacred possession, isn't it, Doctor? Oh, how they guard it! How they delight in making men pay for it. I paid the whores for theirs." He chuckled, "Well, there was nothing pure about them when I was done, as you well know. Thus, it was a weakness of my blood that has drawn me to bathe in that of others. Women's blood, preferably, for I have yet to kill a man. We shall see if that remains so after tonight. Time to draw our little drama to a close, so please pay attention.

"I am about to give you two choices, Doctor Doyle, so do listen carefully. Miss Harkness," he said softly, while returning the blade to her throat, "you should pay particular attention.

"Here are your two choices. Option one: I slit Miss Harkness's lovely throat in front of you both. You attack me in a vain attempt to save her or at least to avenge her. Too late, of course, but very noble."

My heart was hammering like a steam engine.

"But I said there was a second option now, didn't I? If your thoughts stray, you may miss the crucial difference. I slit Miss Harkness's throat as before, but this time . . . you do nothing. You walk away, and you live. If Professor Bell feels his honor is at stake, I can easily wound him sufficiently to satisfy the demands of chivalry. My exile to Merry Old England was to be for one year, and that year has nearly expired. I return home, no more 'unfortunates' in the East End die by my hand, and you live the rest of your life knowing your incompetence cost Miss Harkness hers."

I had no more words to bandy about. I could tell Bell was poised to spring forward at the slightest chance, but the knife at Margaret's throat still held us back.

"I must admit I rather prefer option two," Graff purred. "The memory of her dead body gazing up at you will ensure you never pen another frivolous story about this 'Sheerluck' Holmes for the rest of your miserable life. I so like the thought of you left twisting in despair that I am willing to give you a significant incentive."

Graff reached into his inner uniform pocket with his knife hand and withdrew a thick envelope that he threw at my feet as one tosses scraps to a dog, and as he did so I noticed Margaret reach into her coat pocket.

"Here you are, Doctor Doyle. The remainder of the money due you, plus a substantial bonus. Payment for services rendered, and a life. Pick it up, and we have a deal."

CHAPTER FORTY-SIX
DANSE MACABRE

Sunday, November 11, cont.

I tensed to rush forward, knowing it would be too late, when Bell placed his hand upon my left shoulder to restrain me.

Graff laughed, and his hand swung back toward Margaret's throat. As it did, Margaret's left hand lashed out and grabbed him by the forearm.

The moon broke free of the clouds at this moment, and I beheld a macabre tableau, frozen in my memory for all time. Graff was looking puzzled and standing over Margaret, his right hand grasping her hair, his left hand momentarily arrested by hers.

Then there was the flash of steel and a scream of surprise and pain as she slashed his left wrist with a razor.

Graff wrenched his injured hand free and stared at it in horror, the knife dropping from his nerveless fingers.

Margaret swung blindly over her head, cutting the back of Graff's right hand, causing him to release her and severing some of her braided hair.

He screamed as the dark blood ran glistening down both arms in the dim moonlight. Then, snarling, he backhanded Margaret in the face before dropping to his knees, fumbling for his fallen blood-slicked knife with his injured, though still functioning, right hand.

We rushed forward just as Margaret recovered from the blow and lashed out again, this time slashing the right side of Graff's exposed neck.

Graff shuddered as he slapped his hand over the wound, then, in pure terror, looked up at Bell, pleading like a frightened child. "Make it stop, Professor! Dear God, make it stop!"

Bell stood there silently for a moment, then responded in a voice husky with emotion, "Ye're already dead."

Graff whimpered, and tried to speak once more. Then, with a soft sigh, his right hand fell away and he collapsed slowly onto his left side.

Margaret leaned over and carefully wiped the razor and her hands on Graff's trousers, then slowly folded the razor with shaking hands. She tried to stand but fell back to her knees, unable to rise.

I found myself suddenly there, holding her.

"I'm sorry, Mary," was all she said, weeping.

"For God's sake, Margaret!" I exclaimed, "Are you all right?" I could feel her rapid heartbeat against my chest, such was the force of my embrace. Then, after a long moment within the damp London fog, I stood back slowly, as I had to. As I always had to.

She smiled softly as she held my hand a moment longer. "I am fine, dear Porthos, though I think I'll need a new hairstyle." The last said with a wan smile. Then she held the razor up to me, her voice weak and uneven. "A little keepsake from our first meeting. Remember the fragrant gentlemen who threatened us with it? When I began leaving my derringer with Molly, I got into the custom of carrying it. Luckily I continued that habit tonight."

She slowly bent over, picked up her derringer, and slid it back into her coat pocket along with the razor. She suddenly embraced Bell, and although surprised he returned it fiercely.

"I knew you two could not restrain yourselves from rushing him," Margaret said, after she and the professor stood apart once more. "As charming as that would have been, Graff was entirely correct; it would have served me nothing."

Margaret patted the coat pocket containing her weapons, and shook her head. "Remember what I told you, Doyle, about my envy of men and their pockets? Thank goodness your fashion allows them!" Turning to Bell, "Thank you, Professor, for restraining Doyle long enough for me to pull out the razor."

Bell nodded, unable to speak for the moment, and Margaret continued, looking at Graff's body with disgust. "He always underestimated women; that was my one advantage. Believing I was about to die, I decided I wasn't going down without a fight. Just once, I wanted *him* to feel the knife. When he left his neck exposed, I had no choice.

"But he has damned me with his blood!" Margaret spat. "As surely as his family curse damned him. I shall live the rest of my life knowing I have taken a human life, though he well deserved it." She looked at her still-bloodstained hands. "I have a sudden empathy for Lady Macbeth."

"Justice was well served, Margaret," I said. "The killer of women died by a woman's hand."

The body was lying beneath the moonlight in a pool of blood, as so many of his victims had. His face was distorted by the terror of his final moments, and I readily admit the image gladdened my heart.

Margaret nodded without speaking, looking at Graff's remains, when suddenly, without warning, she kicked Graff's face as hard as she could, grunting with the effort.

I was shocked, and before she could kick again grabbed her shoulders, exclaiming, "He's dead, Margaret!"

"Yes," she said through clenched teeth, then roughly shrugging my hands off her shoulders, gritted out, "but he will never be dead *enough*!"

She followed her exclamation of "enough" with one final kick, delivered with such ferocity that I heard the crunching of broken bone, the face now clearly distorted. Then she stood there silently, weeping, and in an uneven voice gasped out, "That was for Mary, you bastard. And all the others. Now go to HELL!"

Bell stepped over to Margaret and softly laid his hand upon her right shoulder but said nothing. We stood there silent and looked at one another, savoring breathing deeply.

CHAPTER FORTY-SEVEN
A TRAIN TO CATCH

Sunday, November 11, cont.

Finally, Bell cleared his throat, finding his voice once more. "I am overjoyed you survived, Margaret, but I doubt the killing of a German noble and the grandson of the Queen will be well received by the authorities. I expect the German ambassador would press for our prosecution, if only to rebut the allegation that Graff was the Ripper. We are in treacherous waters, my friends," he said, shaking his head slowly. "We should avoid becoming officially connected to his death."

"I agree," Margaret replied, slowly returning to us from wherever she had gone. "We do not have conclusive proof of his guilt, even now. We have a false constable with two knives. Suspicious, but a prosecutor could argue he was trying to catch the Ripper and had the knives to protect himself. If a director of the Bank of England can masquerade as a workingman in an attempt to stop the murderer, a German noble could easily disguise himself as a bobby. Besides, I do not wish to be known for the rest of my days as the woman who killed him, as it would define me in ways I could never control. But we cannot leave an obviously murdered body here. Scotland Yard would be forced to investigate, and there's no telling where that could lead."

The professor turned thoughtful for a moment. "I think the solution is right before us. Indeed, it is right beneath our feet."

"The track?" I asked. "How does that resolve our problem?"

"I have, on occasion, been called in to treat the victims of rail accidents," he replied, "and I have seen the remains of those who were run over. Trust me, though the wounds Margaret inflicted on Herr Graff were telling, they are small. The trauma inflicted by a train often results in the body being torn to pieces, which would leave the incisions Margaret made scarcely noticeable. If we remove any identifying information from his clothing, when the remnants are found he may well be thought a suicide or a drunkard who fell asleep on the tracks. There will be no murder investigation, as there will be no discovery of murder. Are we agreed?"

While Margaret concurred at once, I had some difficulty reconciling my sense of justice with the disguise of a homicide, but, in the end, I saw the necessity.

"We are standing on the local track," said Margaret. "Let's move him over to the farther track. That's the freight line. As those trains run continuously, the body won't lie here until morning, when it is apt to be discovered intact."

"Capital idea," agreed Bell, "and we should remove the constable uniform, as it might draw more notice in the press and among the police than we desire. We can rub some mud on the white shirt, and coupled with the dark pants that should render him sufficiently obscured for our purpose."

"Before we do," Margaret urged, "let's see what information his belongings provide."

She proceeded to rummage through his clothes, producing an expensive gold pocket watch, a small batch of keys, and a battered brass ring, identical to the two I had received in the mail. There was also his thick sealskin wallet. To my surprise Margaret loudly proclaimed, "I hereby declare myself executor of Herr Graff's estate. All ye who have claims against his earthly possessions come forth now or hold silent henceforth!" Turning to us, she said more seriously, "I think I'll take the watch, since Pennyworth's is not fit for formal occasions." She collected the envelope Graff had tossed at my feet, which revealed a sum of five hundred pounds, and a penny.

"A final taunt," observed Bell. "He would buy your surrender with the exact amount offered for his capture by the City of London, plus a penny. I suspect the penny was to deepen the insult by paying the least amount more than the reward for his capture. While I despise his morality, his subtlety was remarkable. Introducing you to Miss Harkness to provide him with a victim for whom you would feel compassion, however, was utterly fiendish."

"I have an alternate explanation for the penny, Professor," Margaret said, her lips compressed into a thin smile. "Remember how Graff said the money was 'For services rendered, and a life?' I believe the life he was referring to wasn't his, but mine. He must have somehow known of my alias as Pennyworth, and intended to mock your impotence by paying you one penny for my life."

Then, shaking her head, she continued, "But I cannot imagine why he would believe you, Doyle, would ever accept his bargain."

"I think I understand," I answered slowly. "He saw only what he required of me: a prop for his drama—an excuse for his butchery. He grew up in a world surrounded by servants and those who owed allegiance to his family. He believed other men were as shallow and grasping as he needed them to be in order to control them."

Bell nodded approvingly, a satisfied smile on his face. "Welcome to a larger world, my friend," he said. "I believe you have mastered your final lesson from me."

Margaret opened the wallet and, after adding up the contents of the two, gave a low whistle. "Six hundred and eight pounds, and a penny, gentlemen. As executor, I award two hundred to each of us and beg your indulgence to claim the remaining eight pounds and one farthing, for I find myself in sudden need of a new hairstyle and a lady's hat to go with it. To you, Doyle, I bestow the wallet, knowing of your history with seals. To you, Professor, I bequeath his knives. May you use them to heal, and thus redeem the labor of those who forged them."

To our surprise, the constable's jacket was reversible, the opposite side an unremarkable dark wool men's coat. Beneath the coat we discovered a leather harness with sheaths for his knives and a pocket containing a flat, lozenge-shaped stiff hat. When we withdrew it from the pocket, it expanded, revealing a collapsible police helmet.

"That explains much," remarked Margaret. "After murdering someone, he merely reversed his tunic, with his bobby's helmet assumed the guise of a constable, and walked calmly away. Even if he got blood on the civilian coat, the reverse side with the uniform would be clean. The leather harness he wore underneath with the knives gave him the appearance of being heavier than he was, further altering his appearance."

"I noticed he held the knife in his left hand, Professor," I said. "That must give you some satisfaction."

"It does," Bell replied. "While we do not need further proof of his guilt, it is always gratifying to see one's deductions confirmed."

I went back to retrieve Bell's cane and the cricket bat, while Margaret and the professor applied mud to Graff's white shirt to make him less noticeable. As I returned, we heard the whistle and saw the light of a westbound train, shining dimly through the gathering fog, headed toward us on the far track.

Bell hooked the cane over his arm, while I, in my rush, dropped the bat. We hurriedly picked the body up, Margaret and Bell each holding a leg, while I carried the upper torso with one arm under each of his, and we staggered to the track in a manner that would have been comical were it not for the gruesome burden we bore.

The fog was now so thick we could not tell how far off the train was, nor how quickly it was approaching, so we moved with a purpose. We positioned the corpse so the traverse of the wheels would pass over his neck and arms, then hid behind a maintenance shed as the train came roaring past.

I offered to go alone to inspect the result, but Margaret would have none of it. "I need to see," was all she said, while Bell followed, as silent and solemn as a pallbearer.

We found his head resting face up, separate from everything else, three feet from the rail. The wheel had cleanly severed his neck where Margaret's incision had been made, obscuring the initial wound perfectly. The face was frozen in the terror of his final moments, and the intermittent moonlight reflected dully in his dark eyes. "This is how I wish to remember him," Margaret said, with grim satisfaction. "*Now* he's dead enough."

We looked at one another, nodded, turned our backs on the Ripper's scattered remains, and walked slowly side by side through the thickening fog toward the station.

CHAPTER FORTY-EIGHT
A FINAL VOW

Sunday, November 11, cont.

To my surprise, I heard a church bell toll three times as we walked. So much had happened, yet it was still over three hours until sunrise. We reached the station platform greatly fatigued, finding it as deserted as when we arrived. Margaret, taking pity upon us, invited us to her flat, saying Miss Jones could brew us some tea while we made our preparations to greet the day.

"What do we do now?" asked Margaret, swaying on her feet in weariness.

"I have learned as a surgeon that I make my worst decisions when exhausted," said Bell. "Let's recover our strength and our wits and make a proper ending of our alliance. I would be of no use back in Edinburgh at the moment. I shall require a decent holiday before I return to therapeutic bloodletting." The last said with a genial nod toward Margaret.

"Odd," she replied with a faint smile. "I believe the bloodletting I performed tonight was most therapeutic."

Dawn found the men dozing fitfully in chairs in Margaret's front room, while the ladies slept in their beds. I dreamt of Margaret and Graff struggling beneath the moonlight. On both sides of Margaret, and behind her, were the vague shadows of women, the one to her right discernible as Mary Kelly.

Some of the figures were helping Margaret rise from Graff's second blow, while others were moving his knife to and fro among the stones, making it more difficult for him to grasp.

When Margaret lashed out the final time, the faces of the women glowed, and I saw Miss Kelly's right hand reach for Margaret's. As their joined hands sliced his neck, the faces of the apparitions grew brighter still, and then, with a soft sigh, they faded away. I awoke with a deep sense of tranquility, never to dream of that moment again.

Later that morning, in a moment of inspiration, I asked Margaret to meet us at the Fenchurch Station at seven o'clock that evening dressed in her finest male attire. Margaret could tell I intended some mischief, but agreed, smiling.

Bell and I hobbled like two old men as we left Margaret's apartment. Prolonged encounters with unyielding furniture seemed to be my lot for much of this adventure, and I was looking forward to returning to my own bed. We boarded a cab at the now bustling railway station, and both of us made an effort not to look too far to the west to see if anyone had discovered our handiwork.

Once our hansom was underway, Bell asked me mildly what I had observed of our driver.

"A former jockey, I believe," I responded, puzzled by his inquiry.

"How did you arrive at that conclusion?" There was a slight smile at the corners of his mouth.

"Surely you noticed his size and the way he grasped the reins," I answered, confused why he should ask me such an obvious question. "Given the stiffness of his right leg, I assume he suffered a fall, with the horse landing atop him and resulting in a hip fracture. His knowledge of horses continues to provide him with a living, however, and he still dreams of his days astride the finest of stock as demonstrated by the overhand grip with which he holds the reins, instead of the usual underhand grasp of your average carriage driver. Why do you ask?"

Bell said nothing, looking oddly pleased with himself.

We were silent for the remainder of the ride back to the club, agreeing to meet around six o'clock in preparation for our call upon Margaret. When Bell asked me what was afoot, I smiled and said he would see soon enough. We parted ways to sleep some more and to bathe, while I made some private arrangements.

Margaret was in her West End dandy attire when we boarded our cab at the station, and I made sure to compliment her on her gold pocket watch. Her smile was warm, though her eyebrows showed she was bemused by my secretive manner. I had refused to tell Bell of our destination, either.

"We made the paper today," Margaret said with an innocent expression. "See?"

She handed me the afternoon issue of the *Star*. At the bottom of page six was a small article circled in red, describing the body of a man discovered on the tracks that morning, identity unknown. It was presumed the man was a drunk who had fallen asleep; the only mystery was a cricket bat found nearby.

I blushed at this. "In the heat of the moment, I must have left it behind."

"All the same," Margaret teased, "You owe me a cricket bat."

Bell shook his head like an indulgent parent, and we laughed together.

Margaret said nothing more, though the glow in her eyes warms me still when I recall it. I realized acutely how much I would miss her.

Margaret colored slightly when she saw how her gaze had affected me. The moment passed, as sadly such moments always do.

"We seem to be retracing our steps," Bell said, to no one in particular.

I knew I could not keep my plan secret much longer, but I was savoring it until the last possible moment. "I believe we are," is all I said.

Margaret looked at Bell, then down at her attire, and I could see the deductive process ongoing as plain as any formula drawn upon a chalk board. "You daren't!"

"I dare!" I replied, my plan now revealed.

Our growler stopped in front of the Marlborough. "Mister Pennyworth," I said in my most formal voice, "would you care to join us for dinner at our club?"

"Delighted!" she said, giggling like an errant schoolgirl.

I felt the Three Musketeers deserved a fitting final meal together, so with considerable pride led them to the private dining room I had reserved. Here we could speak freely, and make a proper ending to our alliance.

The meal itself was nothing extraordinary, but I could tell for Margaret the act of penetrating this male bastion made the beef Wellington a veritable feast. We laughed as we celebrated our victory, though we knew we could never share our tale for fear of prosecution.

At meal's end, we vowed to keep our secret for the remainder of our lives. Then there was a pause, none of us wanting to say goodbye. To break the silence, Margaret said, with perhaps a bit of false heartiness, "Well, gentlemen, spending time with you has been both instructive and profitable, but I suppose it is time to prepare for your departures. I shall always have a spare chair for you to sleep in, if I can't find a cot." The last said with a smile, tinged with sadness.

Our task done, Bell and I had our mundane worlds awaiting us to the north and south.

We concluded our evening by standing tall around the table, an ale in our hands, as we renewed our vows with fervor: "All for one and one for all!"

CHAPTER FORTY-NINE
JOURNEY'S END

November 1888 to August 1889

Time is often described as a wind, and in this instance the description seems most apt, for I was quickly whisked away from a life-and-death struggle with the Ripper and back to publishers' deadlines and patients with lumbago.

As to my parting with Margaret, I will not speak of it, even now. We knew each other's hearts. That had to be enough.

With the passage of time and absence of further murders, the police presence slowly dwindled, and the residents of the East End returned to their difficult, though less hazardous, existence. Although I cannot truthfully say the anti-Semitism within London entirely dissipated, the threat of riots faded over time as all of London slowly returned to a life without the Ripper.

I never saw Inspector Abberline again, and I regretted the manner of our parting given the admiration I held and still have for him. I often wondered if he ever linked the cessation of the Ripper murders with my admittedly insane-sounding proclamation that I knew who the murderer was, followed by our abrupt disappearance.

We Musketeers vowed to keep in touch but, as usual, the woman among us was a more faithful correspondent than we men. Margaret's book about the Salvation Army was published a short time later, at first under her pseudonym John Law and entitled *Captain Lobe: A Story of the Salvation Army*. It did moderately well and was subsequently reissued under her true name and with a new title: *In Darkest London and The Way Out*, in which she added elements of Jack the Ripper, careful to cast him as a gentile.

Bell returned to his surgery practice and teaching. Some years after our affair with the Ripper, he was consulted in a suspected case of murder and, by the absence of gunpowder deposition in the victim's wound, determined the alleged shooting accident was a deliberate case of homicide.

Given his powers of observation, the growing affection between Margaret and myself could not have escaped his notice, yet he never alluded to it in any way, not even by way of a raised eyebrow. I believe his affection for the two of us, and trust in our sense of decency, assured him we would behave honorably. In the end, his trust was justified.

Meanwhile, I continued my writing of historical fiction. *Micah Clarke* did moderately well; I believed my best work lay in this genre. My interest in spiritualism, already kindled by an earlier study of hypnotism and attending séances, was strengthened by my experiences during the Ripper investigation. My dreams of the murdered woman with their portents of the final confrontation left an indelible impression upon me.

I also began my studies in eye surgery in earnest, going to Vienna for a time to enhance my knowledge. I was straddling two careers, wanting to commit to writing but fearful of deserting my medical career given my growing family. This state of affairs might have continued indefinitely if not for one fateful evening in August 1889, at the posh Portland Place Hotel in London, when I and a young Irish author named Oscar Wilde met with an American publisher named Stoddart.

I was fascinated with the wit of Mr. Wilde, and quite flattered to learn he had read *Micah* and was sincerely complimentary of it. I was also well pleased with the conclusion of our meeting when we each were given a healthy check for some unspecified work to be published in one of Stoddart's magazines. Wilde's commission resulted in *The Picture of Dorian Gray*.

I was preparing to leave when Mr. Stoddart made it clear he was expecting more Holmes stories, and this brought me up short. My jaw clenched as I recalled the odious Mr. Collier, sneaking into the morgue to sketch the bodies of those who had died violently, and of the crowds leaving the Lord Mayor's procession in hopes of glimpsing a mutilated corpse.

"I'm sorry, sir," I said to Mr. Stoddart, "but I want nothing more to do with crime stories."

"I quite agree, Doctor Doyle," said Mr. Wilde. "Crime writing would be most distasteful for anyone with decent sensibilities."

Then leaning forward and placing his hand upon my shoulder, he said, "Write about Justice."

My jaw slowly relaxed as I thought of the dedicated Inspector Abberline, the Jews who had been in danger of being killed merely for being different when their neighbors were frightened and angry. I thought of Mary Kelly, whose murder I had in some small way caused, and then helped avenge. And, finally, I thought of Margaret, kneeling in the dark with a knife to her throat. I realized one could write a crime story focusing on the horrific nature of the crime, or one could focus on the victims and on putting the scales of justice back into balance.

The Ripper's cruelest act may have been his theft of hope. Perhaps my Mr. Holmes, like some modern-day knight errant, could restore the belief that there could indeed be justice for all, not only for the rich and powerful but for any man or woman who found their way to his consulting room.

"Excellent suggestion, Mr. Wilde," I said, smiling as I considered his words.

I turned to Stoddart and extended my hand, which he clasped warmly. "Agreed, sir! We have a deal."

And thus was my consulting detective reborn. I certainly gained much experience that would inform me in the coming years as I wrote his adventures, but I believe my greatest reward was gaining the insight I needed to enter into the larger world that Bell inhabited. I learned that doormen, bobbies, and, yes, "laundresses" were also human beings worthy of my notice and sympathy.

Truly, I could never have contrived a woman as intelligent or resourceful as Irene Adler, the only woman to ever equal Sherlock Holmes both in intelligence and resourcefulness, had I not found my way to a shabby flat on Vine Street.

THE LETTER

January 1, 1924, Windlesham

Thirty-six years have passed since we faced and ultimately defeated one of the vilest men to ever cast a shadow. Professor Bell left us in 1911, dying in his beloved Edinburgh. To my great regret, I was afflicted with a severe case of rheumatism at the time, and was unable to travel. I sent flowers, and Margaret later wrote to me movingly of the service. There are few men whose heart and intellect are grand in equal measure, but surely he was one.

Margaret would suffer from some illness, the nature of which she never shared with me. Apparently, she fared better in warmer climes; thus she lived at times in Australia, America, the South of France, and Calcutta, India. She published various works, never losing her ardor in defense of the poor and, at one time, managed and owned her own periodical. Her final work was a novel entitled *A Curate's Promise: A Story of Three Weeks, September 14 to October 5, 1917*, published in 1921. She died in modest circumstances in the Pensione Castagnoli in Florence, in the year just past, and was buried the following day in the Allori Cemetery in a *tomba di seconda classe*.

I never told her, but when I refreshed my memory of Dumas's classic, *The Three Musketeers*, I decided Bell must be Athos, the older man who was a father figure for d'Artagnan. Since I was obviously Porthos, that left Margaret as Aramis, the Musketeer conflicted by his desire for the sacred and the profane but passionate for both—similar to her desire to better the life of those at the mercy of the powerful, yet with a fierce enjoyment of life no matter what challenges fortune threw her way.

Following her death, I was surprised to receive this small cardboard box. It came from one of the nursing sisters who tended to Margaret in her final days. But now, finally, I must open it and consign the past to the past, however unwillingly.

There are two items, each with a note attached. The first I recognize immediately. A straight razor: the very one Margaret wielded that night on the railway track. Its note reads:

> Dear Doyle,
>   Never forget:
>   I am the Master of my Fate,
>   I am the Captain of my Soul.
>   Margaret

The second item . . . is unfamiliar to me. Is it a religious symbol? . . . No. On closer inspection, I recognize it as a Queen Victoria penny, dated 1888. A hole has been drilled, and a tricolor ribbon of red, white, and blue runs through it, such that one could wear it as a pendant.

With it is a letter, containing Margaret's final words:

> Dear Porthos,
>   As self-appointed executor of Herr Graff's estate, I took the liberty of fashioning this medallion from the penny he offered in payment for my life. I then bestowed upon myself the honorific of Monster Slayer, First Class. I have worn this beneath my garments often when faced with a difficult situation, as a means to remind myself of far graver challenges I have successfully overcome. It has been more than a penny's worth to me, if you'll forgive my little joke, my friend. But I now bequeath this to you and authorize its wear upon any and all suitable occasions, but most of all on each twenty-fifth of September, the anniversary of the founding of our stalwart band. All for one and one for all, dear Porthos. May you raise a glass in our memory for many years to come.
>   M

I am wearing the medallion now as I finish my tale, while the glass sits patiently beside me.

I miss you, dear friends.

Happy New Year.

Arthur Conan "Porthos" Doyle, MD

AFTERWORD

This book is a work of fiction, though mostly grounded in fact. It began one day as I was reading about Conan Doyle and realized there was a four-year gap between the first Holmes story and the next. In the middle of this break were the Ripper murders. I immediately saw the opportunity to write a story that would use the Ripper as a means for Doyle to solve the murders and return to Sherlock Holmes.

Some events, particularly news articles, were moved in sequence from their actual date of publication to facilitate my storyline, but only the report of the body found with a cricket bat was fabricated.

Professor Joseph Bell

Arthur Conan Doyle met Professor Joseph Bell at the Edinburgh Royal Infirmary while a medical student and became his clerk. Impressed by the professor's ability to render diagnoses and insightful observations regarding occupation and travel history, Bell became the inspiration for Sherlock Holmes. Bell was in fact the surgeon in attendance to Queen Victoria whenever she was in Scotland.

An article in the *Irish Times*, dated November 4, 2011, states that Bell was consulted by Scotland Yard during the Ripper murders to perform handwriting analysis of the letters signed Jack the Ripper, a fact I learned only after I had already written it into the story.

Margaret Harkness

This image is the only likeness of Margaret known to exist, and I'm grateful to Professor Deborah Mutch of De Montfort University, and editor of a recent reprint of Margaret's book, *A City Girl*, who verified it. She in turn credits her former graduate students Doctor Lisa Robertson and Doctor Flore Janssen for unearthing it.

I do not know if Margaret was in the habit of wearing men's clothing or carrying a derringer, but everything else I have written in the book regarding her literary career and biography, including her father's attempt to compel her to marry, is true.

In the summer of 1888, Margaret helped organize the Matchgirls' Strike to better the working conditions for the women who worked in the factories. Sadly, these efforts were unsuccessful, but in 1889 she persuaded Cardinal Manning, the Bishop of London, to intercede in the London Dock Strike. This resulted in the formation of trade unions for unskilled laborers and vastly improved working conditions for approximately a hundred thousand workers.

To my knowledge, Margaret and Doyle never met. When I began writing this tale, she was intended as a minor character I meant to use in only a couple of scenes to highlight the social status of women at that time. Margaret had other ideas, and you know the rest.

My favorite Holmes story has always been "A Scandal in Bohemia," and I can think of no finer inspiration for Irene Adler, "the woman," than this remarkable lady, who lived a life far ahead of her time.

Those interested in knowing more about her can reference the excellent article about her on the Victorian Web, a website for researchers into that era: http://victorianweb.org/gender/harkness.html.

Sir Arthur Conan Doyle, MD

There is not enough space for me to relate Doyle's literary accomplishments, but I can mention that he made a couple of forays into detective work in later years, resulting in the ultimate release of Oscar Slater, wrongly convicted of murder, and clearing the name of George Edalji, accused of animal mutilations. When the crime writer Agatha Christie mysteriously disappeared in 1926, however, Doyle hired a medium, who accurately predicted she would emerge on the following

Photo credit: Walter Benington.

Wednesday, prompting him to advocate for a psychic to be employed by every police department.

In answer to Margaret's query regarding Holmes—"Wherever did you get that name?"—fans of the Great Detective will be surprised to know the original name was Sherrinford Holmes, and the loyal companion and narrator of his adventures was Ormond Sacker. I, for one, am glad how things turned out, and I think most readers would agree.

The epitaph on Doyle's headstone reads:

Steel True
Blade Straight
Arthur Conan Doyle
Knight
Patriot, Physician & Man of Letters

The words in this story are my own, but they are hopefully true to the spirit of the man who gave us that champion of justice, Sherlock Holmes.

ACKNOWLEDGMENTS

If it takes a village to raise a child, it took a tribe to write this book. First, I'd like to thank my inspiration, Mary Roach. I was fortunate enough to work with her on her latest book, *Grunt*, and seeing the nuts and bolts of storytelling made it less frightening. She inspired me to "give it a go," so it is all *her* fault!

Next, I would like to thank my editor and mentor, John DeDakis (www.johndedakis.com). He convinced me that my early scribbles had something of value buried within my run-on sentences and meager descriptions. Like a gentle gardener, he pruned and fertilized as called for. I had the vision; he taught me the craft.

I would also like to thank my agent, Jill Marr with the Dijkstra Agency, and her reader, Derek McFadden. Derek forwarded my story enthusiastically, and that made all the difference. Jill believed in me, and helped make my dream come true. There is no greater gift, and I am indebted to them both.

To my loyal readers who have, each in their own way encouraged me, foremost of them would be my old boss, Col. (ret.) Doctor Holly Doyne. She was tough but reassured me that within my early mess I had "the bones of a good story."

Others of my tribe include Jimmy "two-bits" Ethington, Petra Winters (a wonderful editor in her own right,) Sarah Davis, Milyn King, Larry Philips, Chris Miguez, and my Mexican brother from another mother, Gustavo Ramirez de Toledo, a well-known author and educator in Latin America, who also encouraged me.

I would also like to thank my friends Henry Chambers and retired Major General David Rubenstein, for the use of their names, and my

British friend Harvey Blair, who taught me "the difference between chalk and cheese." Writers really are the most shameless of thieves.

Next on my list would be my patient editors, Mr. Dan Mayer and Sheila Stewart at Seventh Street and Prometheus Books. Their enthusiastic involvement got me across the finish line.

I would be remiss if I failed to thank my wife, Chere, and my mother, Mary Elizabeth Shwiller, who were my first editors, and my daughter Linnea Harper, who gave me the book that led me to Mary Roach, and my daughter Dawn Skye DiComo, who was my research librarian.

The map at the front of the book was created by Mr. Geoff Cooper (jacktherippermap.info), and I am indebted to him for his meticulous attention to detail and patience with my shifting requirements.

Finally, I would like to praise Mr. Richard Jones. His book, *Jack the Ripper's London*, was a revelation. I might have been able to write a book about the Ripper, but it would never have been as rich in detail nor as sympathetic to the denizens of Whitechapel as this work attempts to be. He patiently suffered from my many unsolicited emails over the early course of the composition, and his generosity of spirit shaped this novel to a vast extent. The night we spent together walking through Whitechapel allowed me to experience the Ripper's hunting ground in a way a book could never do, and I heartily recommend his walking tour (information available at https://jack-the-ripper-tour.com). His book mentioned Margaret Harkness, whom I had never heard of before, and I decided to research her further. I shall *always* be in his debt.

As always, any errors in the story are my own. Thank you for joining me on this journey into Victorian England and the fog-enshrouded alleys of the East End.

Bradley Harper MD, Fellow, College of American Pathology
Col. (Ret.) US Army Medical Corps
Williamsburg, Virginia, USA

ABOUT THE AUTHOR

Bradley Harper graduated from college in May 1973, and went directly into the welcoming embrace of the US Army Infantry School at Fort Benning, Georgia. His career plan to be a high school history and Spanish teacher was altered forever by an unpleasant encounter with an army doctor. Deciding he could do better, he attended Uniformed Services University of the Health Sciences, graduating in May 1983, with an MD degree. He became board certified in anatomic and clinical pathology, and ultimately served thirty-seven years of active duty.

Photo by Chere Harper

During his Army career Doctor Harper performed approximately two hundred autopsies, twenty of which were forensic, and this experience informs his writing. In addition to his clinical experience, he had four commands, beginning with the 67th Combat Support Hospital (Forward), in support of the Bosnian peacekeeping mission, and culminating as Commander, Vicenza Army Health Clinic, Vicenza, Italy. In Italy he received an award from the Knights of Malta (the only non-Italian to ever receive this award) for his support of the Italian Army.

His most notable staff assignments include Command Surgeon, US Army South, where he briefly served in support of US Special Forces in Colombia. During that time all US military personnel had a $1.5 million bounty placed on them by the FARC. Colonel Harper made sure that check was never cashed. His other staff assignment of note was on the personal staff of the US Army Surgeon General, in the Pentagon. He represented MEDCOM (Medical Command) at various recurring meetings of the Army General Staff and was always given the same two instructions: Take good notes, and don't agree to anything!

He earned an associate's degree in creative writing from Full Sail University in March of 2018, graduating as valedictorian of his program.

Doctor Harper and his wife met in junior high and have been married forty-five years. They live near Williamsburg, Virginia, have two grown daughters and one freshly hatched grandson. The two of them take a break from the authorial life in November and December, when they portray a happily married couple from the North Pole. A kindly soul, he only threatens those on the Naughty list with burnt cookies.